Advance Praise for P.

"Historical fiction readers and Colorado history buffs will enjoy *Prairie Truth* by Marilyn Bay. Challenging us to examine ideas and standards, Bay transports the reader to another time and place, but she causes us to examine the effects of that history on the here and now. *Prairie Truth* immerses the reader in good story, well-crafted characters, and accurate history. So much so, that it is difficult to put the book down and return to an era of cell phones and technology. From the comfort of our armchairs, *Prairie Truth* transports us to Colorado's past with vivid descriptions and settings. Galloping through a compelling story, Marilyn Bay demonstrates that reading about yesteryear is exciting and has import for modern society."

–Alice Longaker
author of *Wren*

"Marilyn's writing is majestic, swooping yet gentle—like the landscapes she uses as the backdrops for her stories. She is to be commended for working hard to present a vibrant story in a historically-accurate ambiance. She bravely took on the theme of a Hispano story line knowing it would not be easy, but she embraced it and the result is stunning."

–Richard de Olivas y Cordova
historian and genealogist Los Fuertes, Colorado

"Captivating characters combine with historical accuracy to create non-stop entertainment. Bay's writing style pulls readers in and takes them on a wild ride!"

–Jaydine Rendall
author of the *High Plains Heroes* series

PRAIRIE TRUTH

a novel

Marilyn Bay

CLADACH
Publishing

Published by
CLADACH Publishing
PO Box 336144
Greeley, Colorado 80633
http://cladach.com

Prairie Truth is a work of fiction. The characters are both actual and fictitious. With the exception of verified historical events and persons, all incidents, descriptions, dialogue and opinions expressed are the products of the author's imagination and are not to be construed as real.

Cover photo credit: Twyla Walker-Collins
Cover photo likeness: Julie Goodnight http://signin.juliegoodnight.com

ISBN: 9781945099090

To
my father, Marvin Bay, who
believed in me, taught me, and
always told me I could
accomplish anything I wanted
to accomplish.

PART I

Chapter 1

Sanchez Estate, San Luis Valley, Colorado

Spring 1886

When she passed the statue of St. Jude, a favorite saint of Señora Sanchez, Caroline gave it an irreverent, farewell kick. Then she hoisted her bulging saddlebags onto her right shoulder and raced down the steps, away from the sprawling adobe estate house ... and away from her brief marriage to Carlos, a disaster in more ways than one.

"You may take a carpetbag of clothing, acquired during your marriage, *no más*, and the saddle, bridle, and lazy horse you rode in here with when you presented yourself as a *señorita*," Señora Sanchez bellowed after Caroline signed the annulment papers. "You're nothing more than a half-breed. How stupid of you to try to trick me. Surely you knew the truth would come out!"

Caroline sprinted to the barn. What an ignorant woman her now ex-mother-in-law was to call her horse "lazy." The woman knew nothing of horses. The bay mare did exactly what she was bred and trained to do. She worked hard, could pull down any steer and stood still as a rock when that was required of her. She was no high-stepping parade horse, but ranches needed strong, good-minded horses, and the bay was that indeed. Caroline's ma had given the bay mare to her for her sixteenth birthday. Had Señora Sanchez told Caroline she couldn't take the mare with her, the woman would have had a fight on her hands.

"I expect it'll be one of the last births for my sorrel mare, Cheyenne. I want you to have her," Ma had said. "Train her like I taught you and she'll serve you well. When you find the right stallion, you can raise a string of fine cattle horses."

She jerked open the barn door, nearly pulling it from its hinges. "Azúcar," Caroline called to the bay mare as she walked to the tack room to fetch her saddle, saddle blanket, bridle, and grooming tools. During training, the mare had loved the lumps of sugar Caroline fed her—hence the name. Now Azúcar nickered, swinging her head toward Caroline. *How long since I groomed her?* Much too long. The Sanchezes placed little value on grooming horses, except for trips to town, or festival days when the Hispanos paraded their high-stepping horses down Main Street. Caroline would have groomed Azúcar, and the other horses also, but Señora Sanchez insisted such activity was not fitting for a woman of her standing.

Not only had Azúcar been neglected, Caroline still felt the sting of Señora Sanchez's attempts to transform her into a dutiful daughter-in-law. For her mother-in-law, a proper woman excelled in embroidery, discarded her personal opinions, rode only when required and then only side saddle in a full skirt. Riding astride was unladylike.

At first, Caroline had tried. Her ma taught her the basics of sewing. She could hem a dress or sew on a button; but why every towel and handkerchief had to be stitched with ornate designs was beyond her. She would never have agreed to marry Carlos had she known marriage would require her to become someone she was not—just one of the reasons she regretted marrying the spoiled, mama's boy.

She brushed and saddled Azúcar. *I wish I'd left this dress in the house. Trousers and shirts are so much easier for riding and working.* She would have enjoyed her mother-in-law's outrage at seeing her former daughter-in-law riding, in men's trousers, at a gallop down the lane. *At least I had the presence of mind to pull on my sturdy leather boots before Señora Sanchez threw me out.*

Saddlebags tied in place and her oiled canvas duster secured behind, Caroline swung up onto the saddle. *Thank goodness I didn't forget how to mount a horse on my own.* With the exception of yesterday, Caroline hadn't ridden a horse in months. When she went to town or to a social event, Señora Sanchez insisted she ride in a carriage pulled by high-stepping horses. As she turned Azúcar to exit the barn, she felt a slight twinge of guilt for leaving the barn door open; but she didn't want to waste another minute at the Sanchez estate. All the animals were stalled or tied, so her inaction would not endanger them.

She reveled in her vindictiveness—until she noticed Carlos heading into the barn, his head hung low, as if searching the ground for lost coins. What does one say to an ex-husband upon departure?

"Adiós, Carlos."

He raised his eyes no higher than her stirrups. "Adiós," he said, then dropped his head again and pushed past her into the barn.

Why should I expect anything different from him? He's never stood up for me during his mother's systematic control of my life. Whenever Caroline and Señora Sanchez argued, Carlos shrank away like a coyote confronted by a gun-slinging cowboy. He never helped her feel a part of the family and refused to demonstrate any responsibility for her, his wife. Now, as Carlos summed up their marriage with a single 'adiós,' she realized he had never loved her. She had given him the prestige of being a married man, but he didn't love her. He was still a child, despite the fact that he was nearly a decade older than she. Her disdain for him couldn't have been greater than at that moment.

Caroline pressed her heels into Azúcar's sides, urging the bay mare to lope. She didn't know where she would go, but she knew she wanted to put distance, lots of it, between her and Carlos, between her and her mother-in-law, and between her and the pretentious Sanchez Estate. She had agreed to marry Carlos, had convinced herself she was in love with him, but the truth was she had married him because she thought it would take her away from the reality and horrors of Sand Creek, away from being half Cheyenne. She felt she had lived her entire life under the shadow of the massacre at Sand Creek that had occurred in 1864, the year before she was born. Many of her father's people had been murdered at Sand Creek, and she had allowed it to weigh on her, to define her.

"I should have been there. I should have stopped it," her father said once. He was a good man and a good father yet he could never quite leave behind the guilt. "Why am I alive and they are dead?"

Caroline's ma carried her own guilt. "I'm so ashamed of our people, of the soldiers who did this," she said before bursting into tears. Caroline was only six years old but, like Ma's kitchen sponge, she absorbed the guilt. When she entered her teen years, the guilt didn't lessen, so she stuffed it deep within her soul, determined to ignore it.

She thought escaping to the other end of the state would make her forget, but she was wrong. *Now here I am, running away again.*

Azúcar's pent-up energy paralleled her own urgent yearning for freedom. When the Sanchez Estate was no more than a speck on the horizon, the mare's gallop slowed to a lope, and Caroline breathed the brisk, clean mountain air. The tension in her jaw and neck abated, as she moved in unison with the mare's smooth strides. Her mount had led a sedentary life since she and Carlos wed eight months prior.

"Easy, girl. We both have to get into better shape." The mare slowed to a trot. Her exhilaration with her newfound freedom dulled, and the reality of her situation began to sink in. She was a young woman, alone, with few prospects for supporting herself in a land still foreign to her. Tears sprang to her eyes and streamed down her cheeks. The choices she had made over the past eighteen months, pretending to be someone she was not, had brought destruction to herself and to those around her. But she could now see, as clearly as she saw the imposing Sangre de Cristo Mountain Range to the east, that her downfall had been created by her unwillingness to listen to the counsel of others and to face her problems instead of running from them. *Pa was always cautioning me about those character flaws of mine. Now this is what two years of rebellion have got me.*

Her parents' ranch in the Bijou Basin, forty miles southeast of Denver, was protected from the harsh winter winds by the line of bluffs to the west. Her grandfather, Thomas MacBaye, had chosen a prime spot close to the Bijou Creek to build the ranch house, barns, and corrals. Their well supplied the house and animals with all the water they needed. The irrigation system brought water from the creek for the garden and corn patch. Further away, the dryland pastures and wheat fields did well, most years, with the meager Colorado rainfall. Overall, it was a good place to live, a good way to grow up.

Ah, the ranchland in late spring! Caroline pictured it now: the pastures and prairies covered with delicate wildflowers in brilliant purples, oranges, and golds; prairie grasses waving in the ever-present breezes. *Why was I so anxious to leave?* She wished she could return now, but how could she admit to her family that she had erred? She had to try again. *Maybe I'll have better luck posing as a señorita elsewhere in the San Luis Valley.*

A darker memory presented itself. She was eight years old. Her shiny, black hair was neatly-plaited. She was lifting her small hand to grasp Pa's hand. She felt proud in her store-bought, pink-and-white checked, gingham dress and white pinafore. Pa swung her up onto his sleek, black stallion, Wise Heart. He had used a saddle that day and was dressed in white-man's clothes. He stepped into the stirrup and swung with ease to sit behind her. Wise Heart lunged forward at Pa's signal and carried them without effort northwest to the schoolhouse.

Caroline's ma had taught her to read, write, and cipher, but when the settlers decided to build a schoolhouse and employ a teacher, her parents agreed she should attend.

Pa slowed Wise Heart to a walk as they entered the school yard. Children were playing outside on the warm fall morning. Now they stopped playing and stared at Caroline and Pa. *They must be looking at our beautiful stallion*, she had mused to herself. Then Pa reached for Caroline's hand again and lowered her to the ground before he dismounted. She felt his grip firmer than usual. His walk was stilted and cautious, like when he, a Cheyenne Indian, walked the streets of Denver. When they reached the stoop of the schoolhouse, Pa pulled open the door. The schoolmarm was writing on the blackboard, her back to them.

"I'm here, ma'am, to enroll my daughter, Caroline," Pa said. His English was as good as any settler, better than some, Ma had told a shopkeeper when they visited Denver. It was true, Caroline knew.

The schoolmarm must have thought so as well. She spun to face them. "Good morning. I'm Miss Foster." She suddenly stopped midway to the door, eyes wide, mouth agape. "I didn't know we would have ..." Miss Foster over-enunciated her words. "I mean, I'm not certain we're ah, equipped to—"

"Caroline speaks fluent English," her father said, looking resigned, but determined to remain polite. "She can read, write, and do figures. She brought her own slate and chalk."

"I see; yes, indeed." Miss Foster wrung her hands. She looked no higher than his throat when she spoke next, and it wasn't because he was so much taller than her. "Well, perhaps your daughter could sit here." She patted a desk in the back row.

Pa breathed an almost imperceptible sigh of relief. She felt his grip on her hand soften. "That will be fine." Pa turned to her. "Caroline, I know you will do everything Miss Foster asks you. I will return in the afternoon to fetch you." He looked deep into her eyes, a softer version of his own. "Behave yourself." He gave her a peck on the cheek and headed for the door.

Before stepping through the door, he turned to her again. "Caroline, no racing the boys." Though he was speaking in English, his voice became lower and quieter, like when he spoke Cheyenne to her. "No fighting."

"I'll be fine, Pa."

He smiled then moved through the door without a sound. At the mention of fighting, she saw Miss Foster's eyes widen and her shoulders stiffen.

"Caroline, would you like to go outside and play with the other children? When you hear the bell ring, it will be time to come inside and begin lessons."

Caroline looked at the door. Next to it stood a broom. If she answered "no," would Miss Foster whisk her out the door with the broom?

"Yes, ma'am." She ran outside and found three girls playing with homemade corn-husk dolls. She didn't tell them she had a store-bought doll with a china head, hands, and feet. Her Uncle James had brought it to her on his last visit. When Uncle James left, Ma laughed. "That doll will be brand new ten years from now. Caroline would rather do a week's worth of chores than be caught playing with a doll!"

Azúcar's hoof caught a stone and sent it flying, bringing Caroline's attention back to the path ahead of her. Sagebrush, yucca, and an occasional soaring crow or hawk reminded her she rode the high desert of the San Luis Valley. She had traveled miles with no recollection of the scenery she had passed. Caroline's posture and able hold on the reins required little concentration, allowing her mind to drift back to that first day of school.

Chapter 2

Because Caroline preferred boys' work and pastimes, people called her a tomboy. And true to form, at recess on the first day of school, she watched the boys kick a bound-cloth ball. One of them lost control with his kick, sending the ball in her direction. On impulse, she kicked the ball back toward the group of boys. An older boys beckoned her to join them.

So far in her life, Caroline's only playmates were her siblings—and the Indian children in hunting camp when her family helped her father's people hunt meat for the winter.

Caroline got in a couple of good kicks to the *oohs* and *aahs* of the boys. Then Miss Foster rang the bell, and they filed into the school-house and found their seats. Caroline sat alone in the back row.

"Children, the first step in learning to read is to learn the alphabet." *I learned the alphabet years ago*, Caroline thought.

"Now watch as I write the letter A … the first letter in the alphabet." Miss Foster wrote a capital "A" and a small "a" on the blackboard. "Can anyone tell me why we have two?"

No one else raised their hand, so Caroline did. "Capital letters are used for starting sentences and for proper nouns."

The boy who had invited her to play ball turned and stared at her. Miss Foster stared, too, seemingly unable to speak. Finally she stammered, "Your father was right. You know your letters."

"I can read, too!" Caroline didn't intend to boast, but seeing the admiration of her classmates stirred her on. "My mother taught me. Taught my brother and sister, too."

Around noon, Miss Foster announced it was time for the students to eat. They went outside, each student with the food they brought from home. Caroline's mother packed her a piece of fried chicken, a slice of bread slathered with butter, and carrot slaw, left-overs from Sunday dinner. She noticed that most of the children had far less hearty meals. One ate a crust of bread without butter. Another nibbled on fried potatoes.

"You're lucky t' have meat."

Caroline turned.

The boy who invited her to play ball added, "My name is Andrew. What's yours?"

"I'm Caroline Thomas."

"I didn't think Injuns had last names," said an older girl. "I don't mean no disrespect. My name is Emma."

"I'm only half Indian." Caroline remembered with pride the summers spent with her father's people at their early summer celebrations and fall hunts. "My pa's Cheyenne. My ma's white."

"Was that your pa's horse?" Andrew's eyes were wide with admiration. "Sure wud like t' own one like that myself someday."

One of the other boys—the teacher had called him Teddy Blackmore—cut in. "My pa could train 'em fur ya if ya want. He says them Injun ponies don't know nothin'."

"Wise Heart's his name. He's my pa's stallion. Broke to ride just perfect." She gestured with her hands for emphasis. "He will do anything my pa asks of him." It was all true, but she knew her mother would chide her for putting on airs.

"Will you be ridin' Wise Heart to school by yerself?" Emma slid closer to Caroline.

"Naw. He's Pa's horse," Caroline shrugged. "We kids have to ride the mares."

"You have more'n one horse?" Andrew's enthusiasm for horses was clear.

"We have a lot. At our ranch we breed and train them."

More admiring sighs came from the other children.

After the noon meal, which these settlers' children knew as "dinner," Miss Foster rang the bell to call the students back to their desks. She told them they would be learning arithmetic.

Caroline was eager for arithmetic lessons. She wanted to learn something new. Miss Foster wrote the numerals 1 through 20 on the blackboard and asked the children to copy them on their slates. She followed directions, even though she had known how to do this for years.

ooooo

Caroline was not the only smart child in Miss Foster's class. By November, many of them could read simple sentences. They progressed even faster in arithmetic. Settler children learned when they were very young to cipher, as Caroline's mother called it. Girls could calculate how much flour their family would need to keep them through the year and how many yard goods required to buy a new dress or shirt. Boys could figure how much feed they would need for their animals, and their fathers taught them how to measure lumber to construct their homes and barns.

Once the students learned how to write the numbers, they had great fun competing to be first to answer Miss Foster's equations.

Caroline managed to win most of the competitions. Her father always said, "My Caroline is a good one to do figures." But when she noticed the others' frustration at not being able to win, she became slow to raise her slate or didn't carry a number to the next column, so that her answer was incorrect. She was especially inclined to do this to let her friends, Andrew and Emma, win.

The students were involved in a ciphering contest when Caroline noticed Teddy's pa slip in the door and lean against the back wall. Anxious to impress his pa, Teddy raised his slate to answer Miss Foster's arithmetic questions before he had worked the problem. He guessed three times and each time Miss Foster said, "That is not correct, Teddy."

Mr. Blackmore's face reddened. The man looked like her pa did the time she and Chance had been careless and broken two-dozen eggs they were supposed to deliver to the neighbors. She wished Miss Foster would dismiss them or ask them to practice their letters instead, but she didn't. Rather than allow Teddy to offer a fourth incorrect answer, Caroline's hand shot up.

"Five multiplied by eighteen is ninety." Caroline hoped Miss Foster was finished; but she continued to pose problems, and Caroline was the only student who could come up with the answer before Teddy shot his hand into the air.

Anger like hot coals boiled out of Mr. Blackmore's mouth. "Blasted idiot of a boy, haven't ya learned a thing at this here school?" He moved toward Teddy. He was much angrier than Caroline's pa was when she and Chance broke the eggs. "You are so stupid that this here half-breed can beat you."

No one moved a muscle.

"You go on home, boy. I'll not abide an Injun sitting in this here white school."

A sobbing Teddy ran outside, Mr. Blackmore hot on his heels.

Wide-eyed, her voice trembling, Miss Foster whispered, "Class dismissed."

After supper that night, Caroline relayed the story to Ma, leaving out the man's rants about Teddy being beaten by a half-breed and not allowing Indians and whites to be educated together. She wondered, since she was half white and half Indian, how she might divide herself in two and study in two separate schools, one for whites, another for Indians. She wanted to continue going to school. She liked the other students, and she liked feeling smart. Even Miss Foster gave her grudging respect.

"I don't like the sound of that one bit, Caroline. Maybe you should stay home," Ma said, sitting down across from her at the kitchen table. "We can continue your studies at home." Ma smoothed an errant strand of hair back into Caroline's braid.

"No, Ma, please let me go." She knew it was hard for Ma to say no when her oldest daughter was courageous. "I will be fine."

ooooo

Just in case it wasn't as fine as she had proclaimed it would be, the next morning Caroline decided she would take the store-bought doll—that had china head, arms and face—with her to school. The doll had blonde hair, and wore a beautiful crimson, silk ballroom dress. Perhaps the white doll would make her seem no different than the all-white students.

She saddled the mare and secured the saddlebags, which contained the doll, her slate, and her dinner. Arriving in the schoolyard, Caroline tied the mare and retrieved her belongings. She joined the children playing outside in the cool air. The girls' eyes went wide with admiration when she pulled the doll from the saddlebags.

"She's so beautiful!" Emma touched one finger to the silk dress.

"Would you like to hold her?" Caroline thrust the doll into her friend's hands.

"I do declare, I've never held anything so dazzlin'."

Caroline shrugged and ran to join the boys at a game of tug-o-war using a lariat. Play time ended when Miss Foster rang the bell.

During lessons, Caroline's tummy began to growl, signaling that dinner time must be around the corner. About that time a knock sounded at the door. Teddy's pa and two other men entered the classroom and stepped to the side opposite Caroline's seat.

"Miss Foster, a word with you, please." Mr. Blackmore's words sounded polite, but he scowled at the teacher and the students.

Why were the men angry? Caroline wondered, but she couldn't hear their words to Miss Foster. Then the teacher left the conversation and walked over to Caroline.

"Caroline, please come with me."

When Caroline looked up, her teacher looked away.

"Yes, ma'am." Caroline stood, and Miss Foster grabbed her hand. She spoke in a low tone, so that only Caroline would hear. "You are a fine student, but you will have to continue your studies at home … with your ma."

Confused, Caroline said, "But, Miss Foster, I like school." She had done everything her father had told her to do and avoided every-thing he had asked her to avoid. "I promise to work harder and not put on airs." Her voice was loud enough for everyone to hear.

"Oh, that's not it at all." Miss Foster dropped Caroline's hand and began wringing her own hands. "You see, the board, the people who built this school, don't want me to teach—" She swal-lowed hard. "Indians. They are telling me I cannot even teach smart Indians like you, Caroline."

"But I'm half white," Caroline pleaded.

"Ain't no matter. It's the Injun blood we're concerned with," one of the men with Mr. Blackmore bellowed. "Leave now, and we won't scalp ya." The man chuckled like it was a joke, but no one else laughed. "Git yer things and git outta here."

Caroline stuffed her slate into a saddlebag and ran out the door to the hitching post where her mare stood. Miss Foster and the three men followed her outside. She hoped her teacher would stand up to the men and tell them Caroline should stay at school. But the teacher just stood there wringing her hands.

Caroline fumbled with tightening the saddle. She had loos-ened the girth to give the mare breathing room while she waited at the hitching post all day, but her shaking hands prevented her from performing the simple task.

"Caroline, wait! You forgot your doll." Emma ran toward Car-oline with the china doll cradled in her arms.

"What's that ya got there?" Mr. Blackmore's friend grabbed for the doll, but Emma jerked it back from his grasp. Enraged, he lunged at Emma, and wrested the doll from her arms.

"Give it back, mister! It's Caroline's doll!" Emma's scream ended with gulping sobs.

The man swung the doll like a lariat. "The little half-breed is doing her best to show all the white kids she's got a doll nicer'n anyone else." He stepped toward Caroline. "Who do you think you are, girl?" As he said 'girl,' he let the doll fly. It hit the ground next to Caroline's feet. She jumped to the side as the fragile head shattered into pieces.

Miss Foster gasped, and Emma shrieked.

Caroline prayed the cinch was tight enough. She stepped up into the stirrup then shoved her right foot into the opposite stirrup. Ma had taught her to loosen the cinch when not in use and to always, always check and tighten it before remounting so the weight of the rider wouldn't pull it to the side of the horse. She was relieved to find it held her small body without slipping. Taking care not to ride too close to Emma, but not caring if her departure kicked dirt into the faces of the adults, she spurred the mare into an all-out gallop and didn't slow her down until she reached the south pasture gate at the ranch. She dismounted and wiped the tears from her cheeks with her sleeves. She walked the mare through the gate, turned to latch it, and took a deep breath.

She did her best to be nonchalant when Ma and Pa questioned her. "Nothing happened. I can learn more at home, that's all."

She had tried so hard to be a good student and to make everyone like her; but she had failed. She had best hide the truth from her family and save them the disappointment. Never again did she talk about her three months of prairie school.

That was the first time she had not told the truth, but it would not be the last. Looking back, Caroline realized that was when she began to lose her freedom.

Chapter 3

Mauricio Córdova de Medina had heard Señora Sanchez screaming insults at Caroline earlier that day, so he wasn't surprised to see her hightailing it away from the Sanchez Estate. *Good for her*, he thought, when he saw her running the pretty bay mare headlong down the tree-lined lane, away from the pretentious estate.

Señora Sanchez cared much more about appearing wealthy than seeing that the property remained profitable. Instead of focusing on spring work of bringing in the cattle to wean and brand the calves, she had the vaqueros pave her receiving room with intricate tiles imported from Italy. Next, they were instructed to build a grand ballroom (which had yet to be used). Last year's sheep shearing was delayed for two months while the señora sent the vaqueros to the mountains to dig pine trees to line the entrance of the estate. The men had tried to tell her that the larger the trees they transplanted, the less likely they would survive. She called them lazy and sent the vaqueros to find even larger trees.

Mauricio could see great potential for prosperity in this new land. It frustrated him that the Sanchezes, or more specifically, Señora Sanchez, was squandering her resources. Señor Sanchez had died before Mauricio came to work at the estate. The foreman wondered if she had nagged her husband to death. Carlos was nothing more than a pawn in his mother's hand. He knew nothing about ranching and had more than once expressed disinterest.

One day the previous fall Mauricio had met Carlos on the veranda of the house and persuaded Carlos to accompany him to evaluate breeding bulls and decide which to keep and which to cull. On Sangre de Cristo ranches owners normally knew as much or more about their stock and their land as their ranch managers.

While the two men walked toward the corral, Mauricio removed his medium-brimmed, leather, vaquero hat and wiped sweat from his brow. "I think we … er … you should cross your cows with Hereford and Angus bulls … the bulls I've told you about, that have British origins. We can buy good quality bulls from Anglo ranchers and—"

"I cannot concern myself with the work of peasants." Carlos was dressed in gold-embroidered black satin. His boots and hat, good choices for a Madrid bull ring, were ostentatious and impractical in the remote valley ranchland.

"Humor me, Don Carlos."

When Mauricio addressed him with the title reserved for upper-class citizens, Carlos finally looked him in the eye. Mauricio had a hard time trusting a man who wouldn't look another man in the eye. Early on, he had tried to give Carlos the benefit of the doubt. Maybe he had developed the avoidance behavior because Mauricio was at least a head taller than him, and it was awkward for a boss to look up at his employee. Later he concluded that Carlos's behavior was nothing more than arrogance.

"I'll abide this conversation for only a few minutes longer, Miguel."

Mauricio slapped his hat against his thick, practical leather leg chaps, irked that Carlos couldn't even remember his own ranch manager's name.

They were outside the corral that housed the breeding bulls. One of the new Hereford bulls Mauricio had persuaded Señora Sanchez to purchase from an Anglo rancher trotted toward them. Carlos bolted toward the house.

"The 'peasants' have more ranching talent in their little fingers than you'll ever have," Mauricio muttered, out of earshot.

The Sanchez Estate was headed for ruin. Mauricio's suggestions fell on deaf ears. *I only regret that I brought Carolina into this quagmire,* he thought.

Less than a month after accepting the position of ranch manager of the Sanchez Estate, he traveled seven miles north to a small ranch near San Pedro. The Sanchez pastures had a good supply of fine-boned, high-stepping carriage horses, but Mauricio knew he had to acquire lots of steady, sturdy ranch horses quickly or the vaqueros would not be able to work. Señor Martínez was known throughout the San Luis Valley as a breeder of good horses. He bought, sold and bred all sorts of horses, but he specialized in working ranch horses.

Mauricio and six of his most dependable vaqueros left before sunrise. He wanted plenty of time to see the horses in the corral and under a saddle—to determine a horse's disposition and soundness—before he made his decision. The seven men would be able to drive the two dozen horses back to the Sanchez Estate by dark. Other ranch managers would have bought any animal available for a good price, ignoring the horse's work readiness, but Mauricio would buy broke, or at least green broke, mounts. He didn't have time for the vaqueros to break new horses. There was too much ranch work to do.

"¿Cómo está tu mamá?" Señor Martínez's outstretched hand was firm and warm. No matter what, the people of the valley always asked about a person's mother. And, much to Mauricio's chagrin, everyone in the valley knew about him being deserted by his wife.

"The neighbors look after Mamá and she is busy with the sheep." Mauricio knew managing the ranch was not what his mother wanted to do, but he thought not to burden Señor Martínez with this detail. "I've come to buy horses for the Sanchez Estate."

"I heard you were running the Sanchez ranch." Señor Martínez shifted his weight to his other leg and cast his eyes downward. "I regret that you must hire out your services. A man who owns a fine-looking and prosperous rancho like yours shouldn't have to work for someone else." He glanced upward at Mauricio. "I guess you didn't have much choice when your papá died."

Mauricio looked away and kicked the ground with the toe of his boot. "It wasn't Papá's death that put the ranch in financial jeopardy."

Señor Martínez waited, but Mauricio said no more. "Was it your wife, your ex-wife?"

"Sure. When she moved back to Santa Fe and filed for the annulment, her family demanded I pay her a lot of money." Mauricio didn't like to display his dirty laundry, but he had known Señor Martínez a long time; the man would keep the details to himself.

"She left of her own accord?" Señor Martínez shook his head. "Then why would you have to pay her?"

"I didn't have to." Mauricio looked straight at Señor Martínez. "I wanted her family to have no reason to malign the Córdova name."

"A wife is supposed to stay with her husband. And you are a good man, Señor Córdova."

"Gracias." It was important to Mauricio that people thought he had been good to his former wife. "No use dwelling on the past now, is there? Show me some good working horses."

"My men are working dawn to dust to break horses for ranch work, but there's been such high demand since the Anglos started moving into the valley up north. I don't know if I have two dozen good horses that meet your high standards, Señor Córdova."

The two men moved to one of two small arenas. A vaquero Mauricio judged to be in his late teens lasted through four-and-a-half hard bucks before half-jumping, half-falling to the ground. The young man cursed loudly.

"We'll not have that language here, not in front of a fine customer."

Mauricio guessed that for Señor Martínez it was less a reprimand and more his way of letting his vaqueros know they needed to be on their best behavior. But Mauricio had heard worse.

The buckskin that just dumped the vaquero was a fine horse but not ready for ranch work. "Where are your broke horses?"

"Well, that's just the thing." Señor Martínez removed his hat and scratched above his right ear. "Not many are better trained than the buckskin." He pointed at the horse still snorting and crow hopping around the arena.

It was true that a ranch horse of the right breeding and disposition went from unbroken to dependable mount in a season, but Mauricio didn't have a season to get the horses where they needed to be. They were already weeks late weaning and branding calves and moving the cows to the high meadows. Ranch horses had to stand patiently while vaqueros dismounted to mend fences. He could not imagine using one of these horses to transport an abandoned lamb or calf to the barn. A horse as wild as this bucking horse would jeopardize the rider and everyone around him.

"There's another option, but I'm not sure I like it." Señor Martínez replaced his hat, adjusting it so the polished silver conchos sat at the front of the brim.

"Señor, I'm open to suggestions."

The older man gestured to the second small arena. "See that little vaquero over yonder? His methods are, well, different. My first thought was that it would take him forever to break a new horse. He doesn't even saddle a horse for the first week, but once he does, he gets the job done real fast. I've sold horses he has broken to three different ranches. Two returned within a week to buy more."

"I can't wait two weeks for each horse." Mauricio turned toward the barn where he'd left his horse tied to the hitching post.

"Oh, no, he'll train a dozen horses in that time. He works with one right after another. A hard worker but a recluse. He doesn't say much. He may not be all there." The señor tapped his finger above his right temple. "You should watch him work and try to talk to him." Señor Martínez swept his hand toward the little vaquero. "Let me know what you think. I'll be in the barn."

Mauricio stood outside the small arena, but the vaquero didn't acknowledge him. It must be week two for this horse. The vaquero placed two heavy blankets and a saddle on the paint horse's back, but instead of rushing to tighten the cinch that held the saddle, he tightened it a bit and then led the horse halfway around the small arena before stopping to pull the cinch a bit tighter. He repeated this several times. Mauricio noticed that the horse walked beside the vaquero with complete willingness, moving forward when he moved forward, and stopping when he stopped.

Next, the vaquero loosened the lead line, stepped back toward the paint's hip, and clucked. Like an old wagon horse, the paint moved forward, keeping the vaquero in his side vision. When the man lifted the lead line, the paint stopped. The vaquero put the lead in his other hand and with minimal pressure, pulled the paint toward him in a semicircle. He stepped back toward the horse's hip and repeated the exercise in the other direction.

Mauricio was mesmerized. Horse and vaquero worked as partners. There was no shouting or jerking by the vaquero, no kicking, bucking or rearing from the horse.

The vaquero brought the paint to the middle of the arena. When he stepped toward the horse, it backed up. Next the vaquero put slack into the rope and the paint breathed easy and licked his lips, lowering his head relaxation like a seasoned ranch horse. The little vaquero dropped the lead and walked round the horse, rubbing him and talking to him in a voice too low to understand. Returning to the paint's left side, the vaquero looped the lead rope over its neck and tied it to the right side of the headstall. He returned to the left side, squared the stirrup in front of him and, without fanfare, stepped into it and onto the horse.

What would happen when the man spurred the horse? Mauricio felt more suspense than children listening to an exciting story told by a favorite uncle. If the man did spur the horse, Mauricio didn't see it. The horse moved in a circle to the left, nearly as nonchalant as it stood when the vaquero mounted him. Then they moved to the right. Next, the vaquero, through movements of his reins and legs, asked the paint to trot in each direction. The paint gave perfect, easy gaits and worked in partnership with its rider.

This was the kind of horse Mauricio needed to work the massive Sanchez Estate. He was glad he hadn't made his purchases and left an hour ago.

Mauricio watched the vaquero approach the gate, the only way out of the small arena. His relaxed shoulders tightened, and the paint started to prance.

"Easy, boy." The prancing lessened. The vaquero tapped the side of his boot, not the heel, against the paint's side, and the horse stepped away from the pressure. "That a boy. Just a few more steps."

The steps were intentional, part of the training. Mauricio moved to open the gate for the twosome.

"No, señor, I must teach him."

Mauricio watched, stupefied as the vaquero side-passed the paint to the gate, opened it, moved the horse's hindquarters around the gate, exited, and side-passed the horse back toward the gate to latch it. Imagine, opening a gate without having to dismount and remount! He would make a deal with the vaquero.

Señor Martínez was only half right. He was a hard worker and socially inept, but there was nothing wrong with this horse trainer. He was brilliant.

At the barn, Mauricio found the little vaquero unsaddling the paint. Mauricio watched him return the tack to its place. Next, he brushed the paint, patting and murmuring to the animal.

"I need to talk to you." Mauricio moved closer. Was the man deaf? "Will you train horses for me?" Mauricio reached toward the cowboy's shoulder to get his attention, but before his hand landed, the vaquero spun around.

Chapter 4

Sí, señor, I will train your horses." The slim vaquero met Mauricio's eyes, then looked away. He was taller than he looked in the arena. He wore pants covered with chaps, and a vaquero—some called it Western or cowboy—hat pulled down low.

"How soon could you be finished with a dozen horses?" Mauricio was drawn to this very young vaquero. There wasn't even a trace of stubble above his lip or on his chin. Probably hadn't even started to shave yet.

"It is best if I can work with a horse for a month, but if your men are good with new horses, I can green break them in two to three weeks." There was sweat at his hat line. It was nearing noon and the day was hot, yet he made no move to take off his jacket or leather work gloves.

"That paint, how long you been working him?" Mauricio could only hope to have a working string of horses like the paint.

"One week, three days." No boasting. Only explanation. "Today was my first time to ride him. It took longer to get him ready." A hint of contempt entered his voice. "Señor Martínez's vaqueros scared him. He's a sensitive horse."

"Seems you're a good judge of horseflesh. Will you come with me to the corral to choose the horses to buy for my ranch?"

"There's this black and white paint, a tri-color paint with a white coat and big brown and black spots, and a blue roan. Those three are the only horses I'd bother with, the only horses in the corral that the vaqueros haven't soured." There was something different about his speech. He pronounced every syllable like a young child, and he didn't roll the "r" quite like the San Luis Valley people did. "In the vega, Señor Martínez has some nice horses. They're strong and heavy muscled."

Mauricio knew exactly what he meant. Most people wanted the finer boned horses, but he sought steady, hard-working ranch horses. It was worth a trip to the vega, the communal grazing land that connected all the San Pedro ranchos. "Let's go."

The vaquero headed to the corral and emerged with an ugly little gray mare. The mare looked to have a bad disposition, her ears perpetually pinned back. "Frost is a sweet mare. Got her ears frostbit off as a foal. No one wants to buy her, because she always looks like she's going to bite. But it's not her fault." He swung lightly into the saddle. "Frost is a great riding and working horse. I can't imagine a gentler animal. Children can hang all over her. She wouldn't hurt a flea."

Ten minutes later, Mauricio and the vaquero were loping toward the vega, a short ride. The vaquero pointed to a selection of paints, several sorrels, and a brown horse with a nice blaze and three white stockings.

Mauricio nodded. "What about the palomino?"

"I don't know much about that horse, señor, but in my opinion, it is best to stick to horses with common coat colors." They had slowed their mounts to a walk, and he looked Mauricio square in the eyes for the first time. "Everyone wants a palomino, and so they tend to breed animals with inferior conformations and dispositions just because everyone likes the coat color."

"You are absolutely correct." Mauricio stared back at the vaquero, noticing him smile for the first time. "My papá had a palomino mare once, and she was a nasty animal. Never occurred to me why that might have been." Why did he find this vaquero so intriguing? Well,

the horse knowledge, of course. But there was something else about
the vaquero. Something he couldn't quite put his finger on.

"We can cut out the ones you want and head them back to the
corrals." The vaquero loosened his lariat from the leather strings
on the pommel of his saddle.

Mauricio did the same, but he was not focused on the task. He
was thinking about the vaquero when the brown horse tried to dart
through the space between them. He threw his lariat hard to dissuade the horse but overshot his target. His lariat thumped against
the vaquero's head, knocking him and his hat to the ground. Long,
thick, black hair tumbled down his … er … her back. Smooth skin,
heavy, bulky clothes, reclusiveness. Now it made sense.

She got up and ran to retrieve her hat. Then she turned toward
him with large eyes full of tears. And a creamy complexion.

"Please," she said. This time holding his gaze. "I have nowhere
to go. I just needed a job." She wiped the tears off her face with
her sleeve.

If Mauricio was mesmerized watching her work the paint, he
was speechless now. A woman—a young, beautiful woman. Her
eyes begged him to keep her secret.

"They will find out, if not today, someday soon." He dismounted and stepped toward her. She was trembling.

"I know." She gathered and twisted her hair, so she could stuff
it back under the oversized hat.

"Have you considered working as a maid or caring for children?" As soon as the words left his mouth, he knew the answer
to his question. He shook his head. "No, that would be silly when
you're so talented with horses." He sank to the ground, releasing
his horse to graze. She sat across from him.

"I can offer you employment as a maid or a cook, but Señora
Sanchez would never allow a young lady to train horses, to do the
work of a vaquero."

"What about as a teacher? Do the Sanchezes have children at
the rancho?" Her scared eyes softened.

Mauricio felt her distrust melt. He had always had a talent for gaining a stranger's trust. Or maybe it was because she was forced to confide in him.

"First, we are not allowed to call it a rancho." He chuckled. "It is an 'estate,' the Sanchez Estate." He pursed his lips and moved his shoulders stiffly from side to side.

"Carlos Sanchez is the only child, and he is an adult; but I believe I can make a case for hiring a teacher. Most of the vaqueros have wives and children living with them on the estate. And, should you have time after lessons, there are plenty of horses to train."

"I have a confession. I'm not from here. I learned Spanish as a child and have spent the last year moving from rancho to rancho. I know how to do arithmetic, and I read and write English very well, but I never learned to read or write Spanish very well."

Mauricio groaned. "How about if I get you some books? As long as you stay a chapter ahead of the children, you would be able to teach them."

"I am a fast learner." Her eyes twinkled like a mischievous child's.

"Where do you come from, and why are you here alone?" It was his directness that got him into trouble. He could feel her retreat.

"I was born up north." Her eyes left his. "My ma is white, but my pa…"

An awkward silence followed. He wanted to spare her embarrassment. "Some folks here in the valley don't look kindly on whites and Spaniards marrying. I understand your reticence."

She looked surprised. "Thank you … for understanding."

Mauricio stood and flipped his hat into place. "Here's what we'll do. I will inform Señor Martínez that I intend to buy the horses you helped me choose and that you and I have a deal to train them." He extended his hand to help her off the ground. "I will return three weeks from today to retrieve the horses … and you. What do I tell your new employer is the name of the teacher she is hiring?"

"Carolina, señor. Carolina Thomas."

"Thomas? Is that your Hispanic father's name?"

She looked like a rabbit caught in a snare. "It's my mother's family name, the name we go by up north." That sounded unconvincing. Her eyes widened with panic, and her gaze darted to and fro like a penned wild horse looking for a way to escape. "Espinosa, that's his name. My name is"—she hesitated—"Carolina Thomas de Espinosa."

"Carolina, it matters little to me where you came from or who your parents are, but it will matter to others, especially Señora Sanchez." He sighed, cocking his head sideways to look at her. Why did he feel she was only telling a half true? "With a name like—"

"I know, Thomas is an Anglo name."

"I was going to say with a name like Espinosa, you will raise suspicions."

"Why, señor?"

"Have you heard of the Espinosa brothers?" Her blank stare told him she had not. "In 1863, when I was a young boy and you probably weren't even born, the brothers went on a killing spree here in the valley. They, like many New Mexicans, were angry with the Anglos for taking our land and livestock. In addition, the sister of the Espinosa brothers was raped by soldiers from Ft. Garland."

Carolina frowned. Seeing that, Mauricio hesitated, then continued.

"The Espinosa family was unable to support itself, and two of the brothers, Felipe and José, turned to robbing freighters to feed their families. No one here would justify what they did, but they understood why they did it. They wore masks when they held up the freighters, but one time, one of the freighters recognized the brothers anyway. From that time on they became fugitives. And they started killing Anglos. A contingent was sent out from Ft. Garland to bring them in, but they killed the corporal and escaped. In the spring of that year, the brothers were tracked to their home in the Sangre de Cristo Mountains, and José was shot. Rather than stop, Felipe, the older brother, recruited his twelve-year-old nephew to join him in the killing. Some Hispanos feared being mistaken for the Espinosa brothers or that Anglos would assume all Hispanos were violent."

"My pa told me never to judge a group of people by the actions of one member of that group. He said it was an important lesson my Grandfather Thomas taught him." Carolina smoothed her hair and tossed it back over her shoulders. "I wish more people lived by that creed."

"Me, too." Mauricio nodded.

"What happened to the Espinosa brothers?"

"U.S. military authorities offered a large sum of gold to anyone able to bring in the dead bodies of the Espinosa brothers, or rather the uncle and his nephew. Tom Tobin, a well-known Indian fighter and tracker, and his men tracked the Espinosas to a cabin, where they shot both of them. Tobin cut off their heads and delivered them to Ft. Garland to collect his gold."

Mauricio expected Caroline to be appalled, but her lack of reaction told him she either was cold or had experienced a lot of violence in her young life.

"So, maybe I better rethink the Espinosa surname," she said.

"How about Carolina Vargas de Garcia? There are so many people in the valley and New Mexico by those surnames that people will not associate you with any one family."

"Carolina Vargas de Garcia. I like it."

Who was this woman to adopt a new name and a new identity without a thought? Mauricio hoped he would not regret walking through this door.

"We have horses to round up." She headed to find Frost but turned back after a few paces. "Señor, you have not told me your name."

"Mauricio Córdova de Medina." He tipped his hat toward her. "Con mucho gusto."

"Igualmente, Señor Córdova." Carolina tipped her head in acknowledgement. When she did, her smile showed a dimple in her right cheek.

Chapter 5

Judging from the moon, it was close to midnight when Caroline rode Azúcar into San Luis. She was dead tired. The long ride and being out of shape wearied her, but mostly it was the drama and sense of failure. She knew she should worry about where she would live and how she would support herself, but … what was it her ma always said? "Don't be visiting tomorrow's worries on today."

She pulled her mare to a walk, hoping not to awaken any of the town's dogs. Her time in the San Luis Valley had taught Caroline that no Hispano town was without a plaza. It was the center of the town's social life. When the settlers from New Mexico first came to the Culebra River area thirty-five years ago, the people from each settlement constructed mud-plastered log homes called jacals that adjoined to create a large square or plaza in the center. The jacals were built by erecting hundreds of small, rough logs side-by-side vertically and anchoring them into a trench. This construction created the outline of each family's house. Each small home had its own door and sometimes windows opening to the plaza. The wall opposite the plaza wall was without doors or windows to protect the settlers from Indian attacks. Rough-hewn logs formed the ceiling beams, and grass and willows filled in the skeletal frame before being packed with dirt and mud. The new home was then covered with layers and layers of mud, both inside and out, on the ceiling and on the roof, to form thick walls. The walls facing outward were thickest.

As the Hispanic population grew and Indians left or were forced onto reservations, the threat of attacks lessened. Ten years ago, residents had started to create doors and windows on the outside of their jacal walls, and off those they built individual courtyards, garden spaces and animal enclosures. Often their cropland, which they had been promised as part of their agreement to settle in the savage land, extended directly behind their jacals. Here they planted corn, pinto beans, wheat, barley and other grains. A man typically raised enough to feed his family, give to the church, and trade for supplies like coffee and sugar. Some families eventually left their jacals and built larger, free-standing adobe or wood houses away from the protective plaza but still within walking distance. Nowadays most of those still living in the plaza, ran businesses out of the front of their homes and lived in the back. Those who raised animals and crops for a living moved farther away.

The sizeable central plaza was still the center of the settlement's religious and social life. It was large enough for animals to be brought into the courtyard when the settlement had come under attack by Utes or, on occasion, by Plains Indians. At the urging of Sangre de Cristo land grantee Charles Beaubien, the U.S. government established Fort Massachusetts and shortly thereafter, moved it to a more effective and strategic location which they called Ft. Garland. This lessened the need for the fortified plaza. Someone had explained this history to Caroline when she first came to the Culebra River region.

Caroline hobbled Azúcar, so she could graze in the courtyard but not wander away. It was too late to find lodging. Even in spring, nighttime temperatures in the high desert still dropped below freezing. She was glad she had grabbed the wool blanket and her vaquero duster. They would keep her warm and dry while she slept outside. Her last thought as she drifted off to sleep was an ironic one: What would the residents of San Luis think if they

knew the structure built to protect them from Indians was itself
now protecting an Indian, or at least a half-Indian?

ooooo

When Caroline opened her eyes the next morning, three
young faces stared back at her. For a terrifying few seconds, she
couldn't remember where she was. Then it came back. She would
never again sleep in the feather bed at the Sanchez Estate. She
now lay on hard clay inside the San Luis Plaza.

"¿Está bien, Señorita?" A young girl patted Caroline on the
head. "Me llamo Ana."

"Yes, I'm fine," she said in Spanish. She scrambled to her feet,
the blanket and duster falling to the ground. "Thank you." She
was relieved to see Azúcar grazing nearby.

A boy, perhaps an older brother to the girls, followed her
gaze. "Is the bay mare yours?"

Caroline nodded.

"She's a beauty. I'll fetch her for you." He approached Azúcar
from the side and patted her on the neck. When the mare was
comfortable with him in her space, he bent to remove the hobbles.

Caroline watched as the young man cautiously but confi-
dently led Azúcar to her. He handed her Azúcar's lead rope,
and she gratefully greeted her horse then folded her blanket and
stuffed it into the saddlebag. She stretched and groaned. It had
been a long time since she slept on the ground.

Ana reached for Caroline's hand. "You must come to our
house for breakfast," she said. "My mamá is making tortillas,
and we have fresh goat cheese. Gloriana made it yesterday." She
beamed at her older sister.

"Sí, you must eat with us, Señorita. I'm Felipe."

Caroline smiled and allowed him to help her saddle the mare
and secure the saddlebags and duster.

"You look tired, and a little sad," Felipe said.

Am I that easy to read? And by children, no less. "Well, if you're
sure it will not inconvenience your parents."

"My parents run the mercantile." Gloriana pointed to the storefront on the opposite side of the plaza. "They like visitors." Gloriana was as matter-of-fact as Ana was solicitous.

The mercantile had a courtyard on the plaza side with sets of tables and chairs. Two were occupied by older men enjoying their morning coffee and tortillas. Each table was decorated with a vase of fresh wildflowers. The hard-packed earthen floor was clean and tidy.

"If you trust me to take your horse, I can put her in the barn. I'll give her some hay and water."

"Thank you, Felipe. Her name is Azúcar."

Caroline followed Ana and Gloriana inside. As her eyes adjusted to the dark interior, she saw shelves packed with containers. If it was like other mercantiles in the valley, the containers held coffee, sugar, flour, dried fruit, and other necessities. On the floor were hoes, rakes, and other hand implements, as well as several plows. The counter displayed jars of peppermints and lemon drops. Bolts of calico fabric and muslin caught her eye. The smell of cheese wafted in the air.

"Gloriana made breakfast before we came to the plaza—and found you!" Anna's cherubic face beamed. Gloriana nodded calmly.

As they approached the counter, a stout, balding man with a wide face came through the door from the family's living quarters. He beamed at his children.

Felipe had returned from securing Azúcar in the barn. "Papá, we found this señorita sleeping in the plaza, and we invited her to have breakfast with us." The slightest crease showed on the man's forehead, but his smile remained. "Papá, you know what you tell us about the importance of welcoming strangers."

Caroline felt bad for putting the father in an awkward situation. "Señor, you have the most fetching children. They really are very lovely. They insisted I come to meet you, but the last thing I wish to do is to inconvenience you and your wife."

"No inconvenience whatsoever. It's not every day we find a señorita sleeping in our plaza." He inclined his head, inviting her to explain.

"I arrived very late last night. I didn't want to wake the town."
Caroline didn't mention that if she had found lodging, she would
have been unable to pay for it.

"I see," the man said in a slow, drawn-out way that indicated
he really did not see. "I'm Señor Cohen."

Without thinking, Caroline extended her hand, the way
Anglo men greeted one another. Some habits died with difficulty.
A lady might extend her hand to a gentleman to kiss, but such
formalities were rare in the valley. Women who knew one another
greeted each other with a kiss on each cheek, but those being
introduced for the first time inclined their heads when introduced. "I'm Carolina Vargas Garcia."

Señor Cohen, clearly uncomfortable, shook Caroline's hand
and then released it quickly. "Please join us for breakfast." He gestured toward the door from where he had come into the store a
few minutes earlier.

"Venga." Ana pulled her by the hand toward the door.

Señora Cohen, a small woman with an abundance of jet-
black hair pulled into an elaborate knot at the back of her head,
reminded Caroline of Señora Sanchez, minus the haughtiness.
"I'm pleased to meet you, Señorita Vargas. ¿De dónde es?"

Caroline winced at the standard question of where she was
from. She was not ready to give personal information. "I'm a
teacher. I grew up to the north, but was recently teaching children
south of here." Though she wanted to remain vague, she couldn't
help adding, "I'm also a horse trainer!"

"¿Really?" Señora Cohen pursed her lips, eyebrows arching.

Caroline found it amusing that people questioned what was
true but easily accepted untruths and partial truths.

"Please, have a seat. Señora Cohen has prepared a lovely
breakfast." Señor Cohen pointed at a sixth chair at the table, an
expertly-handcrafted oblong table. From the characteristic knots
in the smooth-sanded wood, Caroline supposed the furniture was
made from the Pinyon pines found in abundance in the surrounding mountains.

As Caroline took her seat, she realized how very hungry she was. She had not eaten for over a day. The whole wheat tortillas straight from the outdoor grill were perfectly browned, promising that delicious mix of soft and crispy. The señora placed a steaming bowl of frijoles fried with eggs and onions in the center of the table. Dried plums, a delicacy, were likely added because of the Cohens' guest. Señora Cohen brought her a steaming cup of dark, black coffee, and placed a small pitcher of steamed milk next to it.

The food tasted every bit as good as it looked and smelled. "¡Excelente! Everything is so very delicious. Thank you." Caroline smiled at Señora Cohen.

The gracious lady nodded her reply. "Will you be staying in San Luis, Señorita Vargas?"

I haven't even thought what I'll do next. "I suppose I'll move on, in a day or two, unless there are horses that need training or children that need teaching."

This caught Señor Cohen's attention. "We haven't had a teacher here for a year. When we do get a teacher here in the valley, she rarely stays more than a year, sometimes less. 'Too primitive,' the last one told the school board."

Señor Cohen refilled his coffee and leaned forward, cradling it with both hands. "Of course, now the children are busy working in their parents' farms and shops, but come October we would like to open the school again."

I thought my teaching days were behind me, but maybe it's something to consider. Was it a way to make yet another new start? She had no trouble studying the books she taught from to stay ahead of the students at the Sanchez Estate.

"I hadn't thought about settling here. October is a ways off."

"Doña Maria said she was looking for a vaquero to train her two and three-year-olds." Felipe chimed in, not quite finished with the tortilla he had stuffed into his mouth. "She told me a few days ago when she came to buy supplies."

"Those are tough ranch horses, son." Señor Cohen put his coffee cup down, and his wife poured him a third cup. "I could not in good conscience send a young lady out there. She'd be killed or maimed for life." He gave a slight nod toward Caroline.

She chuckled. "You underestimate me, Señor Cohen. I would appreciate an introduction." She knew that no one in the valley hired anyone without the crucial introduction.

"Señorita Vargas, these are not parade horses." The volume and intensity in his voice had increased.

"I understand, señor." She gave a soft answer to allay his outburst. "But I must support myself. And," she added as an afterthought, "my pa and ma taught me well how to train horses. I am good at it."

Señor Cohen looked at Caroline for a long time. She hoped she had not tipped her hand, told too much about herself and who she really was. *He must be wondering why I'm not living with my pa and ma.*

"Very well. I will give you a proper introduction to Doña Maria the next time she comes to the mercantile." He rose from the table to return to the store but then paused and turned to face her. "In the meantime, I hope you will accept our invitation to stay with us. You can help Señora Cohen with her work."

Felipe followed his pa. Gloriana and Ana rose from the table and began gathering the dishes from the table. Caroline filled her arms with the empty platters and followed the girls into the kitchen. Señora Cohen scraped pieces of leftover food into a wooden bowl. The dirty dishes were placed in the sink and the girls began to scrub each dish with a soapy cloth. When all the dishes were rubbed with the soapy cloth, Gloriana rinsed the soap from the dishes by dribbling water from a metal bucket over each dish. The rinse water drained from the sink with a pipe that was threaded through the wall to the outdoors. When she first came to the valley, Caroline had been surprised that dishes, even greasy ones, could be cleaned this way. At home, Ma would have heated water on the stove top and poured half of it into the sink with some lard soap. Each dish would have been rinsed in a basin with the other half of the hot water.

Señora Cohen thrust the scrap bowl at Ana.

"I can fill these water buckets for you," said Caroline, picking up the two metal pails.

"The well is in the plaza," the señora said.

"I'll show you," offered Ana.

ooooo

Two days passed without any appearance or mention of Doña Maria. Caroline figured she could find where the woman lived. *But I can't just show up and introduce myself.* No one in the valley did that.

The Cohen family were very kind to her. She shared a room with the girls, who slept in one bed so she could have her own. Señora Cohen was a fabulous cook, and she seemed to appreciate Caroline's help. But she couldn't stay here forever. The Cohens were bound to ask questions she couldn't answer. The lies she told to conceal her identity and make the people here accept her were difficult to keep consistent. At first, the deception seemed freeing. Now it felt like a burden weighing her down.

That evening Señora Cohen told her they would prepare a special meal. It was Friday, and they always ate special foods on Friday night, she explained. The women prepared tortillas, beans, and a soup with round balls of dough boiled—a sort of dumpling.

Gloriana pulled a white wool tablecloth from the hutch in the dining room, and Caroline helped her place it on the table. It had colorful embroidered designs of flowers and animals. She recognized the Colcha embroidery that was distinctive to the valley. Long strands of wool were pulled through the fabric and tacked in place with smaller, perpendicular stitches. This was particularly beautiful, superior to any work she had seen, even in Señora Sanchez's home.

"Such fine work." She looked up to see Gloriana watching her.

"My grandmother made it." Gloriana swallowed hard and looked away. "She brought it with her from New Mexico. She said life in the valley was too hard. She returned to New Mexico, and we have only seen her once since she left."

Caroline was wondering how to reply, when Señora Cohen

entered the room with steaming dishes of food, and they had to hurry to straighten the tablecloth. After several more trips from the kitchen, the meal was ready.

Before they ate, Señora Cohen and the girls covered their heads with a white-on-white embroidered, fine wool cloth. The señora handed Caroline a matching cloth and gestured for her to place it on her head. Señor Cohen began a prayer of thanksgiving. He thanked God for providing for their needs and for sending Caroline to them.

If they knew what a sinner sits in their midst....

The prayer concluded with the words, "In the name of the Father, the Son, and the Holy Spirit." Señor Cohen lit the seven candles held by an ornate brass candelabra gracing the center of the table. Señor Cohen then invited them to sit and eat.

PART II

Chapter 6
Doña Maria's Ranch, west of San Luis

In this valley, there were women older than she. But sometimes Doña Maria felt like she had lived three lifetimes. She had been born in Santa Fe less than a decade after Mexico had gained its independence from Spain in 1821. Optimism over the new republic, where titled gentry and peasants were said to be equals, permeated adult discussions throughout her childhood. But traditions are hard to quell.

On the eve of her quinceañera, her fifteenth-birthday celebration where she, as do all but the poorest Hispano women, had her availability for marriage announced, her mother had declared with gusto, "Surely Maria's beauty will snag a man of noble birth and make life better for all of us."

But much to her parents' disappointment, she had eyes for no one but Roberto, the tailor's son, who was strong and handsome as a June day was long, but untitled. Worse, rumors had swirled that Roberto's family was converso, or converts from Judaism.

"You cannot be serious about this boy." Maria's mother had stomped her foot, as if to jar the thought out of the young woman's mind. "Forget him and find a man of title. One a bit older perhaps, but a man who can give you the kind of life you deserve."

And the life you think *you* deserve, Maria thought, resentment festering.

"Roberto is honorable and faithful. Why marry some old man with several mistresses just to have a title and servants, Mamá?" Her mother had looked shocked at the outburst, but Maria continued. "It's really not about my happiness. Not at all. You and Papá want the things such a man would give you for my hand. You want to be able to brag about your daughter marrying Don so-and-so."

Maria ran from the house, leaving her mother gaping at her.

Three months later, just before Christmas of 1845, she and Roberto were married by a kindly priest. He told them they should seek the approval of Maria's parents, but if it was not forthcoming, he saw no reason not to perform the wedding ceremony.

"You should never walk away from true love," he whispered conspiratorially.

Shortly after that, Roberto's father, who was as happy with the match as Maria's parents despaired of it, sent the couple north to Taos to set up a tailor shop. Roberto, indeed, proved to be a good man, and they lived contentedly.

Early the next summer, change was brewing again. This time, Mexico was at war with the Americans. U.S. General Stephen Kearny marched his 1,750 troops over 850 miles across the plains through Glorieta Pass and invaded the Mexican territory of New Mexico. In late August, the residents of Taos got the news that earlier that month General Kearny's troops had taken possession of Santa Fe.

New Mexico Governor Manuel Armijo attempted to rally New Mexicans to resist American invasion. He requested from Mexico, and was promised, troops to help the New Mexicans defend their territory; but the help never came. The untrained and poorly provisioned New Mexicans assembled at Apache Canyon August 14, 1846, but when Governor Armijo arrived two days later, he told the men not to fight and to return home. He and his people retreated to Chihuahua in Mexico. This allowed General Kearny to take Santa Fe without a battle.

The residents of Taos were all abuzz with the news of the takeover of Santa Fe by the Americans and speculation on how the changes would affect the Mexicans.

One day Roberto was fitting Señor Gonzalez for a new suit, while Maria showed another man suiting styles and fabrics.

"It's hard to believe Governor Armijo ran off to Mexico without putting up a fight," said Señor Gonzalez.

"I think he was scared to death and knew he couldn't win. Kearny had nearly two-thousand well-trained troops, and who knows how many more the Americans would have sent if Armijo had put up a fight," Maria's customer retorted.

It was a common discourse, but New Mexicans had little time to ponder what the change would mean for them. Charles Bent, a foreigner, was named governor of New Mexico.

"We didn't move to America, Roberto." Maria lamented the change of events. "The Americans moved their borders to include our land. I did not cease to be Mexican, but now I am living in another country!"

As fall set in, people grumbled about the Americans taking over their country, but Maria had learned that grumbling was a part of village life. Within a few months the shop had enough business for Roberto to hire two additional employees. This gave Maria more time to tend to her household duties, but she still enjoyed working in the tailor shop in the afternoons.

Roberto's success didn't surprise Maria. She wished her parents could see how he had prospered in such a short time. Roberto was good at business and a genius when it came to dealing with people.

"I thought of you, Don Garcia, when this bolt of fine Italian wool arrived in my shop, and I'm delighted you have decided to order some for your next suit." Other merchants used flattery to sell their wares, but Roberto was entirely honest. If a color or style didn't suit a customer, he refused to tell them otherwise. "While the charcoal grey is elegant, I think a younger man like you would look much better in a suit of dark blue," Roberto said to young Narciso Beaubien, son of a New Mexican businessman the American authorities had appointed Supreme Court justice.

Before Narciso headed back east to complete his final year of formal education, he told the tailor he must have the finest garment money could buy. "You see, my father is an important man. I must show that we are sophisticated and wealthy out here in New Mexico." Roberto nodded, selecting a set of gold buttons he imported from India through a seafaring merchant. Even the likes of Don Garcia had frowned when Roberto told them each button cost an American dollar, but Narciso simply shrugged. "Send the bill to the judge."

Maria could see in the young man's eyes, even if his words were stingy, that Narciso was pleased with his suit.

Before long, Narciso's father, Judge Charles Beaubien, came to Roberto. "My son tells me you make beautiful suits," the judge said in near perfect Spanish upon entering Roberto's shop, his wife on his arm. Maria knew that the judge had been born in Canada and ordained into the priesthood. French was his mother tongue.

The judge, with Roberto's guidance, selected a handsome piece of blue-and-grey Scottish herringbone wool. "I want something different, yet elegant. Not too flashy."

"The herringbone is just perfect for you," Roberto said. "I suggest these leather-covered buttons to complete it." He scooped up the buttons from one of his display cases, and dropped them with practiced showmanship, onto the luxurious fabric.

"Perfecto," purred his wife. Maria Paula Lobato, from a prominent Santa Fe family, had no doubt been accustomed to fine things before she married her husband. Some said it was a marriage of convenience to give Charles Beaubien Mexican citizenship, but the couple appeared devoted to one another.

The judge owned huge tracts of land north of Taos. Before the Americans took over, the Mexican government had granted him and his business partner, Señor Guadalupe Miranda, one of the tracts. A second piece of land, further north, in what they now called Colorado Territory, was owned by Narciso and another of Judge Beaubien's business partners, Stephen Luis Lee.

"Provisions of the grant require that the land north of Taos be settled within two years." The judge explained while Roberto measured his chest, waist and hips with his tape and wrote down the numbers. "It's beautiful land, but harsh."

Maria was surprised to hear the judge talk of the land grants to Roberto. Most men of his stature would find discussing business with a tailor unnecessary, even inappropriate.

The judge stepped back and looked directly at his tailor. "Don Roberto, you seem like an enterprising man. Have you ever thought of going north to stake claim on your own plot of land?"

Maria had been re-stocking bolts of fabric presented to earlier customers. She stopped, nearly dropping the half bolt she held. Roberto was indeed an enterprising man, one never to pass up a good opportunity, but he also was a calculating man. He would never rush into a new venture without learning all the risks associated with it and preparing for them. She hoped his good sense would prevail, as Judge Beaubien extolled the value of land ownership.

"I have thought about acquiring land. The thought of owning land is alluring." Roberto measured the judge's leg length. "But I worry about taking my wife into an area with no cities." He lowered his voice. "And I worry about Indian attacks."

The judge nodded, glancing at Maria, who was standing near the display cases where Señora Beaubien was looking at cuff links.

Maria didn't want the men to know how intently she was listening, so she moved to the other side of the display case. To the señora she said, "Is there anything I can show you?"

The señora whispered, "The cuff links with the small rubies, I adore them." She glanced in the direction of her husband. "It's his birthday next month. I will come back when he is not with me."

"I'll put them aside for you, Doña Beaubien." Maria pulled the cuff links out of the case and took them to the back room for safekeeping.

Chapter 7
Taos, New Mexico, January 1847

The mood in Taos continued to darken, as both Mexicans and Indians grumbled about the U.S. invasion of New Mexico. General Kearny imposed U.S. laws and leaders on the New Mexicans. Overnight, Mexicans technically became Americans, and few were happy about it.

"Didn't we dispense with having our leaders appointed by governments far away when Mexico earned its independence from Spain?" Maria complained to Roberto, using the word "dispense" that she had just learned in one of her new books. Like most young girls, she had attended the primary school at the parish church. She had not been content to end her formal learning there, yet her parents could not afford a finishing school and thought school beyond the primary level for a girl unnecessary. Roberto supported her further learning and joined her in personal book study when he was not busy at the tailor shop.

"They are competent men, Maria. We could do worse." Roberto was as optimistic about American rule as he was about most things. "You'll see, Maria, there is no point in protesting. Eventually, they will either rule well or decide it is too much trouble and leave."

"I hope you're right." But Maria was not convinced.

Unfortunately for Taos, Roberto was wrong. Very wrong.

ooooo

Early one morning, Maria was in the tailor shop, helping Roberto prepare for a busy day when the shop bell sounded and Señora Beaubien entered.

"My husband left town for work, and I came here as soon as I could get away." Her eyes looked as bright and anxious as a child promised a piece of candy. "Do you still have the ruby cuff links? The ones we talked about when he ordered his suit from Don Roberto?"

"Sí, Señora. Immediately after we spoke, I set them aside for you."

Señora Beaubien clapped her hands. "Oh, thank you!"

"Un momentito." Maria held up her right hand and tipped her head ever so slightly toward her esteemed customer before darting into the back room. She must show respect, but her deference was restrained. After all, she was a shopkeeper's wife, not a maid.

She parted the curtain that separated the front, public part of the store from the back where they cut and sewed suits. She found the cuff links in a handsome box exactly where she had left them. She glanced at her image in a mirror of polished brass and smoothed back a strand of recalcitrant hair. Her mother was wrong. Curly hair was not a blessing. One didn't know from one day to the next how it would decide to behave. Maria hastened back to help her customer at the glass display case. Willing her hands not to tremble, she opened the box and took the cuff links out, one at a time, placing them on the black cloth just the way Roberto taught her, so the rubies faced her customer.

"Oh, my." Señora Beaubien brought one hand to her chest, a slight gasp escaping her pretty, painted lips. "They are even more brilliant than I remembered."

"Shall I wrap them for you?" Maria caught Roberto's wink as she smiled at her customer. He was pleased with his wife's social and business skills.

Before Señora Beaubien could respond, an abrupt pop

sounded outside the window. Roberto headed to the front of the store to see what the trouble was, but before he got there, another, louder pop sounded. They watched in surprise as a rock the size of a melon bounced off the front window. A third rock pierced the glass. The window glass cracked and crumbled.

Maria's focus had been on the rocks, but with the window gone, she could see the mob of people moving down the street in front of the shop. Violence in this fashion was new to her. She knew she should do something, but she couldn't seem to move. Roberto, on the other hand, knew what to do. He pushed Maria and Señora Beaubien toward the back of the store. He guided them past the tables of cloth pieces and sewing supplies to the stairs that would take them to Maria and Roberto's living quarters.

"Mí amor," Roberto said to Maria, snapping her out of her disbelief. "As soon as I leave, lock the door and push the table and armoire against it." She nodded. "If you hear them below in the shop, crawl under the bed."

Roberto got down on his stomach and reached under the bed. Drawing out a handgun Maria had never seen him use, he headed to the door of their living quarters.

"Please be careful, mí amor." Maria felt hot, wet tears forming at the corners of her eyes as she watched her husband run out of the room.

Chapter 8

The mob that broke Maria and Roberto's shop window that morning had broken into Governor Charles Bent's Taos home and brutally murdered him and his brother-in-law. Angered by the American takeover of their land and fearing their property and way of life would soon be taken from them, a mob of Hispanos and Pueblo Indians had formed and careened out of control. Those targeted were mostly people put into power by General Kearny the previous August, but innocent people were killed and injured as well.

Roberto, revolver in hand, stood watch in the shop front for several days, leaving the shop only to check on Maria and Señora Beaubien and to eat the food Maria managed to prepare from what they had on hand, since they couldn't go to the market.

By the time the U.S. military troops traveled from Santa Fe to Taos, the resistance had moved to more remote areas of New Mexico. Calm was restored, but the fear and unrest remained. Maria and Roberto, without speaking a word, came to the same conclusion. They could not stay in Taos.

Roberto mailed a letter to his family in Santa Fe. He inquired about their welfare and told them about the recent violence in Taos. He asked if they thought he should sell the tailor shop and equipment or if it might be safe to hire a wagon to bring the equipment and their personal belongings back to Santa Fe.

When Roberto had no reply after three months, he sent a second letter, asking the same questions as the first. That summer he finally received a reply—a shocking one: "Don't return to Santa Fe."

Roberto's father wrote: "There is great unrest. Business is so poor that I am working as a waiter at a hotel. Continue in Taos if you can, or move north."

"Move north rather than return to Santa Fe?" Incredulous, Roberto read the words again.

Business slowed considerably, but Roberto and Maria still had a few customers. Most months they had enough to buy food and other necessities with their earnings but were unable to put coins into the savings box. At the same time, they never had to take money *from* the savings box, which had become fat their first year in Taos.

This meager existence with little hope of change made even cautious Roberto consider Judge Charles Beaubien's proposal.

The judge had remained a faithful customer. He truly liked Roberto's work, but Maria thought he ordered more suits than he needed, surely out of his gratitude to them for hiding his wife during the revolt. The judge's son had not been so fortunate. After his mother left to come to Roberto and Maria's shop, nineteen-year-old Narciso had learned of the brutal murders at the Bent house. He had run from the Beaubien home, desperately seeking a place to hide, but the mob found him under a freight wagon and beat him to death.

"It is hard enough to lose a son; what if I had lost my wife as well?" The judge expressed his gratitude on his first visit to the shop after the uprising. He never again mentioned Narciso. Maria didn't know whether this was because he hadn't been close to his son or because he couldn't bear to discuss it.

During a routine visit to the shop a few years later, under the guise of wanting to see what was new, Charles Beaubien made Roberto an offer he couldn't refuse.

"Don Roberto, I once mentioned my land grant to you and hoped you would be one of the enterprising young people to help me settle it, but at the time you were not interested."

Roberto started to reply, but the judge stopped him. "No need to apologize. It was a lot to ask a young man to leave everything he knew to take his family to a new land far from home." He gestured toward a set of chairs at the back of the shop. "Shall we sit? I have a proposition for you."

When the men moved away from the front of the shop, it was difficult for Maria to hear their conversation. She felt she had to know what the judge was suggesting, so she found the feather duster and began to dust the shelves, inching her way to where the men sat. She hoped Roberto wouldn't notice her dusting or, if he did, he wouldn't remember that she had thoroughly dusted the shelves earlier that day.

"I need a man I can count on to bring good business sense to the settlers of my land grant up north." He shifted in his seat, his eyes wide and steadfast. "Don Roberto, I believe you are that man. If you agree to settle with the farmers, I will give you a rancho. It will not be the small plot of land just outside the village square that the other settlers will get. A man of your talent needs a proper rancho.

"A rancho." Roberto's mouth seemed the size of Maria's tortillas. "But I'm not a farmer or a rancher."

"No matter, no matter." Don Beaubien smiled. "I know this. It will be a large rancho. You can hire vaqueros to do the work. And you will handle the business end of things."

Roberto leaned back in his chair, his lips pursed in thought. His practical side had regained control. "How much land, señor?"

"My men tell me there is a plot of land at the base of the Sangre de Cristo Mountains that is part timber and part open grazing. Water is plentiful; various springs run through the property. The rancho overlooks the valley but is not more than an hour's ride from where the settlers plan to build the plaza."

"Your men? Are you saying you will settle there without ever visiting?"

"My family and I will keep our home here."

"Let me discuss this generous proposition with my wife."
Roberto stood.

Maria didn't know what compelled her to not only reveal that
she had been eavesdropping but to consent to such a proposal
without contemplation. She entered the small room at the back
of the shop and declared, "Roberto, I think we should go."

Later she realized it was her desire to prove her mother wrong
that propelled her compulsiveness. Maria still felt the need to
demonstrate to her family that Roberto was a good husband and
a successful businessman. Maria and Roberto were what people
called 'comfortable,' but if they agreed to participate in the land
grant, they could become wealthy, even titled. Even though she
had been trying to escape society's obsession with class designa-
tion and titles, now she was hoping for that very thing!

"Well, I guess we will accept your proposal, Don Beaubien."
Roberto extended his hand to the judge, and they shook in the
confident, deal-confirming way of Taos businessmen.

ooooo

That was nearly four decades ago. Maria still wasn't sure if it
was a fortuitous or foolish decision. Charles Beaubien was true
to his word. The property was as he described it, and they made
a good profit on the rancho. But Mother Nature hadn't always
been kind, and an even worse peril—the vile, jealous hearts of
men—had taken their toll on the land and on her family.

Misfortune was not something she wanted to think about on
this late spring day, though. Instead, she let her eyes take in the
grazing cattle and the remnant of the horse herd Roberto and her
sons had developed. Just a few years ago, ranchers from throughout the San Luis Valley and beyond had come to buy Roberto's
horses.

How ironic that the prized horses, or one of them, had
changed everything for the Córdova family. On a sunny afternoon nearly three years earlier, Roberto rode a young stallion to a
remote part of the ranch to check on the yearlings. No one knew

what happened—only that the young stallion returned with no rider, and Mauricio found his father dead on the ground.

"There is not a thing we could have done," Mauricio told his mamá. "The stallion probably spooked or bucked, and Pa may have fallen and hit his head on a rock. The only solace we have is that it took him in an instant, and he is in Heaven."

After that, most of the breeding stock, even many of the fine stallions and mares, had to be sold to keep the ranch afloat. She would have to sell the two- and three-year-old horses soon. Selling horses and cattle was the only way she would be able to buy staples for the ranch and hire vaqueros to do the ranch work. She never knew much about ranch work and neither did Roberto. Her sons had loved ranch life, but they had left to seek their own fortunes. If she could find someone to break the young horses, it would double what they would bring, but it was not easy to find someone dependable and skilled.

Maria was delighted with the beauty of the ranch, and the animals it nurtured, but her eyes fell on her greatest delight. To the north of the house in the corral, Maria's grandson pretended to rope cattle and drag them to the fire for branding. Before he left to seek profitable work elsewhere, the boy's father had taught him to rope. Tomás had spent hours watching his father and the vaqueros work cattle from horseback. He handled the rope with finesse, at least for a six-year-old. The boots and chaps Maria's son bought Tomás before he left were wearing out, she noticed.

Gracious heavenly Father, she prayed silently, *what will I do to feed and clothe Tomás and me? I can't sell the ranch. It's all I have to give Tomás some day, and it's the only way I know to make a living in this beautiful but unforgiving land.*

Before her thoughts brought her to despair, they were interrupted by a cloud of dust to the east. A few minutes later, a lone rider came into view. He was making his way up the road toward her house. He looked like a vaquero. Maybe Señor Cohen had sent her a vaquero looking for ranch work. *What is it the Bible says? God answers before we ask?*

Maria's heart sank when she realized the vaquero was nothing more than a girl dressed in men's clothes. She rode well, and she rode astride. Women in the valley riding side saddle with both legs on one side of the horse. But straddling the horse was more natural and allowed the rider greater control. The girl, a young woman, really, looked to be in her early twenties. She wore her dark hair in a single braid down her back. She wore men's trousers. No wonder Maria had mistaken her for a vaquero.

Maria's emotions that morning had fluctuated with the same extremes and abruptness as the weather in the San Luis Valley. Trying not to let her disappointment show, she sang out a greeting to her morning visitor. "Buenos días, Señorita."

The rider removed her hat and work gloves. "Buenos días, Señora." She had prominent cheekbones and smooth skin the color of tanned deer hides. "Me llamo Carolina." She was tall and carried herself with confidence. The visitor was the sort of woman that would turn heads on any street, but there was something else about her, a toughness that belied her pleasant smile.

"Señor Cohen told me you needed someone to train your horses. I should have waited for an introduction. But I need work."

"And lodging?" Maria motioned with her lips to the substantial packs behind the young woman's saddle.

The young woman's expression became one of a child caught stealing an empanada. "Sí, Señora. I don't need much. I can stay in your bunkhouse. It's empty, no?" She brightened.

"Yes, unfortunately, it's empty. Dependable, hard-working vaqueros are hard to find these days with so much work in the mines and up north toward Pueblo and Denver." Maria sighed, gesturing toward the south pasture where horses grazed. "I've not known a girl who can train a horse. You think you're up to it?"

"Oh, yes, Señora." She pointed to her mount. "This one here, she was one of the first I trained by myself. Azúcar is a great horse; she'll do anything I ask of her." She looked straight at Maria. "My training methods are a lot different from the vaqueros, but in the end, you'll have a better trained, more dependable mount than letting them buck you crazy-like."

"I guess it won't hurt to give you a try."

"You won't be disappointed, Señora." Her eyes sparkled with excitement. Maria doubted her enthusiasm would remain when the first young horse pummeled her into the dust.

"You can put your horse in the corral over there." Maria pointed. Then she beckoned Tomás to come to the porch. "My grandson Tomás will show you the barn where you can store your tack. I can't have a young lady sleeping in that unkempt bunkhouse. We've got plenty of rooms in the ranch house. When you've settled your horse, come in and we'll have some lunch."

"I'm much obliged, Señora, but I'd like to get started training your horses. I'll work until dark and then eat." She chuckled. "Unbroken horses are much friendlier when it's hot."

Maria nodded.

Carolina marched back to her horse and unloaded her gear onto the front porch before mounting the mare and heading back down the road to the pasture gate.

"I don't know whether that young lady is crazy or highly enterprising," Maria muttered as she walked inside to prepare lunch.

Chapter 9

Caroline wasn't sure what to think. On one hand, the property looked to be a fine ranch where she'd expect to find well-bred horses and fine cattle. On the other hand, the ranch looked run down. She couldn't quite see Doña Maria or her young grandson having the acumen to breed good horses. She chided herself for making this judgment based on appearances. *Don't I hate it when people do that to me?* Yet, here she was making similar assumptions of someone else.

When she got close to the herd, she could see the fine breeding of the horses. They were well muscled, balanced ranch horses with a good eye and intelligent heads. They looked sure-footed and sturdy boned, not the tiny-hooved, high stepping carriage and parade horses favored by the Hispano gentry. In addition, the horses were as beautiful as they were practical.

Caroline had opened the necessary gates on her way to the pasture. She thought the herd would be less likely to become riled up if she kept the horses together and slowly pushed them toward the corrals near the house. She was pleased to see the set up: a large pen where she would keep the horses as a group, and a smaller pen to work each young horse by itself.

She reveled in the freedom of working in the open country and seeing horse manes flying as they loped in the direction she pushed them. Once she had the herd in the large corral, she succeeded in pushing one stallion—a three year old, she guessed—into the adjacent small pen. She was prepared to rope and drag the horse; but when he saw the opening, his curiosity pushed him to explore the side pen. He was a magnificent buckskin with a golden-tan body and long, flowing black mane and tail. And he was smart. She could tell he was thinking about his options, evaluating her as she pushed him away from her repeatedly. Eventually he followed her when she turned her back on him.

Thus she won his trust and was soon rubbing and walking around the horse. Within a half hour, Caroline raised the blanket and set it on the buckskin's back. She did the same with the saddle. When she tightened the girth, he lunged forward and began a loping buck around the small pen.

"Easy, Boy," she cooed. Now accustomed to looking to her for reassurance, he stopped and turned to face her. She repeated the familiar rubbing and talking, and the horse breathed deeply and dropped its head.

"That's it, Pretty Boy." Ten minutes later, she sent the stallion back onto the outside of the small pen, clucking at him to trot. When she made a kissing sound, he already understood she wanted him to lope. The buckskin jumped forward but settled back into an easy, rocking-chair lope.

It was time to mount. She might normally have waited another day, but she wanted to show her new employer that she had made progress. As was often the case when a horse was mounted for the first time, it acted paralyzed, as though it had its feet stuck in quicksand. Caroline took the time to pull first one rein, then the other toward her knee to ensure the stallion would turn when asked. She knew it was sometimes easier for a young horse to move to the side, rather than straight ahead when first asked, so she pulled the right rein slightly and clucked for him to move forward. He did and soon gained enough confidence to walk along the outside fence. Caroline had been so focused on the buckskin's training that she hadn't notice the sun sinking behind the mountains.

"You can turn the horses out into the small pasture." Tomás had been watching her. He swung his rope impressively. "There's some grass there and plenty of water. The stream is running strong now." He looked at her square, like the true cowboy he was. "If you turn them back into the big pasture, they might not want to come back tomorrow."

"You, Tomás, are very observant." Her smile was returned. "And you are very smart. Gracías."

Tomás helped her get the horses into the small pasture.

"Abuela said to tell you it's time to eat."

"You know, I just now realized how very hungry I am."

"Me, too." He smiled, and his face seemed oddly familiar, but she was sure she had never seen him in San Luis. "Abuela makes the best posole. Venga." He reached his hand toward her. She grasped it like a drowning woman holds a rope thrown from shore. Immediately, she lightened her grip. She didn't want a boy, even this bright and capable boy, to know how desperate she was to have a place to stay, to belong, even if only for a few weeks. She was tired. The running and the lying were weighing her down. Her soul felt like those hardy burros the people of the valley used for carrying their burdens. Yet she saw no way to unwind those lies.

Tomás was right. His grandmother made the best posole she had ever tasted. The lamb broth had bits of meat, onion, chiles, garlic and tender, yet crunchy, kernels of sweet corn. Doña Maria set tortillas warm from the stove top before Caroline, and a pica- dillo or chopped tomato salad, perfectly seasoned with cilantro, salt, and vinegar.

Caroline let the flavors tantalize the back of her tongue before she swallowed. "¡Qué rico!" she exclaimed.

"Gracias." Doña Maria smiled. "Eat more. You need energy to work with horses."

When Caroline finished, Doña Maria invited her to the front porch. "Siéntese," she said, pointing to the well-crafted pair of rocking chairs facing the ranch's entrance, where she was sitting when Caroline rode up to the ranch house early that morning.

"I hope you like coffee, Carolina." The woman handed her a steaming mug of coffee, lightened with cream, and kept the second one for herself. "We must get to know one another."

"I like coffee very much." The bitter, dark liquid was smooth and strong. Caroline wondered where the woman, this far from San Luis, had secured fresh milk. "Do you have a goat?"

"I do, though the goat will not kid for a month or more. But we *do* have a cow, a Jersey cow." A sadness seemed to pass over Doña Maria's sparkling eyes. "With proper care, a cow will give milk all but the month before she calves. A nanny goat gives milk for five or six months a year. Tomás's mother left when he was very young. We … I needed milk to keep him strong and growing well, so I bought the cow from a farmer north of San Luis."

'Left'? Was that a euphemism Caroline hadn't heard before? When the grandmother offered no further explanation, curiosity got the better of Caroline. "Did his mother die?"

"No. She left."

What mother would just leave her child? Especially a child as bright and loving as Tomás? And what woman would not wish to live in this beautiful place? Caroline wanted to know more, but it would be rude to ask. And no further explanation was offered.

"What do you think of our horses?" The gaiety had returned to Doña Maria's eyes. "I was surprised to see you doing so well with the buckskin stallion."

"They are fine horses. Well built and smart. Your family must know horses." Caroline sensed Doña Maria did not possess the same love for horses as she had; but obviously, to the older woman horses were a source of income and pride. "They will be worth double the price when I have trained them. Maybe more if we can sell them to a rancher who appreciates the way I train them."

"God sent me an angel today, Carolina." She rose from the chair, empty mug in hand. "Come; my angel needs her sleep."

Doña Maria lit a lantern from the fire in her kitchen oven and then motioned for Caroline to follow her. They passed through the living and dining areas to the side of the large adobe house with a series of sleeping rooms.

"This will be your room." She removed the glass top from the lantern she carried and lit another lantern on a small table. "I will have Tomás bring you water in the morning." Before pulling the door closed, she bid her "buenas noches."

Caroline was surprised at the spacious house and very adequate, though certainly not ostentatious, decor. Like the front porch rocking chairs, the table and bed were fashioned by someone with talent. The furniture was stained and smooth, showcasing the beautiful wood grain. She slipped out of her work clothes and into her nightdress. Later, she didn't even remember pulling the heavy wool blankets over her body before falling asleep.

The following morning, she awakened with a start when she heard a gentle rap at the door. "I have warm water for you." It was Tomás.

"Coming." Caroline sprang out of bed and pulled the door open. She noticed how light and smooth it swung on its leather hinges. Just like the furniture, the door reflected the work of a true craftsman.

She moved to take the bucket of water from Tomás, but he rebuffed her. "I can do it." It was not a defensive declaration, only a statement. He poured the water into the basin on the table. "There, now you can wash up before breakfast."

She reveled in the warm water and the privacy. She had slept better than she had in a very long time. *Could be the bed, the security, or even the wool blankets*, she told herself. But she knew the real reason was that she had not lied one time to Doña Maria or Tomás. She had even told her employer that her name was Caroline, though Doña Maria, who was not an English speaker, had used the Spanish version, Carolina.

Chapter 10

Six days later, Caroline had started training three more young horses, while continuing to work with the buckskin. At this rate, in a month and a half she would have the fifteen two- and three-year-old horses well started and suitable for vaqueros to use in ranch work. She pushed back the question of what she would do then.

She offered to help milk the cow in the morning, but Doña Maria refused. "This chore I can do. Breaking horses I cannot do."

Caroline was amazed by Doña Maria's resourcefulness. Even Ma, who knew so much about growing and preserving food, would have appreciated Doña Maria's early spring garden. On the south side of the adobe house, where the cooking oven was vented, was the small garden. The side of the house and the ground around the garden was lined with black rocks and ceramic tiles, designed to absorb heat from the daytime sun. The vegetables—tomatoes, peppers, onions, and herbs—were planted in a deep trench where the sun and moisture nurtured them, yet the plants had less exposure to the freezing temperatures. At night and when the days were not warm, the vegetables remained covered with a somewhat transparent but insulating animal skin. *Ingenious*, thought Caroline. *Fresh vegetables in April!*

Coffee on the front porch after the evening meal had become a ritual for Caroline and Doña Maria. Perhaps it had been Doña Maria's ritual, and Caroline joined it. During evening coffee, Doña Maria told her that the ranch had been granted to her husband by Sangre de Cristo land grant owner Carlos Beaubien. She said her husband was a good businessman who worked well with people but knew little about agriculture. Her older son had the same tendencies as her husband, but her younger son loved the ranch and enjoyed breeding and raising animals. In addition to horses, they had cattle and sheep. Caroline was less familiar with sheep, but she enjoyed watching them graze in the pastures alongside the horses and cattle. She marveled at how Doña Maria's call to them would bring them running back to the sheep pen behind the house at nightfall.

The abundant coyote and wolf populations were of little threat to the horses or cattle, but sheep were much smaller and unable to defend themselves from predators, so Doña Maria made sure they were locked in the pen each night. The wool was an asset to the ranch, but Doña Maria told her it wasn't always easy to find dependable men to shear the sheep.

One Saturday night the women found themselves on the porch after their evening meal, chatting about food and the personalities of San Luis residents they both knew. They were in no rush to turn in for the night because the people of the valley, like those in the Bijou Basin where she grew up, rested on the Sabbath, on Sunday.

Without notice, the sadness was back in Doña Maria's eyes. "How could a woman leave her home? Her husband? Her child?" When she said 'child,' her voice dropped to a whisper and Caroline could see the moisture gather at the corners of her big, expressive eyes.

"Are you talking about Tomás's mother?" Caroline patted her shoulder.

Doña Maria nodded, pain choking her ability to speak. "He is starting to ask questions, and I don't know how to answer them."

"Why not tell him the truth?" Caroline blurted out before considering the hypocrisy of her suggestion.

"'You shall know the truth, and the truth shall set you free.' Those are the words of our Savior, but I don't know if a boy so young can handle such an awful truth."

Caroline thought God must have been having a good laugh at the irony of her giving advice on truth telling. "What can be so bad that you can't tell him the truth? He's a strong, bright and loving boy."

"Because the truth is his mother chose social status and comfort over him." Doña Maria covered her mouth to choke back a cry. When she regained her composure, the story of Tomás and his mother's abandonment spilled out like the rush of the Culebra River in early summer when the snow melt rushes off the mountain peaks.

"When we first arrived in the valley, I was pregnant with our older son, Roberto, Jr. We struggled the first few years, but soon the ranch was prosperous. We had twenty vaqueros working for us. I even had a housemaid. Imagine that! Me, a simple, poor girl with her own maid!" She smiled and smoothed her skirt.

She continued. "Because of the help we had, we became accustomed to traveling to Santa Fe every summer. We would visit friends and family and shop for things we needed or wanted but couldn't buy in the valley. By the time Mario, our younger son, was born nearly ten years later, our herds had grown and we were wealthy. We attended concerts and theater performances and were invited to many of the high society events on our annual visits to Santa Fe. The year Roberto, Jr. turned twenty-three he met a young lady at a society ball and fell in love. She agreed to marry him only if he would stay in Santa Fe. We were sad to know that he would settle so far from us, but we could see that they were in love and felt the match was a strong one. And my older son had never been a rancher at heart. Roberto, Jr. is a buyer and seller of goods. He has three shops in and around Santa Fe, and is very successful."

She sighed as though finished with her tale, but when Caroline moved forward in her chair to stand, Doña Maria raised her hands in front of her, palms open. "I'm afraid Mario was not so fortunate in love. He also met a young woman during a summer visit a decade later. Teresa was from a good family, although not the high society type of Roberto, Jr.'s wife. Teresa was—still is—a beauty ... and a flirt. She swooned over young society men, and when they confessed their love for her, she dismissed them with disdain."

Doña Maria raised her cup to her lips and sipped the now lukewarm liquid. "I am sad to say that Mario joined the young men who stood in line to be swept into her cruel game. She would bat her eyes at him and invite him to a picnic or a concert. When he showed up, she acted like she barely knew him. Over time, most of the young men first smitten with Teresa tired of her games and moved on to court other young ladies. Mario, however, was devoted. His father and I never understood why he didn't come to despise her for the hurt she caused. He had always been the practical one. She was his first love, and I guess he just couldn't pull away from her. The ranks of young men pursuing her thinned, and soon Mario was her best prospect." Doña Maria's voice was thick with disdain. She circled the top of her now empty cup with her finger.

"Teresa was out to marry as best she could, whether that was money or position, it didn't matter." Her face hardened. "She didn't love Mario. She didn't even care about him."

This time Doña Maria allowed Caroline to take her mug and refill it inside. When she returned with mugs full of steaming coffee and sat down across from the old woman, Doña Maria continued her sad story. "When we returned to the valley from Santa Fe that summer, Mario told us he wanted to ask Teresa to marry him. Seeing his determination, we were reluctant but gave him our blessing. He asked us to immediately write Teresa's father to ask permission to marry her."

Doña Maria shook her head, eyes downcast. "Once her father granted him permission, Mario wrote a long letter to Teresa, confessing his undying love for her. He asked her to marry him the following summer. I know this because I saw the letter on the table in his room. It looked like he had written and re-written it many times."

She gazed straight into Caroline's eyes. "Months later, Mario received her reply. She would marry him if he agreed to live with her in Santa Fe. She also asked for many matrimonial gifts. He agreed to the gifts, but he put his foot down about where they would live. He was a rancher, and they would live in the San Luis Valley, he wrote. It was May and nearing time for our annual trip to Santa Fe when Mario received her response. I found her letter, wadded up on the floor beneath his table." She choked back tears. "It was short but so spiteful that I remember every word."

Dearest Mario,

Although I despise the idea of being a rancher's wife, you are really the only suitor of considerable means. Therefore, I will accept your offer. I must take a month to shop for the things I need to have in the God-forsaken north where your ranch is located. Please do not come for me before July.

Yours truly,
Teresa

Doña Maria straightened in her chair. "I told my husband about the letter. We were jubilant. Mario would be shocked into realizing his mistake in thinking Teresa loved him. Surely, the wedding was off. Mario said nothing of the letter. We left for Santa Fe the first of July, Mario called on Teresa, and they were married within the week."

"Did Teresa return from Santa Fe with Mario?" Caroline was engrossed in the sad story.

"Yes, she did. As difficult as she had been from a distance, she was yet more incorrigible when she lived under my roof. She complained day and night and refused to do any work at all. Within months she was pregnant. I really hoped this would set her mind on important things and coax her into being thankful for her many blessings. I didn't think it was possible for her to be any more rude or insolent, but I was wrong." Doña Maria stood and walked to the porch railing, gazing toward the horizon.

"What happened? Did Mario get fed up and send her back to Santa Fe?" To Caroline, the story was better than a three-act play she had seen in Denver one spring when her parents traveled to the booming city to sell cattle and grain and to stock up on supplies.

"No, even still he did not," the old woman sighed and returned to her chair, collapsing into it like a bag of wheat.

"Aren't you going to tell me what happened?" Caroline felt like a child sent to bed early.

The great sadness returned to Doña Maria's eyes. "There is much more to tell, but it is getting late. Another time."

Caroline went to her bedroom, thinking. *Why did Doña Maria cut short her story? It must have to do with that sadness that comes over her. Maybe she can bear only so much pain at one time.*

Chapter 11

Before morning light, Caroline woke with a start. Someone was knocking with force at the door. She swung her feet onto the floor and ran to open it.

Doña Maria stood there, dressed, still in her boots. "Please, I need your help with a ewe. Come to the barn." She turned and was gone before Caroline could respond.

Pulling on breeches and shirt over her sleeping gown, Caroline hurried to the back door, grabbed her boots, and headed to the barn, thankful for the full moon lighting her path. The heavy barn door had been pushed back just wide enough to enter.

She found the older woman squatted behind a ewe. A lantern was perched on the feed bunk in the small pen. "Carolina, get in front of the ewe and hold on to her while I try to pull out her lamb."

Caroline did as she was told.

Doña Maria pushed her right hand into the womb.

The ewe moaned and lunged forward with surprising strength. If not for the sturdy feed bunk behind Caroline, the ewe would have pushed her over backward.

"There now, that's the problem." She spoke more to herself than to Caroline. "The lamb is breech. And I think there's a second one behind it waiting to be born."

The ewe moaned and pushed forward again as Doña Maria

pulled the breech lamb out, back legs first. "Grab me a piece of burlap behind you," she instructed Caroline, as she used her fingers to clear the lamb's mouth and nose of afterbirth. "There you go," she reassured the lamb. "Now breathe." She stretched her hand toward the piece of burlap that Caroline handed her and rubbed the lamb with vigor. "Pull the ewe's head around here so she can see the little one," she implored with urgent voice.

Caroline did her best to push the ewe toward the newborn. The lamb heeded Doña Maria's urging and let out a weak bleat, spurring its mother into action. The ewe spun around and rushed to the lamb, licking its face, mouth, and body, while she bleated encouragement.

"There you go, baby. I think you're going to make it." Doña Maria wiped sweat from her forehead, as she let the ewe take over cleaning duties.

Caroline had seen calves born and even a few foals. Horses give birth quickly, making it rare to witness the birth of a foal. But the wonder of a new birth never ceased to amaze her. "How did you know the lamb was breech?"

"I saw mucus and other signs of birth before suppertime. When the ewe hadn't given birth by my before-bedtime check, I suspected she had either a dead lamb or breech one." She grabbed another piece of burlap to clean the blood and afterbirth off her hands and right arm. When I first checked her, before I came in to get you, I was afraid the lamb was head back. That is the most difficult position to deliver, and it is helpful to have someone hold the ewe."

"What do you do when no one is here to help you?"

"I tie up the ewe, but it is not ideal."

"I'm very impressed. You know so much about delivering lambs." Caroline smiled in wonder. "I would have thought that was your husband's job."

"The sheep were his idea, and he was very diligent caring for them, but we learned from other ranchers and with our own experience, that with sheep and goats both, a smaller hand is less damaging to a ewe's uterus and better able to maneuver inside it."

The ewe quit licking her newborn and pawed the ground in front of her. "Oh, look, she's ready to give birth to number two."

The ewe lay down and pushed, extending her neck and pursing her lips. After half a dozen pushes, she got to her feet and resumed licking the first lamb. She repeated the cycle twice.

"Looks like she needs help with number two." Doña Maria brought a bucket of water into the sheep pen to wash her hands and arms. "I see the lamb's head but no feet. Lambs shouldn't be born like this." She bent at the waist, put both of her arms next to her head, extending them together and forward. "This delivery could be a bit trickier."

Tricky or not, Doña Maria deftly pushed the soon-to-be-born lamb back into the womb with her left hand, while she fished for the front legs with her right hand. She popped out one leg with tiny hooves and then a second. She pulled firmly on the hooves, holding both in her right hand, while guiding the face of the lamb through the final phase of the birth canal. She again cleared the airway of the newborn and let the ewe take over from there.

"I think they'll both be fine." She fetched a second bucket of clean water for the ewe. When she returned, the first lamb had pushed itself up and was trying to maneuver on its wobbly legs. "I'll check them first thing in the morning to make sure they are eating. We'll dock their tails tomorrow."

"Why do you have to dock sheep tails? Doesn't that hurt?"

"Long tails get manure and urine on them and attract flies and eventually maggots." Doña Maria sighed. "And, if we do it when they are young, the pain is less and short-lived."

Caroline nodded. She wanted to stay up and watch the ewe mother her newborns, but she felt a yawn coming on. The two women walked back to the house in silence.

Chapter 12
Sanchez Estate, Summer 1886

The western horizon was swathed with crimson, deep rust, and brilliant golds as the sun sank below the Sangre de Cristo Mountains. Mauricio watched the mounted vaquero rope and drag the last calf to the fire. He heard the sizzle of burning hair and flesh from the iron applied by another vaquero. He winced at the calf's pitiful bawl, even though he had heard hundreds of calves bawl when the iron touched them. He reminded himself that the pain was short lived and would render no long-term discomfort. It was the way of the vaquero.

The vaquero wielding the S-shaped iron removed it and used a second iron to burn a long, straight line directly below the S iron. The Anglos called the brand S Bar. It was a good brand, easy to read and difficult to manipulate, as cattle rustlers were known to do. Clever rustlers had changed Ps to Bs and Ls to Us by re-branding cattle, adding a line or a curve. In an instant, the rancher's investment belonged to another.

Mauricio had chosen the Sanchez brand to minimize the rustler's scheming and had also taken care to register it with state authorities in Costilla County. Most Hispanos didn't bother, but Mauricio could read the handwriting on the wall. Like it or not, they were no longer Mexicans. They would have to live by the laws of the United States, and those who understood the laws would be less likely to be cheated. This was not something his father had taught him. Mauricio's father would have said that everyone knew the brand was the Sanchez's and that was good enough. Maybe in the old days; but with so many people streaming into the valley, either for short-term work or to settle, Mauricio preferred safe over sorry.

The calf jumped up from its short bout of trauma and bawled in complaint, seeking the comfort of its mama. It was a scrawny bull calf. Some of the calves were larger and beefier, but most were pounds lighter than they could have been if only Carlos Sanchez had agreed to let Mauricio invest in more of the Hereford bulls that the Anglos brought into the valley several years earlier. The Spanish Longhorns were good, hardy animals, but Mauricio had seen the larger calves produced by neighboring ranches crossing Longhorn cows with the new breed of bulls.

Mauricio rode his horse the short distance back to the ranch yard, where he swung his long, sturdy body out of the saddle and onto the ground. Large hands, golden brown from work and summer sun, loosened leather ties on the paint's breast collar and removed the leather latigo that secured the saddle. One powerful arm under the saddle, the other clutching the saddle blanket and bridle, he moved into the small tack shed. He laid his saddle on the stand with the bridle and reins wrapped around the saddle horn. The wet blanket was turned upside down to dry on a nearby rack.

Mauricio brushed the paint, oblivious to his fellow vaqueros, who joked and talked as they unsaddled their horses. He was accustomed to the long summer days and working from dawn to dusk, but tonight he felt a new weariness.

During this time of year each day stretched longer than the one before it, a good thing as ranch work went. In past years, he was grateful for the longer days. The warmth of summer lifted spirits, and the daylight let the vaqueros finish the branding, sorting, and moving of cattle that was inherent to a successful operation. When that was done, there was fence to mend and grain to sow. Señora Sanchez even had the vaqueros working in her garden, a task any other Hispano woman would have done herself or at least delegated to household servants.

This year was different for Mauricio. Each day reminded him that Carolina was gone, and he would never see her again.

"Vengan, vamos a comer," the cook called. Dinner was served.

Mauricio trudged toward the outdoor kitchen, barely noticing the aroma of beef and summer vegetables on the open grill.

"Do you want beans and rice?" The kitchen maid who assisted the cook had her big spoon full of cilantro-and-garlic seasoned beans as she waited for Mauricio to move his plate closer. He did so, grateful she couldn't read his thoughts about Carolina. "Más?" She offered a second spoonful and blushed when he smiled at her.

"Don't pay him any mind, Señorita. The boss hasn't really been himself for months." Rolando, a stocky vaquero whose home was San Pedro, tapped his index finger on his temple. "Now I, on the other hand, will *never* ignore you." His smile showed a chipped front tooth, a battle scar from a frisky horse.

Rolando is right. I'm not the same since Carolina left, thought Mauricio. At first, he had cheered her for marching out, head high, when Señora Sanchez threw a fit. Carolina was not the high-born lady she thought she had secured for her son Carlos. Mauricio knew Carolina's newly discovered parentage would become a social liability for the Sanchezes, but he supposed Carolina's biggest fault was her refusal to be controlled.

Mauricio looked at his now-empty plate. He hadn't tasted a thing.

"Kinda deep in thought, Boss, especially for this late in the day." Rolando looked at Mauricio while sneaking glances at the pretty serving woman. "You still pining away for that woman?"

How could Rolando have known? Carolina was Carlos's wife the whole time this vaquero had worked at the Sanchez Ranch. Mauricio hadn't even known himself that he loved her until she was gone.

Rolando, seeing his confusion, repeated, "That woman. You

know, the one that up and left you?" He put his coffee cup down and leaned over the table toward Mauricio.

"No, no, that's not it," Mauricio stammered, trying to convince himself that he had kept his feelings for the feisty horse trainer to himself. He rose and hurried to the privacy of his bunkhouse room. The vaqueros shared the larger room, but as the boss, he had his own. He lit the oil lamp and pulled out the books. He was behind at least a month on the ledger. His mother had hired tutors to teach him English and French, but his real love was figures. He remembered numbers, like how many cattle were purchased in what years and what the calves netted when sold. He knew how to add, subtract, multiply and divide using paper, but he could calculate most things in his head. He took pleasure in keeping neat and calculated columns. But tonight his mind strayed elsewhere.

He thought about the day two and a half years ago when he had gone to fetch the trained horses and Carolina. She had met him at the end of the lane leading up to Señor Martínez's ranch. She still dressed as a vaquero and glanced over her shoulder as she greeted him.

"Are you going to take me with you?" Rich brown eyes sought his. "I was afraid you…" She glanced back again. "Might change your mind."

"No. I would never do that." How had he ever mistaken her for a boy? "Come, choose a dress." He gestured at the back of the wagon toward the trunk that he had conspired with Señora Sanchez's seamstress to have filled with new dresses. He had purchased cloth, buttons, thread and other items, as well as gloves, hats and boots at the mercantile. He had shopped with his mother many times, so he knew what amounts of fabrics and which notions one purchased to make a lady's garment. When the seamstress had asked what size to make the dresses, he had pointed out one of the young women working in the Sanchez home. "That size, but taller."

Carolina opened the trunk and sucked in her breath. "They're beautiful." Her hand covered her mouth a moment. Then she said, "I can't believe you did this for me. I hardly know you."

"Tell me if there is anything else you need, and I will get it for you when I can." Mauricio headed up the lane, then turned toward her. "The vaqueros will be here soon to drive the horses home, so find a place to dress and wait in the wagon while I pay for the horses."

That afternoon when they pulled into the Sanchez Estate, Carolina had transformed from reclusive vaquero to charming señorita.

Señora Sanchez had agreed to hire a teacher only after Mauricio told her it would be easier to hire and keep vaqueros if their children could attend school. When she met Carolina, she pranced about like she was entertaining the queen of Spain.

"I am delighted Mauricio was able to secure a teacher for our children." She lowered her voice, but Mauricio heard her whisper. "They are a lower class of people, you know."

Mauricio soon learned that Carolina was a very capable and creative teacher. She never made a student feel inadequate, and she made learning fun for the children, many of whom had never attended school before. When Mauricio went to look for additional vaqueros, his claim that having an onsite teacher as an incentive, proved correct.

The day Carlos started attending Carolina's classes Mauricio had a gnawing feeling that something wasn't as it seemed. But he supposed he should be happy that the young heir took interest in the children's schooling. When, a few months later, Mauricio saw Carolina and Carlos walking by the creek, talking and laughing, he had to control an urge to pummel the man with his fists. He hated the picture of the strutting, slothful boy child making inroads with Carolina.

The experience was revealing. He had thought his feeling for Carolina was brotherly concern. But he knew better now.

Either way, he couldn't help worrying about her. Once married, she continued to greet him and the other vaqueros warmly.

Carlos and Señora Sanchez forbade her from continuing to teach, despite having little to do. They also frowned on her training horses.

"Do you want to get hurt? I can hardly even abide you riding that mare, Azúcar." Carlos had stomped his foot, his lower lip thrust forward in a pout. When he spotted Mauricio at the back of the barn, he half smiled, crossing his arms in front of him at his waist. "Don't you agree, Señor Córdova? Riding horses, especially these unrefined ranch horses, is far too dangerous for a woman of my wife's standing."

Before Mauricio could answer—and how could he answer without revealing Carolina's secret—Carlos stormed out of the barn.

"I think I made a terrible mistake." Carolina covered her face with her hands. "I was so flattered that a gentleman would take interest in me."

"Every couple has disagreements," Mauricio said, patting her shoulder.

"It's not the disagreement. It's who he is in here." She tapped her chest with her open hand. "The disagreement is only a reflection of his selfishness. He doesn't love me. He can't love me. He's a child in a man's body." She gulped down a sob. "He needed a woman to play the part of 'wife.' That's all I am; someone playing a part to satisfy the whims of a boy trying to look like a man."

Mauricio didn't disagree. But there was nothing he could say.

Chapter 13

On a cool spring morning a few months later, a blood-curdling scream jolted the entire Sanchez Estate to attention. Mauricio bolted from his saddle-cleaning task, oil and leathery dirt on his hands, and ran toward the ranch house. Carolina and most of the servants were on the front porch of the ranch house, looking in the direction of the scream.

Laura, the wife of one of the vaqueros, ran toward them. "¡Indios!" She shrieked, pointing behind her. "They got some of the children." Her dress was torn, and her face was streaked with dirt and sweat. "They got my baby, my Francisca." She dropped to her knees, wailing her daughter's name and pleading for the Virgin Mary and the saints to protect Francisca and the others.

"The children don't have school anymore, and they wanted something to do." Laura swallowed and looked at the astonished and worried faces surrounding her. "I told them I would take them to play by the creek." Her eyes begged their forgiveness. "We didn't see them until they were close. I yelled at the children to run. Some got away into the hills, but some…" She wrapped her arms around her middle, as if to hold back the pain. "I saw the Indians scoop up the little ones. I'm so sorry."

Voices clamored, asking if Laura had seen this or that child, what children were taken, and what direction the Indians went.

Several minutes passed as the men discussed whether to go after the Indians now or to wait until neighbors could be recruited to join them. Mauricio was in the midst, helping divide the men into two groups—one to track the Indians, another to look for the children left behind—when he saw the barn door fling open. Carolina flew out at a gallop. It was the first time he'd seen her ride bareback, and she rode like her life depended on it.

By the time his group was ready to go after the Indians, Carolina was beyond their sight. He understood that she felt closer to the children than anyone, except their parents, and that she would want to find them, but a lone woman was as vulnerable as a group of children.

ooooo

Caroline drove Azúcar on, stopping only when the trail had to be examined closely. The further the tracks were from the creek, the drier the ground, but Caroline's father had taught her to look for clues less obvious than hoof prints. She had not prayed in a long time, but now she prayed that her heavenly Father would lead her to the Indians and the children. She loved the children. Even if it meant her death, she would do everything she could to secure their freedom.

She continued her trek, always managing to find an overturned rock or a broken tree twig to guide her. When she thought she had lost the trail, she spied a yellow piece of cloth on a twig and recognized it as a fiber from the yellow dress Francisca wore to school. The sun had moved from the eastern sky to the west, but she pressed on, urging the tired Azúcar to keep up the pace. She left the valley clearing and headed up through the trees, where she found fresh horse manure. The Indians had felt safe once they entered the trees and had allowed their horses to slow down and relieve themselves.

Caroline slowed Azúcar to a walk, reassuring him with gentle words. "Just like your name, you are as sweet as sugar." She patted the mare on the neck. Through the thick cover of trees, she saw movement and asked Azúcar to stop. Six braves and five children were resting in a small clearing ahead.

She pulled her long woolen cloak tight around her and rode toward them. She hoped and prayed they would accept her as one of their own and be willing to release the children to her. She was too far away to hear their tongue, but from their dress, she knew they were Cheyenne, her father's people.

Rifles were raised at her approach. Lilting words commanded her to stop. Then, in halting English, the elder of the group, a man in his forties, raised his right hand and ordered, "You, stop."

Her Cheyenne tongue came thick at first. "I come in peace. You are my father's people."

The man who spoke earlier moved his hand down. The braves lowered their guns. "Who speaks the Cheyenne tongue?"

"It is Woman Who Tames Horses." Caroline pronounced her Cheyenne name, pressing her feet against Azúcar to signal the mare forward. "My father is Gray Wolf, nephew of Lean Bear."

"Does your father hide in the mountains, not wanting to leave the land of our fathers as the Great White Father has ordered us to do?" The elder signaled her to come into the clearing, but she did not want the children to recognize her until she told the Cheyenne her mission.

"No, he lives on the plains. My mother is a white woman. They live together with my sister and brother."

"So you are a woman of two worlds." The elder brave had a deep, stilted laugh. "One foot in the white world, one in the Cheyenne."

She liked the man. "Now, I live in neither of these worlds. I live in the world of the Spanish-speaking people. They have accepted me."

The elder pursed his lips. "What can we do for you today, sister?"

Caroline attempted to still her shaking by straightening her back. "These children. What do you want with them?" The children were looking at her.

"They will replace those killed by the white man." He spat. "White men took our children through disease, starvation, and war."

"I know your pain, my uncle. My father has told me many things. He told me about his friends and family killed at Sand Creek. His uncle, Lean Bear, was shot by white soldiers, even though he had a letter and medal from the Great White Father Lincoln showing he was a 'peaceful Indian'. His sister was forced to move to Oklahoma." Caroline's voice cracked. "We never saw her again."

The Cheyenne words came easily now. "But these are not white children. It was not their fathers that killed your children. They and their fathers come from the south. Their fathers have done you no harm, and their fathers and mothers will miss them terribly."

"Come, Cheyenne sister, sit with us."

Caroline slid off Azúcar and led the mare toward the Indians and wide-eyed children. Francisca ran to Caroline. "Your mother is very worried about you. She will be so happy you are safe."

"We were so scared." Francisca buried her face in Caroline's shirt.

An hour later, Caroline and the children began their trek back home. They were met halfway by Mauricio and the children's relieved fathers.

ooooo

"Don't ask," Caroline had said to Mauricio before he could articulate his thoughts of *However did you manage to free the children?*

His suspicions were confirmed the following day. Señora Sanchez hosted a fiesta to celebrate the safe return of the children. She had not been happy that Caroline had ridden out after the children, but it appeared all had been forgiven when she secured their release. Thinking she would do her former teacher a big favor by recounting it, Francisca beamed as she explained how Señorita Vargas had spoken funny words with the Indians and smoked a pipe with them.

"We don't have to bore them with all the details, Francesca." Caroline patted the little girl's hand. "The important thing is that you are safe and back home with your parents."

"But I want to tell them, teacher. You were so brave." Francesca squealed in delight, as she described every detail.

Señora Sanchez was hanging on Francisca's every word. Her face was red.

"You are no señorita!" the woman bellowed, fists balled, arms stiff at her side. "How dare you tell me you're a Spaniard when you're nothing but a disgusting Indian."

"Never did I tell you I was a Spaniard." Caroline held her ground.

"Señora, you may have pure Spanish blood in your veins, but you know most New Mexicans have Indian blood along with their Spanish blood." Mauricio stepped between her and Caroline. He couldn't stop shaking with rage. "Wouldn't a proper Spanish lady say, 'Thank you so very much for saving the children of my employees?'"

But it was the beginning of the end for Caroline.

Chapter 14

Realization of the sizeable amount of work to be accomplished brought Mauricio back to the present. He sat on the edge of his bed, his strong, work-roughened hands tugging to loosen the thick leather loops sewn into the tops of his boots. He stood to push his heels firmly into the bottom of the hardy work boots. The vaqueros in the adjoining room laughed as they teased Pedro and Esteban, fine vaqueros who hated early mornings.

Mauricio chided himself for the late start. He always loved summer even though it meant long days of hard work, but this summer was different. His hands did the work required of him as ranch manager, but his heart was in it no longer. Señora Sanchez and her mama's-boy Carlos were difficult, but it was more than that. He missed Carolina. He missed her enthusiasm, her hard work, and her know-how with horses. He even missed her know-how with people.

Once, when he was frustrated with his vaqueros, he said to her, "They're like children. They have to be told everything. Each morning I must remind them to start their daily chores."

"Let them be in charge," Carolina had counseled. "They act like children because you make them feel like children. Tell them what you expect and let them organize it themselves."

It was good advice. He had followed it and never again had to tell them to get started.

As he reached for his hat, footfalls sounded outside his door.

"Señor, the boss wants to see you," a female voice called.

He pressed the tooled leather hat onto his head.

"She says it is urgent!" the voice added, through the door.

"Tell her I'll be there in a minute." *Hmm. Yes. It must be urgent.* According to the house servants, Señora Sanchez rarely rose from bed before the sun rose well above the horizon. Much less did she want to conduct business this early.

The young woman waited then led Mauricio into the ranch house, where he found the boss sitting at her late husband's ornately-carved, cherrywood desk in the study.

Mauricio removed his hat. "Buenos días, señ—"

"Sit." She pointed to the chair opposite the desk. "Please." The 'please' came off her lips with as much ease as a piglet being drug away from its mother. "I need your help." She shoved a pile of papers across the desk.

Mauricio took the stack of papers and examined the top one. It read *Final Notice* in large, bold type.

"What *is* this?" the señora asked. Her neck was splotchy red. "A man brought this to our estate yesterday, and my imbecile secretary gave it to me just this morning."

"It is a tax notice. You owe the state of Colorado sixty-five dollars." Mauricio placed the paper back on the desk.

She lowered her voice. "I don't have sixty-five pesos to give to the state of Colorado."

"Not pesos, Señora. U.S. dollars." Mauricio skimmed the other papers. All tax notices. "You must pay the taxes, or the government of the United States will take your ranch … er … your entire estate."

Señora Sanchez pulled open a drawer of the massive desk and produced a second handful of papers. "And these?" She pushed them across the desk to Mauricio.

The papers were hand-written in Spanish, but the news was

no better. "Did your husband take out loans from the Banco de Santa Fe?"

"Yes, I believe he told me we didn't have the money for the carriage and the parade horses, so when we were in Santa Fe the summer before he—" She sniffed, dabbing at her nose with a delicate handkerchief embroidered with red roses and a large S. "Before he died, he went to see his friend at the bank."

Mauricio continued to scan the hand-written papers. "It was not just the carriage and horses. Señor Sanchez also had taken out loans for an oriental carpet and a set of silver."

"Just some necessities for the estate."

"Well, now you must pay for all those 'necessities'."

"What?" She stood and stomped her foot. "I can't do that. My husband left me with so little."

More like you have spent every peso he left you, Mauricio thought. "If you don't have the money, you need to sell the carpet, the China dishes, the silver, the horses and the carriage in order to pay back the bank. And you will need to sell other things to pay your taxes."

"What is an estate without those things?"

"If the state of Colorado doesn't get its taxes, there will be no more estate. Authorities will throw you out of your home, Señora."

"What can I do?" She pulled out her fan and began flicking it back and forth in front of her face.

"Talk to Carlos and decide if you want to try to keep the estate."

"Of course we want to keep the estate. It is his inheritance. We are penniless without it."

Penniless, really? He looked around the study. One would never guess it from the tapestry draperies, finely-crafted furniture, and imported rugs. "If you're not willing to sell items of value within the house, another thing you can do is to sell the horses and livestock."

"Yes, let's do that." She walked to the window and back to her side of the desk. "Have the vaqueros round up the stock and sell it for the best price they can get."

"We can't do that if there is no money to pay them." Mauricio waited until her eyes met his. "The vaqueros and all your servants will need to be dismissed."

"No! I cannot abide that!" she wailed. Then she stomped out of the room.

Mauricio stepped outside and breathed deeply. He had held his breath until he was out of the Sanchez house. He felt, not dismay but, relief. For months his heart had not been in his work. The selfishness of Carlos and his mother had worn him down. He no longer need feel guilt about leaving.

The vaqueros had finished morning chores and were headed out to mend pasture fences. Mauricio would tell them that if they chose to stay, their daily rice and beans would be their only compensation. He wasn't even sure there'd be rice and beans for long. He busied himself with corral repairs and tack cleaning, waiting for the noon meal and siesta time, when he could talk with the vaqueros.

He used nails purchased last month at the mercantile to tighten loose corral boards. There was much to despise about the "Anglo invasion" of the San Luis Valley, as many Hispanos called it; but there were good things, too, like store-bought nails. Without them, the vaqueros would spend much time heating iron and forming nails, or repairing loose boards with ropes.

Thank you, Lord, for the restlessness. I didn't understand it before, but now I believe You were preparing me to leave this place. He wiped the dots of perspiration from his forehead with his shirt sleeve. Even during the hottest days of summer, he wore long-sleeved shirts to protect him from the sun and other work hazards, such as barbed wire and splintered wood.

Reality came crashing back into Mauricio's mind. *As much as I'd like to ride out of here tomorrow, I know I must do the right thing for the faithful vaqueros who have worked so hard. God, open a door, and show me the way to pay these men and end my employment here with honor.*

Chapter 15

The dinner bell summoned vaqueros to the outdoor kitchen and dining area. The cook told Mauricio that Señora Sanchez had instructed him to bring the food for her house servants inside the ranch house. "I don't know why she wants me to do this. She has never had the house servants eat inside before, not in the summer."

Mauricio knew the selfish woman was trying to keep the news of the Sanchez Estate's financial collapse a secret as long as she could. In the spring, she told all her employees that she would pay them at Christmas before they left to visit their families for the holidays.

Mauricio appealed to her privately to continue her monthly pay to the vaqueros. "Many have families they support here or at home."

He had prevailed, not because she believed it was the right thing to do, but because she knew the ranch could not function going into summer without the vaqueros. Still, payment for the last two months had been over a week late each time. The house servants were unlikely to see a single peso for their months of work.

He whistled to get the attention of the vaqueros who had gathered to eat. "Men, I have something to discuss with you." They stopped eating, unaccustomed to being disturbed during a meal. "This morning I learned that this ranch has debts it cannot pay."

"Does that mean we won't be paid?" Rolando stood, hat in

hand, shifting from one foot to the other. "We've worked from sunup to sundown every day."

"I know you have." Mauricio cleared his throat and met Rolando's eyes. "I am sorry. A ranch manager could not ask for a better crew of vaqueros."

"You're not going to fight for us?" Pedro's voice was high. "We need the pay. I have a wife and two kids, plus one on the way, back in San Luis. Esteban needs to send money home to his parents, who can't work. Last month he was late, and they nearly starved."

Esteban stared at his feet. "It's true."

"I have a partido and my patron is Anglo." Rolando dragged his fingers through his hair. "My younger brother has been graz-ing the herd of fifty ewes and their lambs in the high mountains while I work here."

"What do you owe your patron?" Mauricio moved closer and placed his broad hand on the man's back. "And when is it due?"

"When I agreed to the partido, I thought it was the normal deal: feed the ewes on the common ground, lamb them out, and return the ewes and half the lambs after weaning." Rolando shook his head. "I don't read, so I didn't know until a Hispano who works for my patron told me it is a new contract. The English contract requires that I return double the sheep I started with and all losses are my responsibility."

Mauricio had heard about the new partidos. In the past, lend-ing one's flock or part of a flock to a penniless young man was a win-win situation. Herding sheep on the open range required constant attention. It was not an older man's work but with the partido, a young man could trade his hard work for a starter flock of sheep, and the established man, the patron, benefited without having to put in the hard work. The centuries-old partido let the caretaker have half the lamb crop. Any losses were absorbed by the patron, and he also provided food for the young man and arranged to have the sheep shorn.

Since the railroads and the Anglos came to the San Luis Valley, demand for lamb, mutton, and wool had surged. Stories abounded of the types of one-sided partido with which Rolando had been duped. Mauricio estimated the fifty-ewe flock would produce about seventy healthy lambs, since many ewes have twins. Keeping sheep in the high mountains led to high death losses from predators and spring blizzards, but it was the only way to feed large flocks without spending cash, something few Hispano families had. The high mountains were common area, equally accessible to all Hispanos in the Sangre de Cristo land grant. Under the traditional partido, Rolando would have about thirty-five lambs to sell or breed for the next year. Under the Anglo agreement, he would have twenty or fewer. If any of the ewes died, he would have to replace these with the twenty lambs left to him.

"I had planned to sell the male lambs and keep the ewe lambs to start a flock." Rolando's face reddened. "With this partido, I have to sell all of them just to help feed my family."

"What about the wool?" Mauricio asked. "You get to keep it, right?"

"Sí." Rolando's eyes brightened. "The sheep are Merino, the best wool. Maybe it is enough to feed us through the winter."

"Go back now. Shear the ewes and bring the wool to San Luis." Mauricio's eyes twinkled, dimples showing. "Find me there, and I will negotiate a good price for you with the Anglo buyers."

"Yes, yes, that is good. I will leave in the morning." Rolando shot off toward the bunkhouse.

Mauricio was famished. He said yes to the cook's offer of a double portion of beans and sat to eat with his men. As he did, the thought struck him. Why not sell the Sanchez livestock to the Anglos in the town of San Luis? They were paying well for livestock, and he would not be cheated.

"Men, what would you think about making Señora Sanchez an offer she can't refuse?"

ooooo

An hour later, for the second time that day, Mauricio was seated across the ornate cherrywood desk from his boss. "One vaquero has left already, and the others will leave soon."

"I don't understand why they would leave." The señora's arrogance was fully restored.

"Because men don't work for free." Mauricio had to bite his tongue to avoid adding, They're not your slaves even though you treat them that way.

"My men and I want to make you a proposal." Mauricio leaned forward, his elbows on the gigantic desk. "We will deliver all your cattle and horses—except, of course, your parade horses—to a buyer in San Luis. We will negotiate a good price and give you half of what we are paid."

"Preposterous!" The woman pounded the desk with her fists. "They are our cattle, our horses. We should get every peso paid for them."

"Señora, you need the vaqueros to gather the animals from summer pasture, drive them to San Luis, ensure they do not wander off, and protect them from thieves. You need me to find a buyer and negotiate a good price. And these men are already owed a month of pay. I would say it is a fair deal." Mauricio rose to leave. "If the men leave tomorrow, as they most certainly will without this agreement, you will have no way to get the animals to a market and no one to negotiate for you."

"How can I trust you to send me the money?"

"Believe me, Señora, if I had determined to steal from you, I would already have done it."

She studied him with cold, ungrateful eyes. "It seems I have no choice. I will send Carlos with you to bring back my share of the money."

Mauricio had to look away, feigning a coughing fit to compose himself. "As you wish, Señora Sanchez." Carlos would be lucky to make it half way to San Luis on the back of a horse, but that was no longer Mauricio's concern.

Chapter 16
Toña Maria's Ranch

Every morning when Doña Maria thanked the Almighty for His blessings, Carolina was at the top of her list. In just ten weeks, the enterprising young woman had broken seven horses to ride.

"Green broke, they're only green broke," Carolina responded when Doña Maria praised her for the accomplishment.

The sun peaked over the horizon as Doña Maria poked at coals in her cast iron kitchen stove, hoping they would ignite the dry bark shavings she tossed on top. She could start the fire anew if she must, but she wanted to conserve the matches she purchased at the mercantile in town.

"Aw, there we go," she said, adding more kindling to the stove. Most people in the valley had to make do with outdoor, clay ovens. She felt fortunate to have the heavy metal oven and stovetop in her kitchen. She pulled the cast iron burner cover over the fire and set a pot on top of the stove to boil water for coffee. The nanny goat gave birth a few days after Carolina arrived at the ranch. She had enough milk to feed her twins and provide milk for coffee and baking. Strong coffee with rich goat's milk was one luxury Doña Maria couldn't imagine giving up.

Now that Carolina had seven horses ready to sell, she would

be able to buy what she needed for the house and the ranch. She also had the Anglo property taxes to pay. Her husband on his deathbed reminded her that if she didn't pay the taxes, she and the boys could lose the ranch. If they were able to get the sheep shorn, she might even have enough money to send Tomás to school in San Luis.

As she poured the boiling water through the cheesecloth bag of ground coffee beans, Carolina bounced into the kitchen.

"Buenos días, Señora." Carolina opened the wooden cabinet to retrieve two mugs.

"Good morning to you, Carolina." Doña Maria poured steaming, strong coffee into the two mugs. "Bring us some milk from the spring house, will you?"

"I'll be right back."

Doña Maria listened as Carolina scampered down the steps outside the kitchen and ran toward the spring house that perched on the edge of the stream. The cool, running water kept milk and cream cold, even amid the heat of summer. She knew the small orphan lamb, Dedo, would follow Carolina to the stream, butting at her legs. The lamb had nearly starved by the time Doña Maria found her and taught her to drink goat's milk from a bottle.

Soon Carolina returned from the spring house with the crock of goat's milk on one hip and Dedo at her side.

"My dear, you have more energy than anyone I have ever known!" Doña Maria poured generous amounts of goat's milk into each mug of coffee. "Just watching you exhausts me."

"Why does Dedo keep butting me?"

"She wants her bottle," Doña Maria said between sips of her coffee. "They butt instinctively when they are being fed or want to be fed. When lambs butt the udders of their mothers, it causes the mother's milk to be released."

"I should have known that. It's the same with cattle."

"Yes, yes, it is. Just one more of those mysteries of creation we ranchers get to see and marvel at."

"Today is the day Señor Hernandez is coming to see the

horses," said Carolina. "I'm anxious to see what he thinks … and what he will pay for them. When I'm excited about something, I can't sit still."

"When Mario was here, we had the reputation for having the finest horses in the valley." She sliced two pieces of bread for Carolina and one for herself. "No one dared cheat us."

"I know it is hard being alone." Carolina's eyes sparkled. "But don't worry. You have good quality horses, and I know what they are worth."

"More bread, Carolina?"

"May I take it with me?" Not waiting for an answer, she smiled her thanks, took up the rest of the loaf, and called over her shoulder, "I have to get the horses into the corral."

ooooo

Several hours later Señor Hernandez knocked at Doña Maria's door. He had his oldest son, his ranch manager, and two vaqueros with him. "So, I hear you have some horses for sale. Can we have a look?"

"They're in the corral." Doña Maria pointed to the front side of the house. "I'll get my hat and meet you at the corral."

ooooo

"We don't want children's horses." Señor Hernandez spoke with impatience when he saw Tomás riding one of the two-year-olds in the larger corral. "We need young, working ranch horses."

Carolina faced the man squarely. "Tell me about the ranch work you need your horses to do."

"Carrying vaqueros to fix fence, rounding up herds, roping, and dragging calves to the fire for branding."

"Ahh. The same work every ranch horse must do, then." Carolina wore trousers and a vaquero's broad-brimmed leather hat, but no one could mistake her for a man. "Don't you need horses that will stand when your vaqueros dismount to fix fences? And don't they sometimes need to bring a stray calf home on the front of their saddles? Ever had yourself or one of your men hurt when a horse spooked for no reason?"

"Sure, but a horse is a horse, no?" Señor Hernandez removed his hat to wipe sweat off his brow.

Carolina whistled to get Tomás's attention and motioned him to ride to her. "This is a really solid sorrel filly with strong legs. See the good slope in her pasterns and shoulder? That tells you she is an easy riding horse. Her trot won't bounce you to death."

Doña Maria noticed the other men zero in on the sorrel filly.

"Sir," said Carolina, as Tomás discounted the filly. "Let me show you what this pretty girl can do and won't do." She pulled off her vaquero duster and slung it up in front of the saddle. The sorrel didn't flinch.

She sprang onto the filly's back with no more effort than most people expend lowering themselves onto a chair. She trotted the filly around the corral one time before moving her into a lope and then a fast lope. With little movement, the filly slid to a stop, turned on her hindquarters, and loped off fast in the opposite direction. Following a second sliding stop, she walked the filly forward, reins loose and natural, and side passed her to the fence, where the potential buyers stood gawking.

Finally, Señor Hernandez spoke, "We could certainly use horses with this training and athleticism. Are all the horses you have for sale trained like this sorrel?"

"I admit, she's my favorite." Carolina stoked the filly's neck. "But, yes, all have this basic training. There are three fillies and four stud colts. In my opinion, all are fit for ranch work and breeding."

Doña Maria saw Señor Hernandez and his son exchange looks, with raised eyebrows.

"We'll give you top dollar. Forty dollars for each of them." Señor Hernandez reached into his pants pocket.

Forty dollars times seven. What she couldn't buy with that, thought Doña Maria. She started forward to thank Señor Hernandez for his generosity.

"Forty dollars might be the going rate here in the valley, but up north ordinary horses are bringing sixty dollars a head; and these, as you can see, are not ordinary horses," Carolina said. She started to lead the sorrel back to the small corral where the other horses waited. Then she turned back toward the men and added, "Please do not insult Doña Maria and her fine horseflesh."

"Wait. Give us a moment, please, Señorita. We must discuss this."

The men spoke in hushed tones. The discussion went on so long that Doña Maria considered going to the house for coffee.

Señor Hernandez addressed Carolina. "We will offer you seventy-five dollars for each of the seven horses." He reminded Doña Maria of a little boy asking his grandmother for another cookie. And Señor Hernandez and his companions had not yet seen the other six horses!

"I think that is a fair price for you and her, but she will have to decide." Carolina turned to Doña Maria. "Señora, can you accept this price?"

Not knowing whether to laugh or cry, Doña Maria exercised great restraint and maintained a business-like tone. "That is acceptable, Señor Hernandez."

The two women and Tomás watched the Hernandez vaqueros herd the seven young horses down Doña Maria's dusty lane.

Chapter 17

Y ou were amazing, Carolina!" Doña Maria squealed like a young lady at her quinceañera.

"Seventy-five dollars!" Tomás jumped up and down. "That's a lot—right, Grandma?"

"To me, it is a small fortune." Doña Maria reached out to Carolina and caressed her cheek. "You *are* an angel sent by God to us." She pulled Carolina toward her and kissed her, first on the right cheek, then on the left. "Thank you." Her eyes sparkled, an aristocratic posture surfacing.

"Grandma, does this mean we have enough to pay the American government taxes?" Tomás stepped between the two women, reached for their hands, and the three walked together to the ranch house.

"We can pay the taxes, hire Carolina and another vaquero full-time, fill our larder with supplies from the mercantile, buy cloth and boots for all of us, and still have money left."

Carolina had been thinking. "I want you to know everything I told Señor Hernandez is true. Ordinary horses in Denver are bringing at least sixty dollars, and your horses are of superior breeding."

"My pa bought the stallion in Denver, and he bought the best mares in the valley." Tomás jutted his chin forward and tugged on the brim of his hat to straighten it.

"Well, young man, it pays to buy good horseflesh." Carolina waited for Doña Maria to climb the steps to the house ahead of her. Tomás flung the door open and swept his hand toward the opening. He had picked up the gallantry of the valley men.

"I made piñon nut and honey empanadas last night," Doña Maria said as Carolina and Tomás followed her into the kitchen. She lifted a cloth from a platter to reveal plump, flaky pastries. "Let's celebrate!"

Tomás downed his first pastry like he had not eaten in days. After the second one, which he ate slow enough to actually taste, he asked, "Grandma, may I go out to the corral to play now?"

She knew the boy could play in the corrals for hours, pretending to ride, rope calves, brand calves, and, now, with Carolina's tutelage, to train horses. "Yes, Tomás, go play."

Carolina reached for a third empanada. Doña Maria smiled. The girl sure could eat. She was tall, perhaps taller than any woman in the valley. There was unmistakably female, but Doña Maria had never seen such an athletic woman. One time, she had looked out her window to see Carolina sprinting toward a gate she must have forgotten to latch. She was as fast as most men. But it was not Carolina's fine, regal, Spanish features that drew Doña Maria to her. It was her caring heart. Doña Maria loved that Carolina was hard-working and skilled beyond words at training horses; but what the woman enjoyed most was visiting with Carolina on the veranda in the evenings. Carolina was a rapt listener. She seemed enthralled with everything Doña Maria told her about the San Luis Valley, the ranch, and Doña Maria's family. She thought it odd the young woman seldom spoke of herself. Carolina was most certainly a Nueva Mexicana, but what young woman never spoke of her family?

Doña Maria had been so lost in her thoughts that she flinched when Carolina put her hand on her own. "Did you hear me, Señora?" Carolina leaned toward Doña Maria. "I said I will not be able to continue working for you. I will ride tomorrow to your neighbor's ranch where the sheep shearers are working and ask them to come here next." Carolina sat up straight. "The shearing has been delayed too long. If you don't shear now, the cold will set in before the sheep regain their wool…. Then I must go into San Luis and set up the schoolhouse for the children to begin school next month." As she spoke, Carolina gazed out the window but didn't appear to look at anything.

"You would leave us?"

"I am good working with animals, but not so good mending fence and all the other tasks vaqueros must do." Carolina sat back in her chair, popping the last bit of the empanada into her mouth. "Señor Cohen at the mercantile is counting on me to teach the children." She brushed her hands together to remove empanada crumbs. "I am hoping you will send Tomás to school. He is young but so very bright. Might he stay with a family in town during the week? I could bring him home during the weekends."

"You are a young lady of many talents." Doña Maria tilted her head sideways. "I had no idea you were trained as a teacher, but I believe it. You were so patient and did a really nice job teaching Tomás your horse-training technique."

"Thank you, Señora." Carolina chuckled. "I didn't set out to be a teacher, although I liked school and was a good student. Most folks would rather me be a teacher than a horse trainer."

"I suppose that's true." Doña Maria rose from the table and slid the platter of two remaining, lonely-looking pastries toward her. "Tomás will miss you. Maybe I can send him to study with you."

"I'd like that very much." Carolina continued to sit at the table. "I'd also like it if you would finish the story you told me the first night I was here—about his mother. It might help me understand him better."

With a sigh, Doña Maria sat back in her chair. "I try to understand folks who don't think like I do; try to see things from their point-of-view. But, try as I might, I cannot think of one good reason Teresa did what she did."

"What did she do?" Carolina folded her hands under her chin and leaned forward on her elbows.

"When we learned she was expecting a baby, we hoped it would give her something constructive to focus on." Doña Maria drew a deep breath. "But, no, she complained even more about having no servants to care for her son. She expected us to provide a wet nurse. What woman doesn't want to care for and feed her own child?"

"I've heard of women with no mothering instinct, but have never known one," Carolina said.

Doña Maria lowered her voice to a whisper. "When Tomás was barely three months, she wanted to wean him off breast milk."

"Three months?" Carolina gasped. "How can a baby live without milk?"

"Fortunately, it was springtime, and my nanny goat was ready to freshen." Doña Maria shook her head. "Gracias a Diós, Tomás took to the goat's milk like a fish to water. When the goat began to dry up, I bought the cow."

"That still doesn't explain why she left."

"One morning, she handed baby Tomás to me—nothing unusual in that—and told me she and Mario were going into San Luis for the day." Doña Maria drew a long breath. "When Mario returned that afternoon, Teresa was not with him." She wiped the tears coursing down her cheeks. "When I asked what happened, he said as soon as they got into town, Teresa bought a ticket and waited at the station for the afternoon train to Santa Fe. To this day, I do not know whether he knew she was leaving before they went to San Luis and had resigned himself to it ... or was it a surprise to him also?"

Carolina got a cloth from the sink to wipe the table. "What an awful thing for your son, for your entire family!" She shook the crumbs out of the cloth into the sink.

"Mario has never been the same since." Doña Maria pushed herself out of the chair. "I don't know what hurt him more: that she spurned his love or that she embarrassed him in front of the entire valley." Doña Maria's eyes glistened with tears. "Tomás has never known his mother. I think her abandonment hurts him more than to have known and lost her. It will be more difficult when he grows older and has no mother, only me, to lean on."

"I'm so sorry." Carolina kissed Doña Maria on the cheek. "Your son had an awful wife, but he's fortunate to have a loving mother."

Chapter 18
The Neighbor's Ranch

The sounds of sheep bleating and men shouting assured Caroline she was at the right ranch. She had never secured a shearing crew, but she had succeeded in other tense negotiations.

Four men and one woman held shearers in one hand and restrained the sheep they sheared with the other hand. She counted seven children, whose job was to catch sheep—one at a time—and lead or drag them to a shearer. The children would help the shearer lift each sheep up and onto its haunches, where the shearer would begin clipping the wool on the animal's underside. The clippers sliced fast and sharp. Caroline heard the woman chide her son to step back as she clipped, lest the sheep kick the shearers out of her control and into the boy.

Once the underside was cleared of wool, the woman eased the ewe onto one side and restrained it by placing her foot on the animal's neck. She continued the rhythmic clipping motion as the wool peeled back from the sheep's belly to its spine. She rolled the ewe to its other side with practiced ease and repeated the process until she had a single piece of wool. The newly-shorn fleece looked like a sheep without head or legs. The woman motioned for her son, and he came and rolled the fleece into a tidy ball. With jute twine he tied the ball and carried the wool to a cargo wagon parked near the sheep pen.

Each shearer's routine varied little. The woman was every bit as skilled as the men, but Caroline noticed the woman's son selected the smaller ewes for her to shear, while the children moving sheep for the men took the rams and larger ewes. Perspiration dripped from the faces of all the shearers. It was back-breaking work. Caroline wondered how the petite woman lifted and moved the ewes. The smaller ewes weighed one hundred thirty pounds, she guessed.

The shearer's hands must be covered with blisters and callouses, Caroline thought. But when the woman opened her hands to stretch, they looked smooth. Then Caroline remembered Doña Maria had told her that wool contained a substance called lanolin that moisturized skin better than the fancy lotions of high-class ladies back East.

Caroline watched, fascinated, as they sheared sheep after sheep without resting. When the sun's position indicated mid-morning, one of the men let loose the sheep he had just sheared and yelled to the others that it was time for morning coffee. The woman directed the children to spread blankets on the ground adjacent to the shearing area. She glanced at Caroline then turned toward the blankets.

"I didn't know women sheared sheep," Caroline said, approaching the woman. "You are very skilled."

"Thank you." Her smile was cautious. "People don't think women are strong enough to shear sheep, but it's like anything else, the more we do it, the better and stronger we become."

Caroline had noticed the woman's biceps and forearms. "How did you get the men to accept you shearing sheep with them?"

The woman arched her back and stretched her arms backward. "My father had a large sheep ranch in New Mexico." She laughed. "But he had nine daughters and no sons. I tried shearing when I wasn't much older than my son and found I really liked it." She twisted her face into a comical frown. "I never much enjoyed cooking and cleaning, though."

"I know what you mean." Caroline chuckled.

A door slammed, and Caroline saw Doña Maria's neighbor lady leave the ranch house with a pot of coffee wrapped in a table linen. Two young girls accompanied her, carrying plates of empanadas and cookies. The trio spread the table linen on the ground and set the coffee pot and goodies before the shearing crew.

Caroline caught up with the neighbor lady as she returned to the house. As instructed by Doña Maria, she introduced herself and explained her errand to find shearers. The lady assured her the crew was good and conscientious, as well as trustworthy. *'Qualified, conscientious, and trustworthy' is what Doña Maria said she wanted. Those must be standard measures for acceptable shearers.* Caroline asked permission to offer the crew work at Doña Maria's ranch.

"Most certainly," the lady replied. "And if there is anything we can do to help Doña Maria, please tell us. She is a lovely woman, who…" The lady looked down and lowered her voice. "Who has suffered much through no fault of her own."

Caroline nodded and turned to seek out the man who had called the break, the crew leader. She found him seated on one of the blankets, sipping coffee and eating a cookie.

He jumped up. "Sí, Señorita, what can I do for you?"

"I want to compliment your shearers. They're very skilled." Doña Maria had instructed her exactly what to say. "The doña who owns these sheep tells me you and your crew are conscientious about doing a good job and not cutting the sheep or injuring them by throwing them to the ground forcefully. She also told me you have shorn sheep for her for many years and can be trusted to complete the job."

The man smiled, revealing a missing front tooth. "Thank you, thank you, Señorita. We work very hard to maintain our reputation with the ranchers."

"My boss, Doña Maria, would like you to shear her sheep." Caroline turned to her left and pointed. "She is the next ranch to the south. Very close to here."

Doña Maria had explained that as long as the shearers met the criteria there was no other negotiation needed. Terms were standard. The rancher provided a rudimentary place to stay, along with food and payment of one-third of the fleeces. A conscientious crew would equally divide good and poorer quality fleeces between the owner and themselves.

"How many sheep does your boss have?" The man popped the last of the cookie into his mouth.

"Fifty-three ewes, three rams, and eighty-some lambs."

The man was nonchalant. "When does she want her sheep sheared?"

"As soon as possible. And she said to tell you," Caroline pulled the word from her memory. "They are mostly Merinos."

"Merinos?" He responded with almost wide-eyed reverence. "I didn't know anyone in the valley had Merino sheep. That's the best wool there is." He glanced at the sheep in the pen. "Tell your boss we'll be there tomorrow, at first light."

"I'll tell her. Thank you very much, Señor."

Before Caroline left to find the shearers, Doña Maria had explained the value of the Merino breed of sheep. The shearer's reaction confirmed it. They were considered a royal breed. Spanish law had prevented ownership of the breed by anyone other than royals and the Catholic church. Because the Merino wool was fine—like silk, some said—Spain developed a reputation for producing very fine wool. It held the monopoly on this wool by outlawing the export of animals to other countries. Furthermore, common people were prohibited from owning Merino sheep. Most Spaniards, including the people of the valley, maintained flocks of Churro sheep, a smaller breed that lacked the fine, beautiful wool. These were the sheep that filled the pastures and vegas throughout New Mexico and up into the valley of southern Colorado, anywhere Hispanos settled. The royal Spanish monopoly of the Merino ended when Napoleon moved into Spain nearly a hundred years earlier, at the beginning of the nineteenth century. Don Roberto, Doña Maria's husband, though he was born in New Mexico, admired the Merino sheep. He always wanted to raise the animals that produced the fine, silky wool.

"Owning sheep that were once owned only by royalty was not a matter of ego for my husband," Doña Maria explained. "Being a tailor, he had sewn garments from Merino yard goods and knew the value of the fine wool."

An American imported a large flock of Merino breeding stock into Vermont after the monopoly was broken. The flock was prolific, and the Vermont farmers who raised them advertised breeding stock for sale throughout the East. Don Roberto, who had become bilingual, read about the Merino stock in an eastern newspaper. He telegraphed the Vermont farmer. "Roberto was so excited the day the answering telegraph arrived. He read and re-read the letter." Doña Maria's dimples showed, and her eyes became misty. "We agreed he should take some of the money we saved over those good years and buy a flock of Merino sheep. That very day, my husband rode into San Luis to send a telegraph to Vermont. He told them he would buy eight ewes and two rams and that he would be there in two weeks to collect the flock. One ram is more than enough, but he reasoned that if the ram was no good, or died, the entire purchase would be for naught; he'd rather spend the money to buy a second ram just in case."

She looked at Caroline like a little girl ready to take her first pony ride. "Three weeks later, Roberto arrived in San Luis with the sheep. They were magnificent. Large, with heavy, beautiful wool. And the horns! The rams had large curled horns, but every ewe had horns as well. Along the way, Roberto also purchased a sheepdog to herd them. My, how people's mouths gaped as he herded those sheep through the streets of San Luis and toward our rancho! The boys and I had come to meet him, and we all followed on horseback, the sheepdog doing most of the work."

Recalling Doña Maria's story now, Caroline's eyes misted. She walked to the hitching post where Azúcar was tied. She removed the mare's halter and slipped the bit in the horse's mouth and the bridle over her ears. Caroline put her left foot in the stirrup and swung into the saddle. Once out of the shearing area, she eased Azúcar into a ground-covering trot.

Chapter 19

The trustworthy shearers arrived just as dawn broke the next morning. Doña Maria, Caroline and Tomás had herded the prized flock of Merinos into the small corral next to the barn the afternoon before. They munched on hay and drank spring water hauled by the trio in buckets. Once shorn, the lambs would be fenced away from their mothers. After weaning, Doña Maria would choose one or two of the best ram lambs. She would turn them and all the strong, healthy ewe lambs back with the mature animals. The remaining ram lambs and ewe lambs she did not want to keep, would be sold to a waiting list of customers who would cross the Merino stock with their own flocks to upgrade their wool quality. Weak or inferior animals would become meat to nourish the Hispanos who bought them.

Other European breeds of sheep had been coming into the valley with the hordes of immigrants. Suffolks, Hampshires, and Southdowns could all be found in the valley, but Doña Maria was still the best-known breeder of Merino sheep.

Shearing proceeded with the Merinos just as it had with the neighbor's sheep the previous day, except it took the shearers nearly twice as long to shear a Merino, Caroline observed.

"It takes longer to shear a Merino, because they are bigger and have double, even triple the amount of wool," said Doña Maria.

Another difference was that the Merino ewes, for the most part, were trained "to lead", like a horse. A few protested by wagging their heads and pulling back, but a couple of pulls by the children on the ropes and they walked along obediently for their haircuts. A good thing, for if the ewes had been as wild as the neighbor's Churro sheep, the children would not have been able to drag the heavier sheep to the shearing area.

"It takes a bit of time when they are lambs, but after I wean, I tie the lambs to the corral rails and let them learn not to fight the rope." Doña Maria's eyes sparkled with pride. "Within a short time, they lead like a horse. That makes it so much easier to move them around for shearing and during lambing."

Caroline helped Doña Maria prepare and serve the morning break of coffee and pastries and the noon meal of rice, beans and green chile stew with potatoes and pork. It was getting dark by the time the shearers finished. Doña Maria told them they were welcome to stay the night in her barn if they liked, since their next shearing job was at a ranch half a day to the north.

As the shearers and their children packed Doña Maria's share of the wool into the barn and laid out their bedrolls, Dedo escaped her pen and butted the children, who stroked her and let her suck on their fingers. The lamb had been weaned and was able to nourish herself on hay and grass, but she still pestered anyone she could in hopes of getting one more bottle of goat's milk.

The next morning, Caroline woke and went into the living room about the time the shearing crew's wagon rattled through the ranch yard. She and Doña Maria peered out the window as the shearers meandered down the lane.

Standing on the wagon between two of the seated children was Dedo, looking as content as a kitten soaking up sunshine. Caroline cried out. "Look! They've stolen Dedo!"

"No, Carolina. I gave Dedo to them." Doña Maria's smile was both sad and contented. "In my opinion, she is not suitable for breeding. I could not return her to my breeding herd, but I couldn't bear to put her in my soup pot. It is the hard thing about being a shepherd or a cattleman, no?" She didn't wait for Caroline to respond. "The children loved Dedo. At least she will give them a nice fleece every year. And who knows, I may be wrong. She may be a suitable ewe for breeding. They will have to decide."

Caroline patted Doña Maria on the shoulder. "It is a decision those who live in cities never have to make."

Chapter 20

Sanchez Estate

Dawn's light was nowhere in sight when Mauricio heard the vaqueros begin to stir on the other side of the bunkhouse wall. They chatted and teased each other with an energy he had not seen or felt in months. He sprang out of bed like a young boy on Christmas morning, but aching muscles reminded him of the week's long days and back-breaking work. He and the vaqueros diligently searched the immense Sanchez Estate to round up every cow, calf, yearling, and bull.

Mauricio's agreement with Señora Sanchez to split the sale proceeds for all the cattle down the middle was hard-earned, and he intended to keep it. This, and not wanting to leave any cattle to fend for themselves, had been great motivation for the vaqueros and Mauricio. More than two-hundred bovine waited in the packed corrals to be herded to San Luis. The low, guttural mooing from frantic cows was answered with higher pitched replies from their calves. Mauricio was reminded of the instrumental warm-ups and tuning before an orchestra performance he heard in Santa Fe.

He pulled on his boots and fastened on thick, leather chaps to provide added protection from the prickly scrub oak and brush. The night before, he had packed his clothes and his Bible into his saddlebags. He glanced back at the room that had been his home for over a year. On the table where he had kept a detailed ranch expense-

and-income ledger for Señora Sanchez, lay the tattered month-old newspaper he read and re-read, with its headline: Denver Union Stock Yard Company Opens Livestock Exchange. The exchange was touted as good for ranchers. Mauricio agreed. No longer would ranchers have only one or two men bidding on their animals.

The exchange would bring dozens of meat-packing houses and other buyers to bid on cattle, sheep, and even pigs. The article told how meat from Colorado ranchers would be shipped east in refrigerated railcars.

"¡Vamos!" Mauricio shouted as he stepped off the bunkhouse porch toward the waiting men. His heart felt lighter than it had in months. "We'll open the corrals and push the cattle hard while it's cool. When the sun is high overhead, we'll stop and rest."

When the vaqueros had saddled their horses, they opened the corral doors. The cattle immediately tried to go south, toward the pasture land from where they had been gathered. The men had to work hard to turn them around and move them north. By day-break, the cattle were moving at a good pace toward San Luis.

Mauricio scanned the horizon for trouble, but saw only a peaceful, quiet morning. The strong bay he rode had an easy trot. He looked to the east and then to the west to assure himself all was well, when out of the corner of his eye he saw movement. He sat back in his saddle and lifted the bay's reins, signaling the horse to sit back on its haunches, while he turned the horse to face the movement. *No, it can't be!* Two seconds later, a rifle cracked, sending the cattle from their dazed trotting pace to full attention.

"Esteban, Pedro, quick, ride to the front of the herd!" Mauricio's voice was urgent, though soothing. "Hold the herd. We can't let them stampede!"

The headers did as they were told, while the rest of the vaqueros pushed in closer to bunch the cattle together and prevent individual animals from breaking out. Despite two more gun cracks, the vaqueros kept the herd from bolting or breaking.

Mauricio's anger rose. "¡Carlos! Quit shooting your rifle or the cattle will break and run."

"You left me." Carlos rode up, bouncing awkwardly in the saddle. "Why did you leave without me?" He fumbled with the scabbard as he attempted to put the rifle back.

"I told you what time we planned to leave and you were nowhere to be seen when we pulled out this morning." Mauricio was standing taunt in his stirrups. "What in the world were you thinking, shooting while we are herding cattle?"

"How else could I get your attention?"

Mauricio was glad to see Carlos had dispensed with his bull-fighting attire. Instead, he wore tight wool pants and elbow-length, shiny leather gloves.

"Shooting a rifle anywhere in the vicinity of a cowherd being moved on open land is never a good idea!" Mauricio grabbed his hat from his head and slapped it on his thigh. "You are lucky we have some of the best cattle handlers in the valley or you'd be headed back to your mother to let her know the herd was lost!"

"It wasn't my idea to come, you know." He blushed. "But what Mamá wants, Mamá gets."

"The only way I will permit you to stay with us is if you agree to keep that rifle in its scabbard and do exactly what I tell you." Mauricio stared intently at Carlos. "Deal?"

Carlos nodded, more with his lips than his head, but he refused to meet Mauricio's eyes. His nose jutted high.

The cattle had settled down once again and now moved in a lumbering jog. Every now and again, an unweaned calf wandered away from its mama until panicked mooing brought the mother cow running. Mauricio scanned the landscape of yucca and scrub oak for danger. He watched a soaring Red-tail Hawk grace the sky with effortless flight. Suddenly the bird dived toward the earth. A few seconds later it emerged from the grass with a writhing snake in its talons. It labored to climb. Other than a jackrabbit darting from one hiding place to another, or a coyote slinking away from the humans who herded cattle, this morning in the high valley was theirs alone.

The unusually harsh winter the previous year had taken its toll

on the cattle herd. Mauricio mentally calculated the calf numbers, figuring the herd size was about eighty percent what it
should be. Still, he figured at an average of only twenty dollars a
head, the herd should bring four-thousand dollars. Half divided
by two shares for himself and eight vaqueros would be more than
a year's salary for each man.

The men needed the income. He would split half the ranch
manager's double share between Rolando and Esteban. It wasn't
that he couldn't use the money himself—he was sure his own
ranch had fallen into disrepair in his absence—but for Rolando,
Esteban and their families, it could mean the difference between
having or not having food for the winter.

Chapter 21

Boss ... Boss!" Pedro was dropping back to talk with Mauricio. "The cattle keep stopping to grab stems of grass. I think they're getting hungry and thirsty."

Mauricio noticed the shadows were gone. "Do you think we should stop for noon meal and siesta?" He held his horse's reins and wiped sweat from his face with his sleeve.

"I think so; but you're the boss." Pedro was his sanguine self.

"See that grove of trees over yonder?" Mauricio waved his hat toward an area to their west. "If I'm not mistaken, a mountain stream runs through the trees. Should be a good place to stop."

"Just what I was thinking, Boss." Pedro spun his horse round and yelled over his shoulder, "I'll let the boys know."

The herd saw the trees about the time Pedro finished making his rounds to tell his fellow vaqueros of their plans. The men loped their horses behind the cattle, confident the herd would stop when it reached the grove. When the men and horses arrived, most of the cows had waded into the swift-flowing stream. The vaqueros moved upstream to wash and fill their water canteens.

Carlos dismounted and for no apparent reason nearly fell to his knees. Without a word, he handed Mauricio his canteen.

Turn the other cheek.... In as much as you are able, live at peace with all men. Mauricio recalled the words his mother had taught him, to dissuade him from fighting with the bullies at school.

He led the bay to the stream's edge. Squatting on his haunches, he poured out the tepid water from both canteens and refilled them from the cold river. He splashed the refreshing mountain water on his face and neck before returning to where Carlos stood.

"All full." He handed Carlos his canteen. "You'll want to loosen your saddle and take off your horse's bridle so he can eat and drink."

"How much farther?" Carlos neither thanked Mauricio for filling his canteen nor acknowledged his instructions regarding the horse. "I can't wait to have a nice bath in San Luis."

"We're less than halfway there; should pull in south of town an hour before dusk, just in time to get the cattle settled with grass and water on the vega, the common grazing land." Mauricio turned to walk away toward his men but stopped and looked back at Carlos. "I don't know where you'll find a bath in San Luis."

The vaqueros chatted, their spirits high as they enjoyed the mid-day rest. The cook had prepared fresh tortillas, farmhouse goat cheese, dried beef, and dried plums for the men to carry in their saddlebags. Carlos sulked beneath a nearby tree. Mauricio ate his food quickly, fearing Carlos had left without food and would ask him to share his. Then again, the vaquero's lunch was probably below the haughty child parading himself as a man.

Bellies full, the vaqueros reclined on their backs, their hats shading their faces. Mauricio enjoyed the quiet but had never been one to take the customary afternoon siesta. Other than the near stampede created by Carlos, the cattle drive north was going well. He aimed to keep it that way. As he leaned back on his elbows, his eyes scanned the horizon. If trouble lurked, he would know.

"¡Ándele!" Pedro jumped up, shoved his hat tight onto his head, and brushed leaves and sand off his clothes. "Let's get going, boys, so we can see San Luis before dark! I hear the señoritas there are mighty fine." He whistled, waking anyone still sleeping.

Señoritas? It had not occurred to Mauricio that the men, at least the single men, saw the trip to San Luis as that sort of adventure. He'd have to keep them in check until the cattle were sold. Mauricio had no señorita to see, yet the thought of meeting one had not passed his mind. When he did think of one, it was not a fine-boned woman with exquisite public manners like his ex-wife. The only woman whose face and presence moved him now was a tall, dark-skinned cowgirl who moved with speed and grace and who was more at home on the back of a young horse than she was at a fine table sipping tea. Why had he let Carlos take her from him? Why had he let Carlos hurt her?

He knew the answers to these questions, but his inaction still haunted him. It had cost both him and Carolina dearly. He knew Carolina was hurt and running from something or someone and that Carlos's attentions flattered her. A part of him hated her for being duped by the man, but when he looked at it from her point-of-view, a woman needed security. Women also needed to be loved and told they were desirable. He had not done that, and he had paid a steep price for his pride. Hadn't Mamá instructed him that pride comes before a fall? He sighed.

Eventually, the shadows lengthened. Mauricio searched the horizon for familiar landmarks. Only because he knew the area so well could he know that the town of San Luis was nearly within sight. It would take another hour to reach the vega. He refrained from telling the vaqueros because he knew their nervous excitement would disquiet the herd and the horses.

The afternoon drive progressed as uneventfully as the morning. The only antic the vaqueros had to endure was from Carlos. He had heeded Mauricio's instructions to loosen his mount's girth, however, Carlos had left it so loose that the saddle swung underneath the horse's belly. Mauricio had retrieved the bucking, terrified horse half a mile behind them on the trail back to the Sanchez Estate. There was no time to repair the broken latigo and stirrups. The mangled saddle was stored in a sheltered spot under one of the trees, and Carlos was instructed to retrieve it on his way back home. Mauricio knew he would not.

The immense San Luis vega had plenty of grass and water for the herd overnight. Mauricio planned to secure buyers the next day.

"Men, I know you are anxious to see the sights and sounds of San Luis, but tonight we stay here." Mauricio waited out the groans of disappointment. "You think we are safe because we are near San Luis, but this is the most dangerous spot on the trail so far. Rustlers know where cattle are held. I need you to work out a schedule where two of you are on watch at all times through the night."

"Then what, Boss?" Pedro was fidgeting.

"Early in the morning, I will take one or two of you and go to the plaza to find buyers." Mauricio shifted his weight to the other leg. "It could take some time to negotiate a good price. You must be patient. It's important to all of us."

The vaqueros muttered their disappointment and discussed the night patrol schedule. By nightfall, all but the two vaqueros assigned to the first watch were snoring under their bedrolls.

ooooo

As the sun peaked over the horizon, Mauricio took Pedro and Esteban, a quiet vaquero that few knew but who had earned the boss's respect, for the short ride to the plaza of San Luis. Carlos had insisted on coming, but was sleeping soundly when the three men rode out. Mauricio felt only a small measure of guilt for leaving him.

Smoke rose from chimneys, where women were likely frying eggs and beans for breakfast. Roosters crowed to welcome the morning. It would soon be the bustling town Mauricio knew. Once at the plaza, he headed for Cohen's Mercantile, where he knew he could find information about cattle buyers. The tidy storefront sporting a series of tables and chairs was as quaint as he remembered it.

"Buenos días, Señor Córdova." The short, balding Señor Cohen greeted Mauricio with affection. "It's been more than a year since I've seen you. Are you well?"

"Very well. Thank you, señor." Mauricio removed his hat. "I have managed a ranch south of here and need to sell some cattle. Any suggestions for who is buying?" He inhaled the smell of brewing coffee.

"Well, I don't know what to suggest. The Anglos are the only

ones with money to buy cattle these days. Many from the valley lost
their cattle and incomes in last winter's blizzards." Señor Cohen
cupped his chin and rubbed the side of his face. Then he brightened. "Forgive my rudeness. Please, sit and have some coffee."

"I'd better not until I've sold the cattle." Mauricio was sorely
tempted, but how could he enjoy a cup of steaming coffee with
cream, while he had told the vaqueros to wait with the cattle until
the business had been transacted. "Have you seen my mother?"

"Oh, yes, she is well. Her spirits seemed better than they have
been for a long time. Do you plan to visit her before you return?"

"I'm not returning to the ranch I managed. It's a liquidation."
Mauricio always hated when a ranch was forced to sell its stock,
even if it was the stock of the arrogant Sanchezes. "I'll work at our
ranch until I can find other work." He pressed his hat back on his
head. "Where can I find the Anglo buyers?"

Mauricio headed across the plaza to the office Señor Cohen
indicated. His long legs and determined stride took him there in
no time. The sign in the window read *Colorado Cattle Buyers*. He
knocked and entered. Two Anglo men, one behind a large, store-
made desk and the other sitting in a chair to the side, looked up.

"Good morning, sir." Mauricio extended his hand to the man
behind the desk. "I'm Mauricio Córdova, ranch manager of the
Sanchez Estate down south." The two men snickered when he
said 'estate.'

The man behind the desk stood, refusing to shake Mauricio's
hand. Instead, he shoved his hands into his front pockets. "Córdova, that's one of them Mexican names," he said, spitting out the
word 'Mexican.' "You are the bastards who bring your sheep onto
cattle land so the cattle smell them and won't graze there. And
your sheep eat the grass to the roots and kill it. How do you have
the nerve to come into the Colorado Cattle Buyers office?"

Mauricio lowered his hand. "You are sorely mistaken, Mister.
We Hispanos raise both sheep and cattle. They graze on the
common land, the vega, or on our private ranch land. If managed
properly, cattle and sheep are complementary grazers."

"What?" The man rocked back and forth on the heels of his shiny boots.

"Cattle prefer some plants. Sheep prefer others. Grazing them together ensures grasses are consumed evenly. Overgrazing is never good, whether by sheep or cattle." Mauricio folded his hands in front of him. "I have come to your office today to inquire what you will pay for a herd of Longhorn cows, calves, yearlings, and five breeding bulls."

The man behind the desk glanced at the man sitting to the side, then back at Mauricio. "Not buying just now."

"Oh, why is that? From what I hear, beef is in demand." Mauricio stared at the man.

Uncomfortable, the man at the desk shifted in his seat. "Well, I could give you two dollars a head if you're really needing to sell."

"Oh, we don't need to sell that badly." Mauricio held the man's gaze.

"Well, alright, I'll give you three bucks a head for the cows, one for the calves and five for the bulls. Yearlings would fall somewhere in between—say, two bucks a head?"

Standing there, Mauricio's eyes caught the headline from a newspaper on the desk. "According to last week's *Rocky Mountain News*, the new Livestock Exchange is reporting prices near twenty dollars a head. Buying cattle for a couple of dollars and selling them for twenty dollars each? Whew, that's quite a profit!"

"I don't know, I can't read." The man was perspiring.

"Well, I can read. The article is right there on your desk." Mauricio leaned forward, resting his palms on the desk. "I know you're not going to pay the same here in the valley for cattle as they pay in Denver, and I know Longhorns bring a little less than the European breeds that are so popular now, but three dollars a head for these cows is unfair. I won't be cheated, and I'll make sure those who don't speak or read English don't get cheated, either." He pushed away from the desk and turned to leave.

"Mister, don't leave. I'm sure we can work something out."

Mauricio let the door slam shut behind him.

Chapter 22
MacBaye Ranch, Bijou Basin September 1886

*C*ould a young man's life be any duller? Chance Thomas moaned to himself and the calico barn cat as he hitched the plodding, patient team of oxen to the harvest wagon. He had cut the grass on both sides of the creek four days earlier. Thanks to the steady breezes, the green stalks were dry in three days' time. The day before, he had gathered the grass into sheaves and tied them with long pieces of grass that Anabelle, his younger sister, braided together. The muscles in his arms and shoulders now registered their protest at being called into action so soon after the taxing work of the previous day.

He led the team hitched to the wagon to the field next to the creek. There wasn't a better team of oxen in the Bijou Basin, possibly in all of Colorado. The steers walked beside Chance, stopping when he stopped and walking when he walked. If he was behind the wagon, they obeyed his voice commands, and they never spooked or ran off. It was almost as if they read his mind. He sighed in resignation as he scooped up the first sheave and tossed it onto the wagon bed.

Despite the cool autumn morning, sweat poured down his face. He wiped it with the sleeve of his cotton work shirt, thinking about his headstrong and rebellious older sister Caroline.

When she was Chance's age, she'd gone off to Denver to find adventure. He supposed she'd seen the new street lights that lined downtown Denver. He wondered if she'd seen the new talking devices. From what he'd read in the newspapers, something called a telephone had been invented that allowed someone in one house to talk to someone in another house clear across town. Imagine!

Chance, the responsible one, never asked to leave home. He stayed on the ranch to plant and harvest crops and care for the cattle. Pa worked the fields with him when he was younger, but when Chance got as tall as Pa and outweighed him by twenty pounds, the older man declared him a most capable crop and cattleman and delegated the ranch and farm work and decisions to his son.

Pa had returned to his true passion of tanning hides and creating leather tack, boots and other items ranchers used. Settlers in Union Colony of Northern Colorado had recruited Pa, renowned for his leather work, to help them improve quality and efficiency in the colony's tanning factory. Now called Greeley, Union Colony had started tanning buffalo hides a decade earlier. Since buffalo had become rare, the factory tanned cattle, elk, and deer hides, as well as sheep fleeces. Chance was left to operate the ranch by himself.

The dinner bell rang as Chance guided the oxen, pulling a full wagon, back to the barn. He longed to leave the oxen as they were and unhitch them after he ate, but Pa and Ma both had insisted that humans took care of the animals that served them before they attended to their own needs. Fighting exhaustion, he unhitched the oxen and removed the harnesses so they could eat and roll in the dirt to scratch their backs.

"I sure hope you're hungry." Anabelle's enthusiasm and perky personality didn't allow anyone to be angry or sad for long. "Elk roast with potatoes and gravy, the last of the bull elk you brought in last week. Ma and I finished smoking the rest of it earlier today."

"Smells divine, Annie." He leaned over the sink and cranked the hand pump three times. Cool water gushed into his cupped hands. He splashed his face and grabbed Ma's towel to dry off.

"And we made your favorite for dessert ... plum cobbler!" Annabelle patted the back of his chair. "I hope you like the flowers. I picked 'em by the creek after I picked the plums."

"They're lovely. Thank you for making the house look so nice." Chance saw his little sister's beaming face. She couldn't train a horse like Caroline or know when to plant and harvest as he did, but she knew how to make things pretty and to put folks at ease. "It makes me forget all about my smelly sweat and aching muscles."

Ma came into the kitchen through the back door. "It's a pile of work your pa left for you, Son. Anabelle needed my help this morning to pack away the smoked elk, but I can manage the team this afternoon while you throw the sheaves on the wagon."

"All done." Chance flexed his biceps for his Ma. "The wagon is already backed up to the barn. I'll unload it after we eat."

"Land o' mighty! That shoulda been a full day's work loading the sheaves. Don't work yourself ragged." She stepped back with her hands on her hips and gave him an admiring stare. "You got your pa's height and agility and my pa's strength."

"And he got your hair, eyes, and freckles." Anabelle brought three plates and three forks and knives to the table, arranging each place setting with care. "Caroline looks most like Pa. I do, too, except I'm smaller and have lighter skin. Chance looks like Ma, except in winter; then she's the only pale one." She giggled.

It was true, thought Chance. His hair was auburn, only a shade darker than Ma's, and he had the same greenish eyes flecked with gold. Strangers always branded Caroline an Indian but few knew he was half Cheyenne. Within a few minutes of meeting Anabelle, strangers were so charmed by her that they were rarely concerned about her heritage.

"Well, now that we've got all that settled, let's eat." Ma sat at her place at one end of the table. "Chance, would you thank the Lord for his provision and the good harvest?"

His prayer was gracious, and by the time he said 'amen,' he truly felt grateful. His life might be dull, but unlike Pa, Chance and his sisters had never had to worry about starving. Pa was a good hunter and had learned to be a good cattleman. Ma was resourceful and a good cook and gardener.

As promised by Anabelle, the meal was delicious. "Later," Chance said when she offered him a second helping of plum cobbler. "I sure hope you dry some of those plums for the winter."

"Already got 'em laid out in the sun to dry." Anabelle began gathering the dishes.

"Is there anything I can do to help you get those sheaves into the barn loft, Son? Your sister can clean up here."

Chance could tell his ma was aching to do some ranch work. She was still a tomboy at heart. "If you'll push the sheaves to the back of the wagon, I can toss them up into the loft."

Ma's face brightened. "You go on out and get started. I'll put on my leather breeches and be there shortly."

Chapter 23

There's some mighty fine hay here, Chance." Ma pushed one sheave at a time to the back of the wagon. "Should be plenty even if we have another bad winter."

Chance loved the way Ma always brought things into perspective. Earlier in the day, all he could think about was the hours and hours of back-breaking work. She thought about the bounty and how it would keep the animals fed and healthy.

"We're about done, Ma." Chance hoisted a sheave to his chest and heaved it into the loft. "You don't ever seem to get tired."

"Oh, I do. I just don't think about it." She thrust the last sheave to Chance and stood, arching her back. "Well, I declare. Look who's snaking down the bluff."

Chance turned to see a buckskin-clad rider on a black horse. "Pa!" Aching muscles forgotten, he ran to the barn and grabbed a bridle from the tack hook before heading to the small corral. Ma and Pa always kept at least two riding horses in the corral. As they had explained to the children, "Ya always gotta have a horse nearby … just in case." Chance knew the "just in case" included the possibility that the Thomas remuda, their saddle-broken herd of horses, would be caught out in a snowstorm or stolen or scattered by a mountain lion. He was glad for the practice of making sure a good horse was readily available. It would be a short ride to reach his pa. He bridled the blue roan mare and jumped on bareback, urging her into a lope toward the bluffs.

Twenty minutes later, Chance met his pa on the winding bluff path. Both dismounted and embraced.

"We missed you, Pa." Chance felt moisture in his eyes.

The older man's jet black hair was just beginning to show gray streaks. "Let me look at you, Son. I think you are even taller and bigger than when I left." He beamed with pride. "I'm anxious to see your ma and sister. Shall we go?"

They remounted their horses and descended the bluff trail as fast as they dared. They pulled up in front of the adobe ranch house next to the hitching post, but before they could dismount, Ma and Anabelle burst from the house. Ma had donned one of her nicer calicos. Pa picked her up and swung her in a circle, kissing her soundly as he set her back down. Then he hugged Anabelle.

"I have news." Pa pulled an envelope out of his inside breast pocket. "It's a letter from Caroline. I stopped by the Denver post office on my way home from Greeley. They had this waiting for someone from the Bijou Basin to pick up and deliver to us."

"Did you read it, Pa?" Anabelle jumped up and down. "Please tell us it is good news."

He glanced at Ma, whose eyes shone. "I'll read it to you right now." He cleared his throat.

Dear Pa, Ma, Chance and Anabelle,

I trust this letter finds you all well and that the entire ranch is prospering. Although I couldn't wait to get away from the Bijou and try out my wings in Denver, I found that the citizens of Denver were every bit as prejudiced against Indians, or 'half-breeds,' as the people back home. Ma's friend, Lucy, where I stayed in Denver, happened to mention that I looked very much like the people of New Mexico and that I would fit in perfectly with the people of the San Luis Valley of Colorado. So I booked passage for myself and Azúcar

*on a railcar from Denver to Pueblo and then I rode into
the valley.*

*In no time at all, my Spanish became fluent. They know
me down here as Carolina. I don't know if they would have
accepted me if they knew I was part Indian.*

*I support myself training horses and teaching children.
There are some other things that I will tell you when we see
each other.*

*This summer, I met a very fine and stately woman named
Doña Maria. She needed someone to train horses, so I became
her employee. Her sons no longer live at home and her husband has passed away. She wanted me to stay on and help her
with her very sizeable ranch. I told her I appreciated the offer,
but my ranching skills extended little beyond my ability to
train horses and use horses to rope and work cattle. However,
I told her that my brother Chance was a very skilled ranch
man and that I would write to ask if he might come to the
San Luis Valley to work on her ranch for a year or two. She
paid me very well, and I am sure she would do the same for
Chance should he decide to work for her.*

*Chance, should you accept this position, I suggest you come
immediately, in time for fall ranch work. You may inquire
about the whereabouts of her ranch by asking for her at the
Cohen Mercantile in San Luis. I hope you can come. You can
find me at the San Luis schoolhouse.*

I feel badly for not writing sooner. I miss you all!

Yours Always,
Caroline

Chance, hardly noticing the relief and joy in Ma and Pa's faces
at news from Caoline, felt the blood rush to his head. Hadn't he
just this morning wished for adventure? And now that it was star-
ing him in the face, he was scared. Maybe Pa would say no, that
he couldn't spare Chance on the ranch.

"Sounds like a perfect opportunity for you, Chance." Ma's gold-
flecked green eyes stared into his. "That is, if your father agrees."

"We'll miss you, Chance, but we can get along. I can see that most of the work for this year is done. If I need help in the spring, I'll hire a neighbor boy."

"Actually, you'll probably have to hire two or three neighbor boys to do all the work Chance does." Ma smiled, holding back tears.

Outside, Pa clapped Chance on the shoulder. "I think you should go, Boy. It's an adventure you need to take. See that big sorrel gelding in the pasture? He'll make a fine mount for you. Your ma gave him a good start. He's strong and needs the miles put on him."

"Really? You'd let me leave and go way down to the south part of the state?"

"Your sister did, didn't she?"

"Well, if you put it that way, I have no choice." Chance grinned and turned toward the hitching post. "I believe we have some horses to tend to, Pa. And thanks for the gift of the gelding. You and Ma and Caroline are all better judges of horseflesh, but even I can see he's a fine animal. ... I think I'll call him Scout."

"Nothing but the finest for my son." Pa pulled on his gloves and turned toward the barn.

My, how things have changed since this morning! thought Chance.

Chapter 24
Town of San Luis

Mauricio chided himself for his temper that caused him to storm out of the Anglo cattle buyer's office and may have cost him the opportunity to sell the Sanchez cattle, though the offer was a rock-bottom price. No one spoke as he and the two vaqueros wove through the narrow streets of San Luis back toward the vega on the south side of town. He dreaded telling his men the herd would bring less than three-hundred dollars. With the cash split down the middle, sale of the cattle wouldn't even pay the vaqueros' wages, much less give him and them a bonus for the extra effort of driving them to San Luis.

"It's not that bad." Pedro forced an encouraging smile.

"Yeah, Boss, the vaqueros will understand you did your best," said Esteban, though his eyes refused to meet Mauricio's.

He'd failed them. He failed to get a price that would allow Señora Sanchez to pay her American property taxes. But of graver concern, he had failed to give his men a decent wage. They had worked from dawn to dusk with barely a complaint, and now he'd have to send them home without enough pay to feed their families.

They were back at the camp in the vega. The men unsaddled their horses and put them out to graze with the cattle and other horses before joining the rest of the vaqueros. Not a word was spoken. Mauricio felt the heaviness of the failed transaction, but the other two moved as though they hadn't a care in the world. Either they were oblivious, or they trusted he'd make it right.

He overheard Esteban say, "You should have seen the boss make those Anglos sweat." The vaquero continued recounting the story. He'd understood completely despite not knowing a word of English. *So much for my thinking he was oblivious!*

"Buenos días," Mauricio greeted the men. Then he noticed a wagon hitched to a team of gray mules. Peaking over the top of the wagon sides, he saw billows of white fluff.

"Hello, Boss." Rolando extended his hand to Mauricio in the manner of the Anglos. "I hear you had the same trouble I had, only a few Anglo buyers, and they don't want to pay a fair price for our goods." Rolando's swagger displayed a new confidence.

"Good to see you, my man." Mauricio shook his hand with gusto. "I see not selling the wool hasn't gotten you down."

"Only a little." Rolando shrugged. "We'll find a way to get fair prices for the cattle and wool." They joined the other vaqueros.

Esteban jutted his chest and chin forward as he continued his story. "Then Mauricio said, 'How can you pay us such a low price when we can get much more in Denver?' That silenced the man!"

"So what do we do?" one of the vaqueros stepped forward to ask. "We can't let them get away with this."

Rolando stepped forward, and the voices silenced. Mauricio wasn't the only one to notice Rolando's renewed confidence. "I'll tell you what we do. We drive the cattle and the wagon of wool to Denver and sell it all for prices that are fair."

Mauricio's head snapped toward Rolando. "What?"

Pedro joined the discussion. "It's not a bad idea, Boss. We know how to handle cattle as good as anyone. Might have to travel a little slower on account of the wagon, but we'd need a wagon for the cook and supplies, anyway."

Hopeful faces focused on Mauricio. "You'd travel all the way to Denver with no promise of what we might sell the cattle for?"

"Most of us have herded cattle or even goats back and forth

to Santa Fe," Esteban offered. "And Denver is not a lot farther."

"Who's in?" Mauricio's eyes widened when every hand shot up. "Let me think on it overnight. You men do the same, and we'll decide at breakfast tomorrow."

○○○○○

Even though Mauricio had pledged to think on the decision to drive the cattle and wool to the Denver market, his decision was made that evening as he watched the eager faces of the vaqueros who, just a week earlier, had been downcast at the prospect of not getting paid.

Early that morning, Mauricio went back into town and re-entered the office of the Colorado Cattle Buyers to see if they had changed their minds. They brought up the offered purchase prices a dollar for each animal. This time, Mauricio minded his manners, thanked them for the offer, and told them he intended to drive the herd to Denver.

"You'll not be able to sell a single cow without a properly reg-istered brand and the signature of the owner that the brand is registered to." The Anglo buyer grinned in triumph.

"Thank you, sir, for the information." Mauricio turned and left the office, closing the door as softly as if his mother was watching.

Gracias a Diós. He had registered the Sanchez brand and ensured that every animal carried it. The only bad news, although he was very glad the buyer had informed him, was that Carlos would have to accompany them to Denver to sign for the cattle.

Mauricio returned to the Cohen Mercantile to purchase cooking supplies and heavy blankets in case of an early fall snow-storm. He also bought a hundred pounds each of rice, beans, and wheat flour. He passed on the lard; they could use fat from game they hunted along the trail. He figured the men could shoot rab-bits or ducks and, if they were lucky, a deer or pronghorn antelope for meat. Fresh berries and plums were plentiful this time of year near creeks and riverbeds.

Señor Cohen, who had outfitted many cattle-drive crews,

suggested Mauricio would need a wagon and team to haul the supplies. A good cook could also provide medical services, he said. Mauricio hoped medical assistance would not be needed. Señor Cohen pointed Mauricio toward the blacksmith for a wagon with wheels equipped for the terrain. He told him to check at the Anglo saloon north of San Luis for Juan, a Mexican man known as a good cattle-drive cook.

"Use your charm and maybe an extra gold piece to convince him to come with you, Mauricio." Señor Cohen winked.

Mauricio came to an agreement with the blacksmith for the wagon and a team of mules. He found the Anglo saloon near the recently closed garrison of Ft. Garland. *Gloria's Saloon~Best Whiskey and Girls in the Valley*, the sign read. Were they really so brazen as to advertise their prostitutes? Mauricio felt his face grow warm.

Loud piano music tumbled through the doors, beckoning men inside. He tied his horse to the hitching post and wiped sweat off his face before opening the saloon door. He was met with a few stares, but most of the men were engaged in drinking or card games or flirting with the saloon women. Mauricio strode to the bar and asked the bartender if he might see Juan.

"That no-good Mexican's shift doesn't start for another hour." The bartender looked up into Mauricio's face. "I mean his English is nearly impossible to decipher; nothing at all like yours, Señor."

"Where might I find him?" Mauricio asked, anxious to leave.

"Aw, I 'spect he's out back in that lean-to he calls home."

"Thank you." Mauricio tipped his hat at the bartender as he backed away and turned toward the door.

Juan was just where the bartender said Mauricio would find him. "Will you consider my offer? I expect to be back in four weeks, six at the most, before the really nasty weather sets in."

"Well, they don't like me much at the saloon, and I work all night." Juan spat a wad of chewed tobacco on the ground. "I'd like to see Denver. I can agree to your terms, Señor Córdova."

"Do you want to come with me now and camp with us in the vega or should I stop by in the morn—"

A woman screamed. Mauricio and Juan looked up to see the angry woman standing—in skimpy nightwear—on the second story balcony behind the saloon. Disheveled hair tumbled around her face and shoulders. With her was an obviously-drunken man. She shrieked, "How dare you stiff me, you dirty Mexican!" She gave the man a shove, and he tumbled down the flight of stairs, landing in a heap not ten feet from Juan and Mauricio.

Mauricio had not recognized the man in skivvies. "Carlos!" "Carlos, wake up!" Mauricio slapped the unconscious man's face until he blinked and slurred, "Angela? Is that you?"

"No. It's Mauricio." He shoved Carlos back to the ground as the hurt in Carolina's eyes flashed through Mauricio's head. "Where are your clothes?"

"My what?"

Mauricio wanted to bloody Carlos's face and leave him lying in the back alley, but as he raised his fist to deliver the blow, he thought about the Anglo cattle buyer's admonition that he would not be able to sell cattle in Denver without the signature of the man to whom the brand was registered.

"Get up and climb onto my horse! It is tied in front of the saloon." Mauricio dropped his fist, still clenched.

As Carlos stumbled toward the side alley, Mauricio turned to wide-eyed Juan. "Under the circumstances, I think we should pick you up in the morning."

Mauricio's annoyance at having to carry Carlos back to camp in San Luis like a sack of potatoes in front of his saddle made him testy. He was pleased to see that the blacksmith had delivered the wagon to the vaqueros' camp. The team of mules grazed with the horses. Mauricio tossed Carlos into the wagon with the supplies. He didn't bother to cover him with one of the winter blankets.

Unburdened, Mauricio moved to the fire. "Men, we move out early tomorrow, those of you still on board with this trip to Denver. We'll pick up Juan, our cook, on our way. Good night."

Smiling faces looked at him.

Chapter 25

At their insistence, Caroline had returned to live with the Cohens in their comfortable living quarters at the back of the mercantile. She couldn't say what woke her so early that morning, but she lay in bed unable to return to slumber. She rose, dressed in the dark, and headed two blocks north to the schoolhouse. It was several weeks until school would start. The children had to help their parents harvest and dry beans, pick and smoke chiles, cut firewood, and finish dozens of other farm chores and housework to keep them and their families fed and warm until the next summer. Only then would they be free to attend school with Caroline as their new teacher.

Caroline sighed with satisfaction as she climbed the steps to the clapboard schoolhouse built in the Anglo style. She wished it was made of adobe, which was warmer in winter and cooler in spring. The Anglo-style, wood-sided houses were now common in San Luis. Caroline supposed they were a sort of status symbol, and where could the Mexicans of the valley better show their attention to style than in their schoolhouse? After all, the schoolhouse and church were where all the public events were held.

She walked down the aisle, imagining students at the rough-hewn, wooden desks. "Boys and girls, we don't have a lot of time to devote to school here in the valley, so I ask that you give all your attention and energy to learning during the months we have for study." She stepped toward the blackboard then stopped and turned again to face the empty desks. "Things are changing for all of us. Already, San Luis is teeming with people, including Anglos, who do not speak Spanish. I am going to teach you to speak, write and read English like they do, so they cannot trick you."

"Now, class, let's get started." She spoke the words in English, but the day school opened she would say the words in Spanish. It had been a long time since she had spoken English out loud. In the beginning, she thought and dreamed in English. Now, her thoughts more often came in Spanish, and her dreams were a mixture of English and Spanish.

Caroline moved to the bookshelf next to the teacher's desk, and ran a finger across the top row of books. The Bible, a history of Spain in three volumes, a catechism book. All written in Spanish. On the second row were books in English, including *The Adventures of Huckleberry Finn, Dr. Jekyll and Mr. Hyde, Heidi*, and *Treasure Island*. All were covered in dust, but she was grateful someone had taken care to stock the classroom with literature.

Rays of light began filtering through the windows, and Caroline opened the schoolhouse door. San Luis was now bathed in sunlight. She stepped onto the stoop, enjoying the sun's warmth on her face and chest. Roosters crowed. Smoke trailed from chimneys. Then came the bawling of cattle, a sound that had become familiar to the citizens of San Luis in the early morning. More valley cattle bought by the Anglos would be on their way north to Pueblo or Denver. She and the other citizens of the valley had been wondering when the exodus of cattle would stop. There was talk every day in the streets and coffee shops of ranchers dramatically underpaid. Caroline had traveled to Denver often enough with her family to sell their cattle to know that the prices paid in the valley by the Anglo cattle buyers were deplorable.

In the distance, Caroline could see a herd of a hundred or more cattle. The animals' angular outlines and horns pegged them as Longhorns. Nothing unusual about cattle being driven north out of the valley. The Anglos would drive them to Ft. Garland, where they would load them on railcars, much the way she had loaded Azúcar on a railcar to travel south.

What was unusual about this herd was that they were being driven by vaqueros. Even at a distance, Caroline could see the distinctive, high-backed saddles and mecate rope reins used by Mexican vaqueros. Anglo cowboys were more likely to whoop and holler as they moved the herd. Vaqueros moved back and forth, seldom yelling at the herd. She guessed the Anglos had decided to hire vaqueros to move the cattle they purchased. It was a good choice. She may have disagreed with the vaqueros she worked with on the best way to train horses—she disagreed with most cowboys about that—but they knew how to handle horses and move cattle.

Her eyes ran over the lumbering cattle and the vaqueros, to the front of the herd. The herd boss was not an Anglo as she had expected. He was a big man with a commanding presence. Even in silhouette, he seemed familiar to her. She couldn't imagine how she would have known him; she'd been in San Luis for only a short time. She watched the herd boss until he disappeared. She sighed with regret that she wasn't on the cattle drive, working the herd with the vaqueros.

Chapter 26
Southwest of Pueblo, Colorado

Cattle lowed and coyotes howled. Both were ordinary, even expected sounds in the pre-dawn morning. Likewise, a horse whinny was no cause for alarm. But the crunch of dry prairie grass predicted trouble, jerking Mauricio from slumber to full alert. He pushed his bedroll to the side and pulled on his boots. The previous evening's extinguished fire offered no illumination in the moonless, early morning. Some of the vaqueros were beginning to stir, but Mauricio did not want to alert the intruder, so he kept silent as he moved toward the open prairie where the Longhorns grazed.

Simultaneous howls of "yippee" split the night. Mauricio saw shapes akin to cattle lunge eastward, away from the camp. He felt dust in his eyes as he struggled to see the rustlers. From the way they moved the cattle with aggression and shouting, he knew they were Anglo. He saw silhouetted men on horses but it was too dark to see faces or horse coat colors.

"Boss, they cut loose the remuda!" Esteban was breathing hard. "Our horses are scattered. I can't catch a single horse to ride after the rustlers."

"How could I have let them steal our cattle right from under my nose?" Mauricio had made it his habit not to curse, but he sure felt like it now.

"Not a one of us heard them, Boss. A bunch of professional rustlers is what this is." Esteban's hands balled into fists.

"Let's get back to camp." Mauricio jammed his hat on his head. "I'm sure the others are wondering what's going on, and we can't inspect tracks or see where they are headed until dawn."

"Yeah, Boss, there's nothing we can do now."

ooooo

A few hours later, Mauricio and his men scoured the area east of the campsite for clues that could lead them to the rustlers. Dust from the movement of cattle and horses had already settled.

"Most of the horses are accounted for." Rolando held the end of a latigo encircling a palomino mare and a tri-colored paint. "Only that sorry buckskin and the brown gelding are missing."

"Tie them up good while we finish here." Mauricio was thankful the rustlers had not stolen the horses, too.

Anglos hung men for stealing a man's horse, because taking a man's horse in the Western wide-open spaces wasn't much short of killing him. It was not from the goodness of their hearts that the horses were left behind. Horses were easily identified. Cattle, on the other hand, could be sold in any town's market and slaughtered within the day. Only if they wanted better prices would the rustlers drive the cattle to Denver. But there, they would have to deal with the problem of not owning the brand.

The tracks from the horses told Mauricio they were shod with metal horseshoes, a practice common among Anglos. There appeared to be at least four rustlers. He also found a patch of cloth. It was a plaid red, black, and tan wool pattern. Likely the tail of a shirt caught and tore when the rustlers moved out the cattle. He stuffed the plaid cloth into his pants pocket.

Juan, the only man whose work routine remained unchanged, rang the bell to call the men to breakfast.

Carlos, who had developed the habit of sleeping in the wagon where he rode with Juan during the day, stumbled toward the breakfast spread, his hair matted from sleep and his eyes drowsy. "It sounded like a ruckus here last night. What happened?"

"Rustlers stole the cattle." Rolando turned away from Carlos, rolling his eyes. "They're all gone."

"What do you mean 'all gone'? I thought they were grazing over there."

"Well they were, but men came in the night and stole them." Rolando struggled to speak without resentment.

"If the cattle are gone, I guess we might as well go back home, no?" Carlos attempted to smooth his wayward hair.

Mauricio could bear it no longer. "Carlos, we can't let the rustlers take the cattle. We ... you, we all desperately need the money from the cattle." He removed his hat and slapped it against his thigh. His brown eyes bored into the nonchalant Carlos. "We'll go after them as soon as we've eaten. Will you be joining us?"

"Naw, I don't care to ride so much." Carlos helped himself to breakfast as if it were a Sunday morning brunch.

The men ate a hasty meal of tortillas and meat left over from the previous evening. Mauricio knew the day would be a long one with a noon meal of nothing more than dried beef and plums eaten in the saddle. The vaqueros ate in silence then saddled their horses for the eastward trek. Juan stayed with Carlos and two others at the campsite.

The tracks led them northeast. On the horizon, Mauricio could see the outline of the town of Pueblo. He had read about the steel mills and railroads that brought manufacturing supplies and workers into Pueblo and carried steel to markets in the eastern United States. The Arkansas River, dotted with dingy factory buildings, flowed east to west along the south side of the town of Pueblo. The readily available river water was essential for making steel. On the banks of the Arkansas River east of Pueblo the cattle and rustlers' tracks came to an end. The men rode along the south side of the river bank for several miles until they saw the muddy trail leading up the north side of the bank of the Arkansas River. The river was shallow and easy to cross.

The vaqueros could see no dust or other signs of cattle up ahead, but the tracks and dung made an easy trail to follow. The landscape was flat, covered in cactus and dry prairie grasses. The day was cool, but the brisk pace caused sweat to form on Mauricio's brow. As he scanned the horizon for movement from the cattle, he caught sight of a rider. The dust cloud grew, indicating he moved toward them. Mauricio could see the man held the reins of the missing buckskin and brown horse from their own remuda.

Mauricio called for the vaqueros to halt. The man on the sorrel gelding pulled the galloping animal to a trot.

"Good morning, gentlemen. Can you tell me if I'm headed in the right direction to reach the San Luis Valley?" He wore leather chaps, a plaid flannel shirt, and the Western style hat of an Anglo cowboy. "I've got work waiting for me."

Despite his suspicions, Mauricio liked the young man. He was large-framed, and the muscling in his forearms and neck indicated a man used to hard work. His hair was reddish brown, and his complexion was light and freckled. Mauricio pulled the plaid cloth from his pocket and felt relief when he saw it was not a match.

"We just came from the San Luis Valley. Follow this mountain range south to La Veta pass, then head west." Mauricio dismounted, and the young man did the same.

"Chance Thomas." The rider thrust his hand forward in the fashion of the Anglos. "Pleased to meet you."

"Mauricio Córdova de Medina." Mauricio was himself taller than average but felt dwarfed by Chance. "Can you tell me why you have my horses, Señor?"

"I didn't know they were your horses. I found them on the trail, probably left behind by the cattle rustlers."

"Cattle rustlers?" Mauricio stepped forward. His eyes bored into the young man's. "What do you know about cattle rustlers?"

"I grew up on a cattle ranch, and it's pretty easy to tell when cattle are being worked by real cattlemen versus thieves." Chance squared his shoulders and stared back at Mauricio. "Less than an hour ago I passed a group of the latter sort. They had the fires burning hot. I 'spect they were fixin' to alter the brands so they could drive them to Denver and sell them for top dollar." He turned toward his horse, then hesitated before again facing Mauricio. "And, sir, I don't take kindly to being accused of being something I'm not."

Mauricio swallowed. "I beg your pardon, Mr. Thomas, for insinuating you were a thief."

"No harm done."

"Did the men you speak of have Longhorn cattle?"

"Yes, sir. Cows, steers, heifers, even a few bulls."

"Can you point us to where you saw them?" Mauricio had removed his hat and now held it in front of him with both hands. "I'd appreciate it."

"Better yet, I'll take you there. It's down in a ravine. Not easy to spot unless you happen across it like I did." Chance stepped up on the big, sorrel horse like he was stepping onto a front porch stoop. "If we hustle up, I bet we can get there before they've messed with your brands."

"¡Vamos!" Mauricio mounted his horse, motioning his men to do the same.

Chapter 27

Twenty minutes later, as they approached a copse of trees, Chance slowed his horse to a walk and motioned the others to stay behind him. He put his pointer finger in front of his lips and cupped his right ear.

Mauricio heard the slightest sound: cattle lowing as they milled about. The vaqueros smiled and nodded.

"Yep, they're still there. Sounds like they might be roundin' 'em up for branding." Chance turned toward Mauricio. "What is your plan to get your cattle back? Do you have pistols?"

Mauricio shook his head. "My men don't carry pistols. We have a rifle back at the campsite to put down injured animals or when we kill one to eat."

Chance sighed. "How about I go in there and ask if I can join them? I'll tell them some sad story about my folks needing money to pay the taxes so they don't lose their ranch." He shifted his weight in his well-oiled saddle. "Give me about ten minutes, then one of you needs to create some sort of distraction in the direction opposite the herd. As soon as they take the bait, the rest of you need to be ready to swoop on in and push the cattle away fast. Real fast. If we are lucky and they aren't mounted, one or two of you can shoo away their horses." He clicked his tongue. "I won't lie. Without rifles, it won't be easy."

Mauricio agreed. It was a risky plan. "How about we ride back into Pueblo to get the sheriff?"

"Assuming he's there and agrees to ride out, the rustlers would likely be gone by the time you return." Chance shook his head. "I don't like the danger, either, but if you don't act now, your cattle will be headed to Denver, and you'll never see them again."

Mauricio translated Chance's plan to his men. They nodded in agreement. Esteban and another man agreed they would ride across the landscape beyond gunshot range but close enough to create a distraction.

"What about our bullwhips, Boss?" Rolando asked. "If the rustlers are mounted and try to come after us or when they draw their pistols, Pedro and I can disable them with our whips, no?"

"It's a good idea, but remember, a gun has a much longer range than a bullwhip." Mauricio felt perspiration on his neck.

Mauricio signaled Chance they were ready. The men walked, communicating only with hand gestures when needed until they arrived in their positions outside the edge of the ravine. Those assigned to herd out the cattle moved into position directly across from Chance. Esteban and another vaquero positioned themselves to ride along the top of the ravine where the rustlers had gathered around the branding fire. Just as two rustlers left the fire to untie their horses from the picket line, Chance rode down into the ravine.

He dismounted, and the rustlers patted him down but found nothing. He had moved his pistol into his right boot. His rifle hung from a scabbard attached to his saddle under his oilcloth duster. He chatted, hands moving in friendly gestures.

When the rustlers appeared fully engaged in Chance's story, Mauricio motioned for the cattle movers to descend the slope of the ravine on the far side of the herd. When they were in place, he looked up the ravine toward Esteban and waved for the distraction to commence. He regretted placing his men in jeopardy while he stood at the top of the ravine, but he knew they needed to see his confidence in their plan.

Because vaqueros did not depend on noise to move cattle, the herd began to move down the ravine just as Esteban and his fellow vaquero rode into sight of the rustlers. The riders held the attention of all five rustlers for about twenty seconds, just enough time for the vaqueros to get the cattle running down the ravine toward where the prairie flattened. The sound of stampeding cattle sent the rustlers running to the picket line, which had been cut by Rolando and Pedro. The crack of bullwhips caused the horses to run toward the other end of the ravine. The two rustlers nearest the picket line drew their pistols just within range of the vaqueros' bullwhips. *Snap, snap!* The pistols went flying as the rustlers wailed.

Chance ran for his horse and yanked away the hobbles as he dove into the saddle, keeping his head low. Mauricio saw him spin his horse three-quarters of a circle to meet the nearest rustler head on. He fired, and the man stumbled backwards before falling.

"Let's go." Chance yelled loud enough for Mauricio to hear.

From his vantage point, Mauricio could see the two uninjured rustlers aiming their pistols at two vaqueros riding behind the moving cattle herd. He heard a *pop, pop, crack* and saw one of the vaqueros fall to the ground. Chance's shot at one of the rustlers had hit its mark, and he writhed on the ground. However, the second rustler's bullet had hit the vaquero. But before the rustler could fire off another shot, he fell victim to Pedro's bullwhip.

Chance spun his horse around and ran it toward the downed vaquero. Jumping down, he pulled the man up and onto his own saddle. He mounted his powerful sorrel gelding behind the vaquero and urged it forward.

Mauricio wondered how he had been suspicious of Chance.

○○○○○

That night over a supper of seasoned beef, beans, fresh tortillas and empanadas, the men recounted their adventure.

"When I heard the crack of that pistol, I sure thought I was dead." The vaquero rubbed his bandaged shoulder. "I think I got hurt more from the fall than the bullet. It only grazed me right here." He pushed up his sleeve, revealing a bloody bruise on the back of his left arm. "I sure am glad the big Anglo picked me up and brought me back." He laughed, then turned to Chance, taking care to pronounce the English words. "Thank you."

"Don't mention it." Chance was stretched out in front of the fire, eating a third empanada.

"Yeah, those rustlers looked pretty surprised when our whips cracked and sent their pistols flying," Rolando winked at Pedro.

The men agreed on a schedule for night patrol of the herd and turned in, tired but satisfied with the day's work.

Chapter 28
Denver, Colorado

Eleven days later, when the shadows were long, the vaqueros saw the buildings of Denver on the October horizon. The weary men picked up the pace, anxious to arrive at their destination. Mauricio called them to a halt when they reached a grassy plain next to a creek within a mile of the city.

"We'll camp here tonight." Mauricio was tired and needed a hot bath, yet he was in high spirits. "The rules are the same for our camp here outside of Denver as they were when we made camp at San Luis. Stay with the herd. At least two men during daylight hours and four at night need to make the rounds, checking that no predators—animal or human—threaten the cattle. Once we've sold the cattle, you will get your share of the money, and you can do with it as you wish."

The vaqueros exaggerated their sighs of resignation. "Aren't you anxious to get into the city and find a hot bath, a whiskey and a girl, Boss?" Esteban giggled like a schoolboy.

Mauricio pretended to sniff under each arm. "I suppose that is a good idea, Esteban. At least the bath and a swig of whiskey. I'll wait on the girl till I find a real woman."

"Boss, you've not been the same since that pretty, tall Señorita Carolina left the Sanchez rancho." Pedro's tone was jovial, but the truth of his words invoked an awkward silence over the men.

The mention of Carolina's name stabbed at Mauricio's heart as sure as if the words were formed of sharpened steel. He felt his face redden. He thought he'd hid his affection for Carolina from the others. He found it strange Pedro had called her a pretty señorita, despite her having been Señora Sanchez, Carlos's wife.

Not wanting to appear bothered by Pedro's comment, Mauricio hurried on with his announcements. "Once we establish the prices we can get for the cattle, you can decide whether you want to use your share of the money to purchase your horse or return to the San Luis Valley by train.

Mauricio still felt his face burning, but he continued. "If you decide not to buy your horse, which belongs to the Sanchez Estate, make sure you save enough money for the train. Your tack is your own, of course." Now he was babbling just to fill the silence.

Pedro, without a doubt cognizant of having trespassed into the boss's private world, spoke to Mauricio without meeting his eyes. "We'll take care of the look-out duty schedule, Señor."

"Gracias." Mauricio felt no ill will against the man.

Pedro stepped back, scratched his head, and put his hat back on.

Mauricio continued, "Tomorrow Carlos and I will go into the city and find the stockyards." A collective grunt of indignation arose from the vaqueros. Mauricio hastened to explain. "Now that we're in Denver, we cannot sell any of the stock without the signature of the brand owner … and that is Carlos."

The vibrating clang of a metal spoon on the huge cooking pot announced supper. The men moved toward the food wagon. Juan was a good cook, but the dried meat and plums had run out over a week ago. The monotony of beans and tortillas with little but salt to flavor them made mealtimes less than exciting. Mauricio had decided that he would spend a bit of his share of the money on a meal from a restaurant—one with white tablecloths and china dishes. He licked his lips at the thought. He had cinched his belt to the last hole. The hard work and limited diet had made all the men skinnier.

In his periphery, he saw Pedro organizing the watch schedule. In the dark, the fire was nothing more than a few tiny embers. Mauricio left the fire to check that the horses were secured. As he moved among them, the horses nickered greetings to each other and to Mauricio, enjoying his pats and rubs as he checked that all were tied to the picket line.

When he returned to the campsite, Rolando and Esteban were tossing the last bit of coffee from their cups, onto the fire, which sizzled and went dark. Mauricio pulled his bedroll from his heavy, dark leather saddle that rested on the gullet end, not far from the cook wagon. As he pulled off his boots, he felt every muscle strain to accomplish the task. Being on high alert over the past week had taken its toll on all of them.

ooooo

Mauricio had anticipated having to wake Carlos the next morning, but that task had been handled by his men.

"It is not your place to tell me the time I should rise," Carlos's voice whined, followed by a shriek. "How dare you douse me with water from that filthy creek?"

A man had to look his best to do business in the big city. The boss smiled to himself, giving a wide berth to the men, as they readied Carlos for his business trip to the Denver Stockyards. Mauricio made his way to the creek, shaving soap and razor in hand. He knew that if the men caught sight of him, they would be compelled to cater to Carlos, as they had the entire trip, albeit often through clenched teeth. He and the vaqueros had abided and waited on Carlos for more than two-hundred hard trail miles over nearly a month's time. He had contributed nothing to the trip, yet had whined and complained, eaten double helpings of the food, and never once thanked anyone for their consideration.

Mauricio felt not one bit of guilt as he took his time bathing. The creek was high, considering the dry summer and fall all of Colorado had experienced. He heard the water gurgle as it made its way around stones and clumps of grass that extended into the water.

Back at the campsite, the spoiled aristocrat was exclaiming, "I will not take advice on how I must dress from a bunch of misfit, low-bred Mexican boys whose social experience does not extend beyond attending a peasant wedding." He spat out the word peasant like it was poison in his mouth.

"When you are alone or representing yourself, we don't really care how ridiculous you look in your jeweled and embroidered matador attire, but out here in the West, in America, it only shows folks you know nothing about ranching." Rolando stamped his foot and stepped to within inches of Carlos, glaring straight into his face. "And, Señor Sanchez, since fifty percent of what those cattle bring belongs to us, I'd say we have a right to tell you how to dress today." Rolando roughly shoved an armful of clothing at Carlos and stomped off.

Chapter 29

Half an hour later, Mauricio found Carlos clad in vaquero attire, down to the leather, fringed chaps. He leaned against the wagon, arms folded in front of his chest, chin jutted forward. From the back of his horse, Mauricio handed Carlos the reins of a good-looking, saddled sorrel. Carlos mounted with effort. Before Carlos could make a derogatory comment about the sorrel mare as he was likely to do, Mauricio made a kissing sound, cueing his own mount to lope. He glanced back to see Carlos following, but bouncing so hard that Mauricio was surprised to see him still in the saddle when they slowed their mounts to a brisk trot at the edge of the city.

The apprehension of being in a strange place gripped Mauricio. He spoke English but understood little about the Anglo culture. He found himself wishing Chance had come to Denver with him.

"I'm not much for the city, and besides, I have a job waiting for me in the San Luis Valley," the big Anglo had told him while clapping him on the shoulder and wishing him an uneventful cattle drive on the remainder of the trail to Denver.

Chance had described to him Denver's electric streetlights. Mauricio stared now at the glass domes on tall poles and wondered how they worked. *I must come back into the city at night.*

Lowing cattle and bleating sheep left no question about the

location of the new Denver Stockyards. From a distance, Mauricio could see the maze of animal pens. He had never seen so much livestock in one place.

He and Carlos wove their way through pens of cattle, sheep, horses, and even a few pigs. They stopped in the center of the matrix of pens where cattle were being pushed one-by-one into a pen so small a cow could not turn around. Mauricio saw a man placing a series of iron disks on a vertical wire. He studied the apparatus and saw that there was another vertical wire with iron disks on it. It was attached to the first wire with a metal bar at the top and a vertical piece of metal between.

When the iron disks were balanced, the man manipulating the apparatus yelled out a number, and another man wrote something in a book. The cow in the small pen was released and another cow was herded into the pen. Mauricio had read about scales large enough to weigh cattle, but he had never seen one in action. When all the cattle in one pen had been weighed, the men working the gates and scale stepped away from their posts while another pen of cattle was pushed forward.

Mauricio cleared his throat and asked, "Who do I talk to about selling cattle?"

"They already in the stockyards?" The man with the weight book squinted into the sun to look at Mauricio.

"No, I came first to negotiate the price."

"No negotiatin' needed. Today's price is four cents a pound for fat cattle, three cents for everything else."

"You buying Longhorns?" Mauricio side passed his horse toward the pen to block the sun.

"Yeah. Back East they's desperate for beef." The man scratched his neck and scowled. "'Spect they'll weigh less than the Herefords, so that's where you'll take the discount."

"Do you pay cash? Same day?"

"Yes, sir, this here's the Denver Stockyards, a right fine operation with bidding from hundreds of buyers. Makes for the best prices for ranchers."

"That is what I read." Mauricio had already run the numbers in his head. The price was more than fair. "Where do I bring them?"

"Just drive them off yonder to one of them open pens. Stay until they are weighed, and you get your bill of sale." He pointed to the book in his hand. "Then take the bill of sale and proof that you own the brand to the stockyards office, and they'll pay you on the spot."

∘∘∘∘∘

Early that afternoon, the vaqueros drove the herd to the stockyards and watched them walk across the scale one by one to be weighed. Mauricio explained the scale and process to the vaqueros. In the valley, people buying and selling livestock agreed on a price per head, not per pound, but he told his companions that selling by weight was fairer and more precise for buyer and seller alike.

They waited outside the stockyards office to complete the transaction.

"Next," a slim clerk with thick glasses squawked as he opened the door for Mauricio and Carlos to enter. "Now, now, we don't need all you ranch hands in Mr. Dunkirk's office." He looked down his nose at the vaqueros as he closed the door.

Mauricio thought the clerk's high-pitched voice could send dogs running and yelping.

The clerk motioned for Mauricio and Carlos to follow him into a spacious office. "Please sit." He pointed in the direction of two chairs across from a large desk piled with paper. "Your bill of sale, please?" Mauricio handed the clerk the bill of sale. He and Carlos sat in the two sturdy wooden chairs.

Carlos gazed out the window then ran his fingers across the edge of the desk in front of them. "Not fine wood. A peasant's desk."

At that moment, Mauricio was grateful that along with everything else Carlos had failed to learn, he was unable to speak, understand, read, or write English.

"So, what do you think of our stockyards, Mr. Córdova?" An olive-skinned, rotund man with black hair thrust his hand forward. "Nathanael Dunkirk at your service."

"Pleased to meet you, sir." Mauricio rose and shook the man's hand with a firm grip. "Impressive, very impressive, indeed. We have read about the stockyards in our newspaper back home in the San Luis Valley, but this is our first visit to Denver." Mauricio nodded in Carlos' direction. "Mr. Sanchez is the brand owner. The cattle belong to him, but my men and I agreed to drive them to Denver for half the proceeds."

Carlos cut into the conversation. "You'd think this fat man would at least offer us tea or wine." He crossed and uncrossed his legs, brushing invisible debris off Rolando's chaps he was wearing.

"I'm afraid Mr. Sanchez is not a very patient man." Mauricio half smiled at Mr. Dunkirk. "Perhaps it would be a more pleasant proceeding if you gave half the coins to him now, so he can leave."

"A splendid idea, Mr. Córdova." Mr. Dunkirk jotted something on his pad of paper, tore the page off the pad, and handed it to the ever-watchful clerk. "Coins," he ordered as the clerk left the room.

While they waited for the clerk to return, a bell rang. It seemed to be coming from a wood and metal box on the wall behind the desk. Mr. Dunkirk stood up, faced the box, and held a piece of metal with a large knob on each end, to his ear and mouth.

"Dunkirk here." The metal piece Dunkirk held to his ear was connected at the other end to a rope that fed into the wall. "Next week's stock prices will be posted by six a.m. Monday, just as always. … Yes, sir, it is something you can count on. You are most welcome. Goodbye."

Before wide-eyed Mauricio could inquire, the clerk returned with a heavy, cloth bag, closed at the top with a drawstring.

Carlos jumped from his seat, snatched the bag from the clerk's hand, and sprinted out the door, insulting Mr. Dunkirk's mother in Spanish as he left.

"My apologies for—"

"No need to apologize for your employer's ... er, I hope it is your ex-employer's ... behavior, Mr. Córdova." Dunkirk motioned to the wall behind him. "That, sir, is a telephone. I take it you've not seen one before."

"I've only read about them," Mauricio said. "May I?"

"Most certainly." Dunkirk removed the handset from the carrier and handed it to Mauricio. "You have to dial zero to get to the operator. She will connect you to the business or home where you wish to place a call."

"Incredible."

"Yes, it is." Dunkirk sat back down and leaned forward, his elbows on his desk. "On one hand it is revolutionizing business, making communication so much faster and easier. On the other hand, I find the telephone to be rather disruptive."

While Mauricio examined the apparatus, the clerk returned with a second bag of coins. "Mr. Córdova, Mr. Dunkirk asked that I offer you a cup of tea or perhaps you'd like a glass of wine?" The clerk smiled at Mr. Dunkirk.

Mauricio stammered. "Oh, no, sir. You've been more than accommodating. Thank you."

Dunkirk winked at Mauricio. "My mother grew up in the San Luis Valley and came to Denver to work as a housemaid before she met and married my father. Spanish was my first language." He straightened in his chair. "There are men of good character as well as bad in any race. I would have let Mr. Sanchez's insult slide, but insulting my mother is another matter, and I'll not have it." His laughter filled the office.

Mauricio shot up from his chair. "I beg you not to punish my men for the outrageous behavior of Mr. Sanchez."

"No need to worry, Mr. Córdova." Mr. Dunkirk stood and tugged on his vest to straighten it. "The stockyards have very strict rules about paying sellers what is due them in a timely fashion."

Mauricio breathed a sigh of relief. "I am grateful for that."

"However, when the money is split between sellers, there are no rules for which seller pays the stockyard fees and which seller pockets any premiums paid for superior animals." He paused. "That is purely up to me, and well, let's just say the number of coins in your and Mr. Sanchez's pouches differ considerably. I don't condone rude or condescending behavior ... in any language."

"Thank you, sir." Mauricio let out a breath he'd been holding.

Mr. Dunkirk stood also. "Your pay is well earned." He handed the bag of coins to Mauricio. "Thank you for doing business with the stockyards."

As Mauricio descended the steps from Mr. Dunkirk's office, he nearly collapsed in relief. Now that the cattle were sold and he could pay his men for their labor, a spring returned to his step.

Chapter 30
San Luis

Estudiantes, I am so pleased that in the first two weeks of school you have mastered your review lessons. You are all intelligent." Caroline smiled at the seventeen faces beaming back at her. "I couldn't be more proud of you."

Luis raised his hand. Caroline nodded to the ten-year-old who wore patched britches and shoes several sizes too big. "What is it, Luis?"

"Why do you say we are intelligent?" He squirmed in his seat but kept his eyes on her. "The Anglo kids call us 'stupid Mexicans'."

Caroline clapped her right palm to her clavicle, remembering the cruelty of her classmates when she was a child. "No, no, that's not true." Her eyes misted a little. "You learn quickly, work hard, and treat me and your fellow classmates with respect. I'm proud of each one of you."

Juan and Felicia both grinned at Caroline. The twins had complexions the color of many people in the valley, but their curly hair, wide noses and generous lips belied their Negro-Hispano heritage. Their Negro father brought them to school each morning on his way to work at one of the Anglo offices in town.

The first morning, Mr. Washington had smiled at Caroline and spoken to his children before he left. He assumed she didn't understand English. "Your ma and I have taught you at home because the other teachers didn't want you in their classes. We have been praying for a teacher who would see you for who you are. Just give this teacher a try. I think she's different. If I'm wrong, I won't make you come back again." Juan and Felicia hadn't missed a day of school yet.

Caroline wanted to ask her students about an idea she had. "We will continue our other studies, but tell me, would you like to learn English?" The silence that followed was unusual for a Friday afternoon. Finally, Gloriana Cohen raised her hand.

"Yes, Gloriana?"

"My pa says the Anglos take advantage of us because we don't know English." She looked down at her hands folded neatly in front of her on the long, rough-cut wooden table that served as a desk. "I don't want to be an Anglo, but I want to speak and read English so I can help my pa."

Three other hands shot up.

"One at a time." Caroline pointed at Lucas, an older boy who rarely entered group discussions.

"It's true what Gloriana said." From the front of the class-room, Caroline could see the muscles in Lucas's jaw tighten. "A man came to our farm in the summer with a paper he asked my pa to sign. He said he was from the government, and we were living on land that belonged to someone else." Lucas gripped the table, his knuckles turning white. "When the man left, my pa took the paper to Mr. Washington. He read it and told my pa the man was lying to get us to sign our land over to him."

"So, then, I guess we're agreed. You want to add English to our lessons?" Caroline looked at her students, heads bobbing up and down.

Juan asked, "Who will teach us English?"

"I will."

"You know English?" Ana Cohen blurted out impulsively before her brother Felipe cuffed her. "I'm sorry, Señorita Vargas."

"You're forgiven, Ana.

"Yes, I will teach you English, and Juan and Felicia can help since their father speaks English and has taught them."

Tomás added, "I want to learn English, too." Doña Maria's grandson was the youngest in the class.

"Perfecto. As long as you continue to be diligent in your other studies, I will add an English lesson at the end of each day. School is dismissed."

The children filed out of the schoolhouse. Those lucky enough, climbed up—often two or three kids at a time—onto donkeys or horses that took the children to their homes. Those without equine transportation walked. Though Lucas lived three miles from the schoolhouse, had yet to miss a day. And after school, he walked with a group of younger children, to see they made it home safely.

Caroline poked at the few remaining pieces of charred wood in the stove. She had learned when to put the last piece of wood in the little stove so that it would burn down by the end of the school day. The valley people worked hard to chop and gather wood from the mountains. Her pile of firewood was always stacked high, but she tried not to waste a single stick.

"Señorita Carolina, Señorita Carolina." Tomás was tugging at her skirt.

"I'm sorry, Tomás. Let me pack my things, then we'll go to the Cohen Mercantile to get Azúcar and ride to the ranch to see your grandmother." She spoke absentmindedly.

Tomás persisted, his eyes wide. "But Señorita, there's a man at the door. He's a really big man."

She rested her hand on the outline of the knife in her skirt pocket as she walked to the only door. She exhaled in relief as the man ducked inside. "Chance!" She ran forward to embrace her brother.

Chance picked her up easily and swung her in a circle. "You haven't changed at all!"

"But you are much bigger and stronger than the sixteen-year-old boy I last saw."

Chance looked puzzled.

Caroline winced. She had spoken Spanish to him! It had been years since she last used her first language, but now when she reverted to English, it spilled out as natural as ever.

In the joy of the moment, she had forgotten about Tomás's presence. He again tugged at her skirt and asked in Spanish, "Is that English you're speaking with that big man?"

Panic flooded over Caroline. Parading herself as Carolina Vargas, she could hardly introduce an Anglo as her brother. Chance didn't speak Spanish, and his light hair and freckled, ruddy complexion would not allow him to pass for Hispano. She would have to introduce him as a friend from up north. This might work until he learned Spanish. The freedom she had felt sharing from the heart with Doña Maria all summer vanished as she again stepped back behind the façade of deception. It felt like a prison door slamming and shutting her in.

"He's a friend from up north." The Spanish words cloyed her tongue like a piece of spoiled fruit. "He has come to work for your grandmother." A half truth.

"Tomás, can you be a really big boy and go back to Tia Anita's house by yourself?" She couldn't look the boy straight in the eye. "My friend and I will go to the Cohens to get my things and fetch Azúcar. Then we'll all ride out to your grandmother's ranch together."

"Bueno." Tomás swept his lunch box off the school table and bounded out the door. "Hasta luego, Señorita."

Chapter 31

Caroline secured the schoolhouse with the hand-hewn key and led Chance past the shops and across the plaza to Cohen's Mercantile. Good on his word, Señor Cohen provided room and board for her and Azúcar as part of her teacher's salary. On this warm and glorious fall afternoon, gold and orange leaves and dry grass crunched under their boots. Caroline linked arms with her brother. "Tell me, how are Ma and Pa and Anabelle?"

"They're fine. Anabelle's almost sixteen now. Fully grown but, as always, she is satisfied to stay inside or work in the garden. But on the last week-long trip we took to Denver, when Pa and Ma were in a hurry to get back home, Anabelle cried about having to leave so soon." Chance huffed. "I wouldn't be surprised if she ended up marrying one of them rich city guys."

Caroline's long legs had to hustle to keep pace with Chance. "Was it hard to convince them to let you come here?"

"No, not at all. Pa said, 'A young man needs some adventure,' and Ma agreed with him."

"What else is new in the Bijou Basin?" Caroline figured if she kept up the barrage of questions, Chance wouldn't have time to ask her what she had been up to for the past three years.

"Some folks have moved out, but a lot, and I mean a lot, have moved *into* the basin."

The townspeople greeted Caroline with "¡Buenas tardes!" and "¿Como estás?" She nodded politely. She was surprised to see a ranch hand from the Sanchez Estate. Unbidden, unpleasant images of life there flashed through her mind; but she responded with obligatory politeness to his "Buenas tardes."

Regaining her composure, she bade her brother to wait outside while she entered the mercantile, passing quickly to the living quarters in the back. She hoped she could slip back out and saddle Azúcar without having to introduce Chance to the Cohen family. But, as she headed outside with her satchel in hand, Señora Cohen called out from behind the counter.

"Who is the man waiting outside?"

"Oh, he's a friend from up north." Caroline quickened her pace. "I'll be back Sunday night. Hasta luego."

She scooted out the door before the señora could respond. Caroline grabbed Chance's arm again and led him around the side to the Cohen's barn. Azúcar nickered at her. Other than a rub and a handful of grain during the week, Caroline's school schedule had kept her too busy to spend much time with the mare.

Caroline ran a brush over Azúcar's thickening coat and picked her hooves to remove debris. "Chance, how about you head over to the schoolhouse to get your horse and meet me back here?" She should have thought of that before.

"Sure, Sis. You never have needed my help when it came to horses."

Caroline threw the saddle blanket on Azúcar's back and then placed the saddle over it. She tightened the girth. When it was time to ask Azúcar to open her mouth so Caroline could put the bit in it, the horse was more than willing. The mare seemed to know tacking up meant she would be able to run free instead of stand in a dark barn.

Caroline tied her satchel to the back of the saddle with the leather saddle strings and led Azúcar outside. Chance was trotting toward her on Scout, a gelding, half draft horse. Scout, whose mother was a plow horse on the MacBaye Ranch, was too mellow for Caroline, but Chance had never liked challenges when it came to a horse. Caroline thought Scout's size and stamina suited Chance perfectly. Ma would agree. Ma was always right when it came to horses. *Ma was right about a lot of things.*

The day Caroline defiantly announced she was leaving, Ma had said, "My daughter, it would be best to deal with your problems here and now. There are people who love you here." Ma was wearing a calico shirtwaist with men's britches covered with leather chaps. "Who knows what danger lies out there for a young girl? Besides, running from your problems will only make things worse." Ma's green eyes seemed to bore into Caroline's soul. Caroline had stomped away in defiance.

She wiped her eyes, hoping no one would notice.

"What's wrong?" Chance noticed.

"It's nothing." Caroline straightened and prepared to mount. "I must've got some dirt in my eye." She rubbed her left eye for effect and then swung up onto the saddle. She felt awkward, sitting in the saddle in a full skirt, but she had not wanted to take the time to change into her britches.

"I guess little has changed." Chance's eyes searched hers. "You never could admit when something ailed you."

Caroline was desperate to change the subject. "We need to pick up Tomás from Tia Anita's house on the way out to Doña Maria's ranch." She reined Azúcar around, and Chance followed.

ooooo

"It was her. I know it was, Boss." Rolando never came back from a business or social visit without some piece of gossip. "Señorita Carolina was on the arm of that big Anglo that helped us get the cattle back." He looked around at his fellow vaqueros to make sure he had his attention. "He didn't recognize me, but she sure did. I don't know why seeing me made her nervous, though."

Mauricio did his best to appear nonchalant. "She has a right to a life after Carlos."

"If I were her, I'd hightail it out of the valley … just to be rid of him." Rolando's tone was teasing. "Of course, if she were my gal, I wouldn't feel that way."

"Now Rolando, I've been trying to get over feeling guilty about leading that girl into Carlos's snare and there you go bringing it up again." Mauricio hoped he sounded jovial.

The vaqueros were enjoying a hot bowl of menudo and a beer. Mauricio had invited them to eat together in San Luis after they got off the train from Denver. All but Carlos, who to everyone's delight had rushed off to the saloon, were seated at the café. Mauricio knew they would soon go their own ways, and he wanted to celebrate a job well done. He also worried some of the men would end up in the saloon if he didn't provide a small fiesta for them.

"We all know it isn't just guilt you are feeling, Boss." Rolando laughed. "You've been sweet on that girl from the beginning, and you should have told her so."

"You're probably right, but that is really no one's business but my own." He didn't mean to be harsh, but the fiesta was over.

Esteban cleared his throat. "A toast to our boss. You've been a great leader to us." The men downed the last of their beer and got up to leave. Again, Esteban spoke for the vaqueros. "We are grateful. We thought *we* would have no pay, but we ended up receiving very good pay ... and a trip to Denver. Thank you."

"Thanks to all of you." Mauricio tipped his hat. The men filed out, and he left a tip in the style of the Anglos.

It was dark. He would spend the night at Tia Anita's and head to the ranch the next morning after he rented a horse from the livery. He and all the vaqueros had opted to sell their horses in Denver where they fetched a much higher price than in the San Luis Valley. In Mauricio's case, he would have many horses to choose from, although none would be broke like the mount from Señor Martínez that Carolina had trained.

The truth was, he couldn't go a day, well, not even an hour without thinking about her. Even Rolando's news that Carolina had a beau didn't keep him from thinking about what might have been if he'd had the courage to tell her how he felt.

Chapter 32

After the party with the vaqueros, Mauricio had tossed and turned all night, finally falling asleep on Tia Anita's straw-filled mattress just before dawn.

People called the widow lady 'Tia' as a term of endearment. She had converted two rooms in her solid adobe house to use as rentals when her husband died. She had no sign advertising the rooms, and no set prices for guests. Only by word of mouth did people know, and only Spanish-speaking people of the valley stayed with Tia Anita when they came into San Luis to conduct business and couldn't get back home before dark.

"Eat," Tia Anita said. She set before Mauricio a hot mug of coffee and a thick slice of fresh-baked bread.

"Gracias." He had splashed his face with the water she placed in his room earlier, but his eyes were still heavy.

"Give whatever is bothering you to El Señor," said Tia Anita, who was known for her piety. Her husband had been a member of Los Penitentes, a Roman Catholic brotherhood or fraternity. "San Pedro wrote that we should cast all our cares on Him, because He cares for us." She gave him a second slice of bread. "Whatever is bothering you, just remember that El Señor sees your trouble and will help you."

Mauricio had always felt comfortable talking to the kindly old woman. "It's this young woman I know. I should have married her, and now it's too late."

"Is she married to another man?"

"No, not anymore."

Tia Anita cocked her head to one side, gazing directly at Mauricio. "Are you sure this is a woman you should be thinking about?" She pursed her lips and let her eyes drop below his. "You found out before that a beautiful woman must be beautiful on the inside or the marriage will not work."

Mauricio blushed. Tia Anita knew about his first wife. It seemed everyone in the valley knew about her. "This woman is different. She is a hard worker and never complains. And she loves children and animals. She's beautiful, too."

"But a divorced woman, Mauricio?" She whistled. "What will the church say? You know you could have any maiden in this valley. Why choose a woman who is divorced?"

"I didn't set out to love this woman." Even in the cold room he felt the heat rising in his cheeks. "It is as though the Almighty put her in front of me. We were friends and co-workers. I think I loved her from the first time I met her, but I never told her. The feelings were more than just an attraction for a beautiful woman. They were deeper, like we could touch each other's souls. You know?"

Tia Anita's smiled a sad smile. "That's how it was with my husband. I thought him good-looking, but there was so much more to our relationship." She placed her wrinkled hand on Mauricio's shoulder, then rose to fetch the coffee pot.

"What would the Penitentes say about me marrying this woman?"

Tia Anita sighed. "Los Penitentes are a misunderstood brotherhood. When most people think of them, they picture men beating themselves in penance. I won't deny that is part of it for some brothers, but for my husband being in Los Penitentes was all about serving the unfortunate and turning people's hearts to Jesu Cristo. We had a good marriage and beautiful children, but my husband said nothing satisfied his deepest longings, except his Savior."

She refilled their mugs then sat down again, across the table from Mauricio. "It used to bother me that I wasn't everything for my husband. I felt like I was lacking because he had to join the brotherhood." She smiled with a far-away look as she cradled the mug of coffee in weathered hands. "But as time went on, I realized he was right. Nothing can complete a person, except intimate fellowship with El Señor."

Tia Anita took the empty coffee mugs to the sink. Then she added, almost as an afterthought, "Perhaps the question you should be asking is not whether you should marry this woman or any other for that matter, but what you can do to grow closer to your Savior."

ooooo

Mauricio thought about Tia Anita's words as he trudged toward the livery to rent a horse. The sun's position in the sky proclaimed mid-morning. He had allowed his thoughts to be obsessed with Carolina and his own mistakes. He needed to quit chastising himself for his failures. The way Tia Anita spoke about the Savior, as if He were her neighbor and close friend … Mauricio wanted that kind of relationship. He rarely went to mass, because the rituals seemed empty to him, but the kind of relationship she described was different. It was one worth pursuing.

Mauricio had just paid to rent a big bay gelding for the week when Esteban burst into the livery. "They shot Rolando! Boss, you gotta come. Quick!"

"Who shot Rolando?" Mauricio was wide awake now. "We just had menudo and beer together last night."

Esteban breathed hard from his sprint to the livery. "Rolando left early this morning to find his brother and his flock of sheep in the high country. Some Anglo cattlemen shot him. They said he had no right to graze his sheep on their ranch." Esteban wiped sweat from his brow. "Boss, Roland needs you! The valley people who are grazing their animals in the mountains are scared to go there to tend them or bring them back home."

Mauricio jumped onto the bay gelding. "Where are they?"

"At the morada north of town." Esteban turned and yelled over his shoulder. "I have to get the doctor to tend to Rolando's wound."

Mauricio slapped his horse with the end of his reins, something he rarely did. He was in a hurry to see Rolando and to know what happened.

Twenty minutes later, Mauricio tied his horse next to other horses, mules, and wagons parked around the morada, a windowless adobe building for religious ceremonies and community meetings. Inside the building, dimly lighted with kerosene lamps, he could see little at first. When his eyes adjusted, there was Rolando slouched against the far wall, clutching his right thigh, blood soaking his pants. He must have tried to stop the bleeding with his hand then wiped his face. His cheeks and forehead were smeared with blood.

"Esteban is bringing the doctor," Mauricio said, squatting on his haunches to be eye-to-eye with Rolando. "You're in a lot of pain?"

"There's a hot branding iron inside my leg."

Mauricio looked up and around at the men and women standing or squatting nearby. He didn't want to overtax the injured man, so he addressed the others. "What happened?"

"It's the stinking Anglos," spat a man about Mauricio's age with broken front teeth. "They come into the San Luis Valley and think they own it."

"They say they do own it," said a woman kneeling beside Rolando. She stood to her feet. Her hair was pulled into a bun and gray showed behind her temples. "My son was headed up into the sierra to find his brother and his sheep. He was excited about the gold he made in Denver from selling the wool and his share of the cattle." She lowered her voice. "And I thank you, Señor, for leading my son and the others to Denver and back safely."

She handed a piece of paper to Mauricio. "They told him 'no Mexicanos' then thrust this paper at him. He couldn't read it, of course, so he put it in his pocket and continued up the mountain. On these mountains we have grazed our animals since I was a child. It is our heritage, no?" Her voice grew louder. "Rolando doesn't remember exactly what happened. He said he heard a gunshot and fell to the ground. A tall, skinny Anglo with a scar from here to here…"—With her thumb she sliced from her upper cheekbone to the corner of her lips—"was holding his pistol and laughing."

"May I see that paper?"

Without hesitation she handed it to him. "Please tell me what it says, Señor."

Mauricio unfolded the crumpled, coffee-stained paper and tipped it toward the light. At the top it read, *Deeded to the U.S. Freehold Land and Emigration Company of Denver, Colorado.* The text described the land that the people of the valley considered the sierra, the hills, and other land people used as common ground. At the bottom of the page was a signature and then the printed name, *William Gilpin.*

Mauricio knew the name William Gilpin. He was Colorado's first territorial governor and the owner of the Sangre de Cristo land grant. Most people in the valley had little interest in who owned the land grant. They had their small farms and the right to use the common ground.

Rolando's mother could contain herself no longer. "What does it say?"

Mauricio exhaled. "It is a deed of sale, indicating Governor Gilpin has sold our common mountain ground."

Everyone in the morada had gathered around Mauricio. Most people of the valley, especially the older ones, couldn't read at all. He was one of the few who could read English.

"The new owners have no right to keep us off that land. It is for all people who live in the valley," said the man with broken teeth. "Everyone knows that."

"Obviously, not everyone does know that," Rolando's mother's voice echoed around the small room. "They shot my boy for trying to use land we have the right to use."

Charles Beaubien had assured the settlers they would keep

their right to use the grant's common land, even after his heirs sold the grant to Governor William Gilpin in 1863, which happened more than two decades ago. When Mauricio was a teenager, his father told him that Charles Beaubien, who had recruited the Córdova family to move to the San Luis Valley, had taken great care to have the legal language drafted to ensure the settlers they would own their ranches and have access to common land, even if the land grant was sold.

Just a few months after the language was drafted, Beaubien died, and his heirs sold the Sangre de Cristo land grant of over five-hundred thousand acres to Governor Gilpin. When news of the sale became public knowledge, no one was overly concerned. They assumed their rights would continue as always. If there were any questions about it now that they were under the governance of the United States, Beaubien's legal document was expected to guarantee these rights.

"Which animals and people from the valley are on the sierra now?" Mauricio addressed the crowd.

"My younger son is there with the sheep." Rolando's mother dabbed at her eyes with a woolen kerchief. "Please, please, Mother of God, keep him safe from the murderous Anglos."

Others called out names of loved ones who were looking after cattle or sheep grazing in the sierra.

Chapter 33

"My friends, we need to pay a visit to the sheriff's office." Mauricio tried not to let his anger at the injustice overcome him.

"That Anglo won't listen to us," spat the man with broken front teeth. "I say we take rocks and throw them through his window. That'll get his attention."

"We'll do no such thing!" Mauricio raised his voice above the riotous shouts. "We are legally entitled to the use of the sierra. We'll ask the sheriff to enforce the law."

"Yeah, right." The man with the broken teeth huffed and turned toward the door.

"Who will go with me?" Mauricio asked, but no one spoke.

Silence. Then an older man, stooped from years of hard labor, stepped toward Mauricio. "I'll go." His blue eyes sparkled with new-found valor. "Señor Alfredo Gonzalez at your service."

Mauricio nodded. Two more men stepped forward. "Vamos," he said, and the four men hurried out the door. They untied their horses and mounted. Mauricio's concern that Señor Gonzalez could not keep up with the younger men was soundly allayed when the stooped man let out a whoop and charged down the path back to town.

On the way, they passed Esteban and the doctor.

The men slowed their pace once in town, where children played in the streets. In front of the sheriff's office, they took a few moments to compose themselves before dismounting. Señor Gonzalez smoothed his hair and ran his hands over his face and beard. Mauricio straightened his hat.

"You speak English, no?" One of the other men asked, wringing his hands.

"Sí."

Mauricio took a deep breath and opened the factory-produced wooden door to the sheriff's office.

The sheriff had his head down, sleeping or reading, Mauricio didn't know which, until he said, "What can I do for you?" He looked up, flustered.

"We're here to report an attempted murder."

"Murder?"

"Yes, sir. A man we know went to the sierra to fetch his brother and his flock of sheep when some Anglos shot him. He has a really nasty wound, but he should live. The doctor is attending him."

"You say the man shot was trespassing on private property?" The sheriff grinned, smug with his legal conclusion.

"I said no such thing." Mauricio stepped toward the sheriff's desk, letting his size and height be intimidating. "He was grazing his sheep on common ground, land he has a right to use. Do you want the description of the man who shot him?" He didn't wait for an answer. "Sheriff, you need to get a posse together now to find the man who did this and ensure no one else's life is in danger. There are boys as young as nine or ten tending sheep in the sierra."

"What did you say was your name?"

The routine question caught Mauricio off guard. "I didn't say, but I am Mauricio Córdova de Medina." He extended his hand to the sheriff.

"Sheriff McCall." The man accepted the handshake half-heartedly but didn't meet Mauricio's steady gaze. "Let me check the files." *Such rotundity in one who is charged with running down criminals.* The sheriff's belly protruded over his belt. He walked stiffly to the four-drawer, wooden file cabinet behind his desk.

"The right of the valley people to use the sierra for grazing, hunting, and cutting lumber is guaranteed within the agreement of the sale of the Sangre de Cristo Land Grant to Governor William Gilpin by the original owner Carlos Beaubien," Mauricio told the sheriff.

On tiptoe the sheriff thumbed through the files in the top drawer marked A-D. "Córdova, yes, there it is." He pulled out a file folder and brought it to his desk, motioning Mauricio to step forward. "Right here is the Córdova de Medina deed, all filed and notarized proper-like. See?" The sheriff pointed to the title of the deed declaring that Carlos Beaubien had granted Mauricio's father eight-hundred eighty acres.

The property was described in the traditional Hispano way—all land between the San Esteban Creek and the crest of the first arroyo. Fortunately, Mauricio noted, it also included the official survey borders that his father insisted be made and recorded.

"Yes, this is my family's ranch, but this is not the concern we bring today, Sheriff."

"You really have nothing to worry about, Mr. Córdova." The sheriff sighed and for the first time, met Mauricio's gaze. "Your property is secure. For now."

Glaring at the sheriff, Mauricio fought to control his emotions. "Pull out the Sangre de Cristo file, please, and bring it here."

The sheriff backed up and opened the second drawer down. He rummaged through files aimlessly, trying to look as though he was searching for something specific.

"Try looking under 'S' for Sangre de Cristo," Mauricio said. He wanted in the worst way to add 'idiot,' but refrained.

"So now, Mr. Know-it-All, you're going to tell me how to do my job?"

"I'm just telling you that files with 'S' are in the bottom drawer." Mauricio felt heat rising in his face.

The sheriff huffed. "Why, here it is." He pulled out a large file folder and with his booted toe shoved the bottom drawer closed.

"Let's take a look." Mauricio stared the man down and pointed to the desk.

The sheriff sighed and dropped the folder on his desk. "Suit yourself."

In the middle of the file, Mauricio found what he was looking for. "Read that." He pointed to the top of a paper titled *Last Will and Testament of Carlos (Charles) Beaubien*. He scanned pages until he found a paragraph in the deed stating that the common ground could be used by the people of the valley and that they would retain their varas. "And read this paragraph right here." With his right index finger in the middle of the page, he pinned down the document.

The sheriff scratched his head. "What's a vara?"

"The long, narrow strips of land that run from the houses of the people into the hills where the irrigation ditches begin. You Anglos call them homesteads."

"What?" The sheriff's face contorted in confusion. "Gilpin sold all the land to that investment company, folks from England and Holland. Two people can't own the same land."

"You're right. That is why I'm directing you to the original contract which says the settlers retain their land and have access to common land for hunting, fishing, grazing, and cutting lumber."

"I don't know," the sheriff sputtered. "I think you need to leave."

"Sheriff, either you form a posse to go after the man who shot my friend and protect the boys and men in the high country, or we will do it ourselves."

The sheriff shooed them out like he was chasing flies off his dining table. "You have no idea what trouble you're bringing on yourselves."

ooooo

The next day while Mauricio ate his noon meal, he decided to have another talk with the sheriff. As he left the café, smoke was billowing from the direction of the sheriff's office. He sprinted to the office to find it fully engulfed in flames. The people ran back and forth between the well in the square a block away, with buckets of water, which they threw at the inferno. Despite the futility, Mauricio joined in the bucket brigade. Joining forces against a common foe, whether human or nature, was what the people of the San Luis Valley did in times of crises. Few, if any, of the people fighting the fire had any idea of the value of the documents housed in the office and what they meant to their own futures.

Mauricio hauled two buckets of water at a time, flinging them as far as he could into the crumbling building. As he turned to head for the well to refill his buckets, he saw pudgy Sheriff McCall across the street, watching the people work to put out the fire. His hands were shoved deep into his pockets. Mauricio was sure he saw the same smug grin on the sheriff's face the previous day when Sheriff McCall had concluded that Rolando was shot while trespassing.

Chapter 34

Doña Maria's Ranch

Doña Maria sat on her front porch, enjoying the warmth of the late afternoon and watching for the arrival of Carolina and Tomás. She was thrilled her grandson was attending school, and according to Carolina, doing very well, but she missed him during the week. She also missed Carolina. The talented young woman was more than thirty years her junior and had very different talents and interests, but Doña Maria adored her. When they were together, it was as if they had known each other all their lives. They never ran out of things to discuss. If Doña Maria had a daughter, she would have wanted her to be just like Carolina.

From the dust cloud emerged two horses. Doña Maria had recognized Carolina's bay mare, Azúcar, but not the large sorrel horse beside her. Had Carolina rented a horse from the livery for Tomás to ride? Why would she do that?

The pair of horses came into view. The sorrel horse carried a man wearing fringed chaps and a hat. She knew from the saddle with its lower cantle and swells that the rider was not Hispano. Tomás was seated on Azúcar behind Carolina. The riders dropped from the easy lope to a trot and then to a brisk walk once they came onto the grassy knoll in front of the ranch house.

Instead of heading to the barn to untack her horse as Carolina always did, she rode Azúcar to the hitching post at the porch.

"Buenas tardes," Carolina greeted Doña Maria, as she lowered Tomás to the ground with her left arm before dismounting herself. "Tomás had another very good week at school. He is such a smart and creative young man. I'm so proud of him."

"Abuela, te amo." Tomás ran to Doña Maria and hugged her around the waist.

"I am so happy to see you. I love you, too." Doña Maria thought it strange Carolina had made neither introduction nor explanation of the young man with her.

Carolina took the lead rope that was secured with leather strings to the back of her saddle and made a simple rope halter for Azúcar. She looped it over the mare's bridle and tied her to the hitching post. The big Anglo, clad in a plaid wool shirt and straw cowboy hat, dismounted and did the same.

Doña Maria saw Carolina draw a deep breath before taking the steps up onto the porch. Tomás had already gone inside to get a chunk of goat cheese. Carolina opened and closed her fists, then turned to motion for the man to join her on the porch.

"Remember when I told you I knew someone who would be a good all-around ranch hand?" Carolina glanced at her and then looked away.

"Is this your brother?" Doña Maria exclaimed with joy. "Bienvenidos. Mí casa es su casa."

"No, no, not my brother. A friend from the Bijou Basin." Carolina's eyes darted back and forth between the Anglo and her host.

"I thought you were going to ask your brother to come and help me?"

Anglo removed his hat and nodded at her, smiling but looking confused. He was the biggest man she had ever seen. "I don't know if I want a stranger living here, and he is an Anglo. How will we communicate?"

"He knows ranch work inside and out." Carolina forced a smile. "Why, I doubt you'll need to tell him much. Just show him the work and the tools, and he'll get everything up and running for you."

Before Doña Maria could reply, her grandson emerged from the house. "What's for supper, Abuela?"

ooooo

Doña Maria showed the tall Anglo to one of the guest rooms before returning to the kitchen to add chunks of dried beef and potatoes to the green chili stew that had been simmering all afternoon. She plopped a spoonful of lard into a pan and heated the oil. Considering the size of the young Anglo man, she decided to prepare refried beans also. Fortunately, she had made a double batch of goat cheese earlier in the week.

Her intuition put her mind at rest about the man being trustworthy. Otherwise, she would not have invited him into her house. The thing that bothered her, though, was Carolina's behavior. She was sure her young friend had said her brother was coming to serve as a ranch hand. If Carolina had asked someone else to come, why had she not told her? Was she nervous about something? This was a new and unwelcome uneasiness between them.

Carolina must have felt the same, because she didn't come into the kitchen to help Doña Maria with supper until just before time to eat.

"Let me set the table for supper." Carolina busied herself with the work, chatting about the students and what they were learning, and the town news, most of which was old. "If there isn't anything else you want me to do, I'll call Chance and Tomás." She left the room without giving Doña Maria a chance to speak.

When Carolina returned, Doña Maria, who had just finished putting the food on the table, pulled out her chair and pointed at the chairs across from her. "Siéntense por favor. It's time to eat."

"El Señor, thank you for supplying us with this nourishing and abundant food. We know that not everyone in this valley has plenty to eat, so we are so thankful. Thank you also for bringing

Tomás and Carolina home safely. And thank you for bringing Chance to help us. Amen." Doña Maria hoped her thanks for the new ranch hand had sounded sincere.

As she had suspected, Chance's appetite matched his size. He seemed truly appreciative for the meal, and with little encouragement helped himself to seconds and thirds. Carolina, though, who normally had a robust appetite, picked at the beans, goat cheese, and half-eaten stew.

"He thanks you for the delicious meal," Carolina said.

Doña Maria knew Chance had said more than that and wondered if Carolina had simply summarized his words or if there was more she didn't want Doña Maria to know.

When her guests had eaten their fill, Doña Maria pulled out of the oven a steaming dish smelling of honey and cinnamon.

"A cherry and plum torta with piñon nuts." She set the dish on the table then brought dessert dishes and spoons.

"My favorite, Abuela." Tomás leaned over the table to smell the steaming torta.

All but Carolina dug into their dessert. "It looks absolutely delicious, but I'm already full from the wonderful meal." She pushed her dish toward Tomás. "Would you like to eat mine?"

After supper, Carolina ushered Doña Maria into the sitting room. "You outdid yourself with that meal. Now, sit here. I'll clean up." The hostess sat obediently, not knowing what to do with herself all alone in the sitting room. She heard dishes clanking against the counter as Carolina washed and put away the supper dishes.

"All done," Carolina said as she entered the sitting room in a rush. "I'm tired. I think I'll turn in now."

Chapter 35

Saturday morning Caroline found Chance in the kitchen eating leftover beans, scrambled eggs, and tortillas. It was still too dark to start working, so she had no choice but to sit down at the table at Doña Maria's invitation. She adored the kindly woman but was afraid she would ask more questions about Chance and how Caroline knew him. She hated lying and she missed the usual warmth between them, but she was afraid Doña Maria, like Señora Sanchez, would learn the secret of Caroline's identity and kick her and Chance out.

After a second cup of coffee, the sun had begun its climb into the sky, bathing the ground in the morning's first light. "It's getting light out, Chance. Time to get to work." Not waiting for a response, she rose from the table and left the house through the kitchen's back door.

She headed to the barn to saddle her horse. Chance was right behind her.

"What is the rush, Sis?" Chance followed her into the barn where the horses stood. "It's not like you to be rude."

"Just a lot to do this weekend. We're burning daylight." Caroline fitted the rope halter on Azúcar's head and led her to the hitching post outside the tack shed.

Chance let out a sigh. He haltered Scout.

MARILYN BAY   177

The siblings brushed the horses and picked their hooves before throwing on and tightening saddles. The morning was crisp, but the silence between them was downright icy.

Once they had mounted their horses and were climbing up into the hills behind the ranch house, Caroline began to relax.

She had turned back toward Chance who was following her on the single horse trail. "I thought it would be best to ride the perimeter of the property, so you'll know its borders."

After a vigorous twenty-minute climb, they reached the top. "The crest of this hill, running north to south is the western border of the ranch." Caroline stopped to catch her breath and give her mount a rest. "The Hispanos aren't big on border fencing, and they also have a lot of vega or common ground that everyone uses." She turned Azúcar to face the ranch house below. "Doña Maria has a nice setup, but the barn and corrals need repairs."

"It's downright pretty, Sis." Chance scanned below, then turned toward the towering mountain peaks to the east. Snow had yet to fall in the lower country, but the peaks looked like they each wore a hat of white.

"Why are they called the Blood of Christ Mountains?"

"The morning sun is behind them now, so they are in silhouette, except for the white caps, but when the sun sets, it casts a dark red hue on the range." Caroline always felt small yet significant, gazing at the Sangre de Cristo Mountains.

"There is a legend about a priest, Father Francisco Torres, who was part of a Spanish exploration here in the early part of this century. That is supposed to be how the mountains got their name." She reined Azúcar toward the south. "Let's ride along the crest of this hill down into that meadow."

"Wait, you've got my curiosity up now." Chance let his face slide into that crooked grin that meant he wasn't budging until he got what he wanted. "Finish your story about Father Torres."

"The exploratory party had reached the mouth of the Rio Grande River, and Father Torres, who had been a missionary to the Pueblo Indians in New Mexico, saw this beautiful valley and named it El Valle de San Luis, or the San Luis Valley as we say in English. It is named after the patron saint of Seville, Spain, his place of origin." Caroline thought a moment.

"The story goes that the Indian slaves that the party had brought with them rebelled and mortally wounded the Father. As he was breathing his last, he saw the setting sun cast the red hue I was telling you about across the mountains. Just before he died, he is reported to have exclaimed 'Sangre de Cristo.' Who knows if that is true, but it's the story that is told around here."

The siblings turned south and continued their trek round the border of Doña Maria's ranch. The sun was high in the sky as they completed the southern loop of the ranch, including the horse and cattle pastures.

"There are seven brood mares and a great-looking palomino stallion. The two dozen cows are plenty to provide Doña Maria and her grandson with beef and give them the cash they need to buy staples, pay taxes, and put away money for a rainy day," Caroline had told Chance as they passed through the pastures. "When the snow falls, you'll need to herd them all into a pasture closer to the house. There is some hay in the loft of the barn, and the grasses will hold out for a while. I know you're not much for working stock, so I can help you move them next weekend."

"I'd appreciate that, Sis." Chance smiled as he pulled Scout in beside her. "It may be a long week with no one to talk to."

"Let's get some grub." With the ranch house in sight, Caroline kicked Azúcar into a run, yelling back at Chance. "Let's see who gets there first." She meant it to be a friendly throwback to their childhood, not an actual challenge. She and Chance both knew that while he was as strong as a bull and had unending endurance, she owned speed on horseback.

They offered the horses water at the well, then used halters to tie them to the hitching post in front of the ranch house. They loosened their saddles enough to give the horses relief but not so much that the saddles might swing under the horses' bellies and spook them.

Caroline entered the house without knocking and called

"Buenos días" to Doña Maria. She tipped her chin toward the interior of the house, urging Chance to enter.

"I didn't know where you had gone or when you would be back," said Doña Maria, pausing to look straight into Caroline's eyes, "but judging from the way your friend ate last night, I guessed you'd be back for the noon meal and siesta."

"I took Chance around the south loop to show him the livestock and the fence that needs mending." Caroline began setting the table for four. "I thought it would help him get a good idea of what needs to be done, since he doesn't speak Spanish, and Tomás and I have to return to San Luis Sunday night to be ready for school Monday morning."

Doña Maria smiled a knowing smile. "I see."

"What do you mean?" Caroline turned to face her, and for the first time since she arrived, she looked the older woman straight in the eyes. "Do you not think we were surveying the ranch and laying out the work that you need done?" Obviously Doña Maria didn't believe her. "Well, we did. And after we eat we're going to ride around the north loop to check the sheep and see repairs that need to be done to the fences and the irrigation system."

"Whatever you say, Señorita." Doña Maria turned to the stove and began scraping seasoned meat into a serving dish.

Doña Maria's behavior befuddled Caroline until it dawned on her. "Chance is not my boyfriend. He's ... a ... someone I grew up with." The words were true, but she was still hiding the truth from an honest and gracious woman for whom she cared very much.

Caroline and Chance enjoyed a meal of seasoned beef, tortillas, and baked squash with Doña Maria and Tomás before heading out to make the north loop of the ranch. That night, Caroline again insisted on clearing the table while their host rested. She had washed and dried all the dishes and was putting the last plate in the cupboard when Doña Maria stepped into the kitchen to announce that she was off to bed.

ooooo

Caroline woke the next morning just as the sun came up. She felt the cold wind bite as she stepped outside. She walked briskly toward the barn. Once inside, she forked hay to Azúcar and Scout and brought them buckets of fresh water from the well. She could see her breath as she jogged back to the house.

She pulled off her duster and hung it on the hook just inside the door before going to the kitchen to make coffee.

"Did you have trouble sleeping, Carolina?" Doña Maria asked, startling her. "Pour yourself a cup of coffee and sit down. I don't like it when you lie to me. Please, you must tell me the truth about Chance."

Caroline filled her cup at the stove slowly, her heart pounding. She sat at the table across from Doña Maria and rubbed together her frigid hands in the cup's steam. *Where do I start?*

"Did you believe I am Hispano?"

"Yes, yes, of course," Doña Maria answered Caroline. "You look like a Mexicana. You talk like a Mexicana. Why wouldn't I believe you are Hispano, Señorita Vargas?

"Living here in the valley is the only time I've felt like I fit in." Caroline wrapped her hands around the warm cup. "After I learned to speak Spanish, people just assumed I was Hispano, and I liked that."

"You mean you're not Hispano?

"No, I'm half white, half Cheyenne."

"You're Indio?"

"Yes, I am, and so is Chance. You were right. He is my brother, but he takes after our ma. Most people never guess he's Indian, but everywhere except here in the valley, people have always guessed I was Indian."

"You lied to me about Chance being your brother so I wouldn't know you're not Carolina Vargas?" Doña Maria's big, light brown eyes searched Caroline's.

"I'll understand if you don't want me around." A hot tear formed quickly and ran down Caroline's face. "It always happens. When people find out I'm half Indian, they always kick me out."

Caroline started to stand, her coffee untouched, but Doña Maria gently took hold of her arm. "Siéntese. I have much to say to you."

"I'm so sorry. I should have never come here. I shouldn't have asked Chance to come." Tears began coursing down Caroline's face.

"No, Carolina, you're not wrong to come or to bring Chance to my ranch." Doña Maria's voice was firm, her gaze steady. "I know you want to help me." She released her grasp on Caroline's hand. "I understand why you did it, but the only thing that bothers me after all we've shared, is that you would continue to lie to me."

Caroline put the palms of her hands over her face. "I know. It was wrong, but I could not bear to have you, especially you, look at me with loathing." Her words were interspersed with sobs.

"I know what a terrible thing it is to exclude or to dislike someone because of the color of their skin, their lack of a title, their religion, or something else they are judged by." Doña Maria patted Caroline's hand. "I only wish you could have confided in me."

She stood and came around behind Caroline. "You see, when I was a girl, I was considered very pretty." She turned Caroline's face toward hers. "My parents said I should marry a titled man because I was pretty enough to attract their attention. But I wanted to marry my Roberto. He was a tailor, not a titled gentleman. The day I married him, my family disowned me. I have determined not to judge people by these superficial things over which they have no control, but to look into their hearts." She took Caroline's hands in hers. "Carolina, you have a good heart, and I love you like a daughter."

Caroline's sorrowful sobs turned to tears of joy.

Chapter 36

Caroline rode back to town with a lightness she had not felt since she was a child playing with Chance and Anabelle at the family ranch in the Bijou Basin. She rode alone. Chance had agreed to bring Tomás to school Monday morning so the little boy could spend more time with his grandma.

Her mind wandered back to a time when Ma told her and her siblings not to play in the creek that ran behind their house. "We've had a lot of rains this spring, and the creek is runnin' way too high for it to be safe for you three," she had explained.

For hours that afternoon, she, Chance and Annabelle had run along the creek, pretending to be cowboys bringing in a herd of cattle. When the imaginary cattle were corralled, the siblings turned to searching the banks of the creek for treasures. Frogs, small snakes, and arrowheads all were in abundance. As Caroline reached for a shiny rock with silver flecks near the edge of the creek bank, she slipped and slid down into the water. The surge of fear turned to delight, as the cool, rushing water washed over her sweaty skin.

"The water isn't dangerous at all. Come on in." She waved at her siblings.

Chance, being Chance, dove in and began testing the current

further from the bank. Anabelle, who was five, timidly tested the water with a toe.

Her eyes grew big. "I want to come in."

The current had pushed Caroline downstream several feet from where her sister stood. "Come on in." She didn't want Anabelle to miss out on the fun, and she also knew that if she was left out, she would be more likely to tattle on her and Chance. She stretched her arm toward her little sister.

Anabelle sprang from the bank into the creek but fell short of Caroline's arm. While the current gently pushed Caroline, it swept petite Anabelle downstream with ferocity.

The previous summer Caroline and Chance had taught Anabelle the basics of swimming, but now the current tumbled her under.

"Help! Chance!" Caroline screamed at her brother, who was allowing the current to carry him downstream. In only a few strokes, Chance moved to the edge of the creek where Anabelle floundered. He snatched her left shoulder and pulled her out of the water. She sputtered and coughed, then began to cry.

"You are fine now, Anabelle," Chance said in the nurturing way he had with his sisters.

The tragedy averted, Caroline concocted—and helped her siblings rehearse—a scenario to explain to Ma why they had defied her. It went like this: Anabelle was walking too close to the bank. She fell in, and Chance and Caroline had to rescue her.

The siblings were not in the habit of lying to their parents, or to anyone for that matter, but this was hardly a lie. It was true that Anabelle had gone into the water, and Chance and Caroline needed to rescue her. Still, when Caroline told the rehearsed story to Ma, her throat felt dry, and she couldn't look Ma in the eye.

"Not only is lying wrong, Caroline, but the truth shall set you free." Ma tipped Caroline's chin up, so that she was forced to look into her ma's eyes. Caroline steadied her jaw and stared back.

"I told you what happened. Why can't you believe me?"

"Don't you think a mother knows when her children are lying

to her?" She paused and looked at Chance and Anabelle, who hung their heads rather than meet her gaze. "*Are* you lying?"

Then Anabelle sniffled. "Aw, Ma, we didn't want to lie to you, but we didn't want to get in trouble, either." Chance stepped forward and looked square at Ma. "Anabelle did fall into the creek, and Caroline and I had to rescue her. But we were in the creek first."

"Is that the truth?" Ma asked keenly.

Caroline nodded. Her cheeks burned with shame, but instead of sorrow, she felt indignation. Instead of repenting, she determined not to get caught the next time.

"Each of you get a switch from the trees at the creek and wait for me in the garden." Ma stood wide, hands on her hips. "Chance and Anabelle, you each get a swat for disobeying. Caroline, you get two swats; one for disobeying, and one for lying."

True to her word, Ma swatted a blubbering Anabelle once, then hugged her and told her she loved her. Chance was already crying when she swatted him. "I'm sorry I disobeyed you, Ma." They embraced, then he and Anabelle ran off to play in the barn.

But Caroline had already steeled her mind and her heart against the punishment. She hardly felt the swat. She wasn't ready to release her defiance. She was determined to show Ma how tough she was.

Looking back, Caroline realized her desire to prove she was right at the creek that day sent her on a journey of defiance that had cost her much. As a result, she had pushed away or run from those who loved her, and married a man she didn't love and who didn't love her.

All these years, she thought she was fooling her ma with her outward obedience, yet she now realized she had not. She remembered more than once when Ma, it seemed out of the blue, had said, "Live in truth, Caroline. The truth will set you free." She thought Ma was accusing her of lying. Now she realized Ma was admonishing her to be truthful with herself.

She had been so caught up in her swirling thoughts, rejoicing in her newfound freedom, that she found herself unsaddling

Azúcar in the barn behind the mercantile without recollection of how she arrived there. She brought the mare an armful of hay and drew a bucket of fresh water from the well outside the barn. She brushed out the mixture of sweat and dirt that lined the area where the saddle blanket and cinch had hugged Azúcar.

When Caroline stepped outside the barn, she closed the door behind her and looked up into the sky, wondering how Ma had grown so wise. Dark clouds covered the sky that was normally decorated with dazzling stars.

"It's me." Caroline knocked on the Cohens' back door.

"Come in, come in," Señora Cohen's voice welcomed her. "I'm so glad you returned before the storm. Old timers say it's going to be a bad one. This has already been a hard winter, and it's not yet Christmas." She set two cups of coffee on the dining table. "Come, warm your hands with some fresh coffee."

Caroline was pulling out the heavy wooden chair to sit when she heard Ana shout to Gloriana. "She's back! Carolina—I mean Señorita Vargas—is in the kitchen, drinking coffee with Mamá."

Ana ran into the kitchen and flung herself into Caroline's arms. "I missed you so much. How is Doña Maria's rancho?"

Caroline pulled the small girl into her lap. "Everything is very good." Caroline patted Ana's cheek. "The man you saw me with earlier…"—She glanced at Señora Cohen.—"His name is Chance. He is here to help Doña Maria with ranch chores." She would level with the Cohens later about Chance and who she really was. Now was not the time.

The stately Gloriana walked into the kitchen, displaying perfect posture and an aloofness Caroline had begun to think was natural. "Good evening, Señorita Vargas. How was your trip back to San Luis?" She pulled out a chair and sat on the front half of the seat, spine as straight as a young cottonwood tree.

"Azúcar was frisky. Animals can always tell when a storm is coming." Caroline held her cup with her left hand while balancing Ana on her right thigh. "I keep forgetting to ask you about that little church I pass each time I go to Doña Maria's ranch."

"That's the chapel of San Acacio. It was one of the first churches built when the Hispanos moved north from Santa Fe to settle in the San Luis Valley." Señora Cohen raised her cup to her lips, then set it down without drinking. "When the people began to settle, they always built houses around a plaza, and in the middle of the plaza was a church. That settlement was known as the Lower Culebra. All that remains now is the church."

"Do people gather there for mass?" Caroline put down her cup and leaned forward, her left forearm resting on the table.

"Sometimes Los Penitentes hold meetings there, but since the new Sangre de Cristo church was completed in San Luis, people attend services there instead."

"Why is it called San Acacio if the settlement was called the Lower Culebra?"

Señora Cohen set a plate of cookies on the table. "The old-timers in the valley tell of the summer of 1853. All the able-bodied older boys and men were in the mountains tending sheep when Ute warriors came upon the Lower Culebra settlement." She took a cookie and pushed the plate across the table toward Caroline, her eyes warning Ana to mind her manners. "The women, children, and elderly knew they were unable to defend themselves from the Ute warriors. They began to pray to San Acacio, a Greek centurion and saint, who was martyred in the fourth century for holding fast to his Christian faith. When they prayed, the settlers said the Ute warriors suddenly halted and fled. The village was renamed for San Acacio and the chapel was built to honor the deliverance of the people from the Ute war party. Years later when hostilities ceased, some of those same warriors told the settlers they had turned back because they saw that the settlement was defended by a bastion of well-armed guards."

Ana could resist no longer. She scooped up a cookie and bit off half of it. "The chapel is sooo pretty. In the afternoon, the sun comes through the stained-glass windows and the light falls on the altar."

"When I get married, I want to say my vows in the chapel of

San Acacio," Gloriana announced, stoic as ever.

Señora Cohen's jaw dropped. She opened her mouth to speak, then stopped. Instead, she reached toward Gloriana and patted her daughter's arm.

"The chapel is so romantic, Gloriana." Ana cupped her cheeks between her palms. "I, too, hope you get married there."

"All this talk of marriage is ridiculous. We're still in primary school." Gloriana blushed.

"It will not be soon, but it is nice to dream, no?" Señora Cohen smiled at her daughters, then winked at Caroline. "Time to wash up our dishes and get ready for bed, girls."

ooooo

Caroline was not surprised to wake up on Monday to a howling wind. There would be no school that day.

Chapter 37

Mid-morning, the self-appointed posse comprised of Mauricio, Señor Gonzalez, Esteban, Pedro, and two additional vaqueros that had worked at the Sanchez ranch, Diego and Antonio, rode northwest from San Luis. The men tugged up the collars of their oiled dusters and pulled scarves up over their faces. The opening between their hats and the woolen scarves was barely wide enough for them to peek out. The swirling snow hid the midday sun.

Mauricio steered his horse toward the peak in the distance. Rolando had described the unnamed peak as the place where he had left his brother with the flock of sheep. It was also where the Anglo had shot him.

"The Anglo who shot me was almost as tall as the boss." Rolando had gestured toward Mauricio. "But a lot skinnier. I'd guess him to be a little older than me. He rode a big, Roman-nosed roan gelding. The man with him was older, the age of our pa," he said. "His horse was brown with no white markings, but he had a distinct circle D brand on its hip."

The men's spirits were lifted when they saw that Rolando was recovering.

"I can't really ask you to go out until after the storm, but I am really worried about my brother." Rolando's facial muscles tensed when he spoke. "He doesn't know how to get back home. I told him I'd come for him before the weather got bad."

The men exchanged glances, confirming their resolve. They assured Rolando they would find his brother, the sheep, and the man who shot their friend.

The people in the San Luis Valley were adept at reading pending weather. They had felt moisture in the air and seen a shift in the direction of the wind. Everyone knew a nasty blizzard was headed their way. The men had discussed waiting in San Luis until the storm blew through, but were anxious to find Rolando's brother and any other boys still out tending sheep. Mauricio remembered an abandoned casita at the base of the mountain, and Diego confirmed it was still there, so the posse decided to try to ride out before the full fury of the storm was upon them. Tonight, they would wait out the storm at the casita and ride up the mountain when the weather broke.

The men rode two abreast in three close lines. Each pair of riders took turns riding in front, providing a break from the brutality of the blizzard for the other two sets of riders. When the lead pair's hands and faces were numb, they would drop back and let the next pair of riders take their turn in the lead. Ice and snow soon covered the legs and faces of their mounts. The howling wind made conversation impossible. The horses, whose instinct would have them turn their tails into the wind and wait it out in the open, had to be pushed to continue pressing into the storm.

Swirling snow obscured the peak most of the time, but the men, who had spent many hours in the saddle in all kinds of weather, knew the horses would take them to the casita. When Mauricio began to worry they had gone off course, the wind would slow just enough for him to see the peak rising straight ahead. The relationship between a cowboy and his horse was symbiotic. Deep down, man and horse knew they needed each other to survive. The horses needed their riders to push them to get out of the storm, and the horses knew where to go to get themselves and their humans out of peril.

After what seemed like an eternity, the wind paused. This was the break the riders needed to catch sight of the casita. Mauricio urged his horse into a trot with a renewed burst of energy.

It was the vaqueros' second nature to secure their animals before seeing to their own comfort. The shed was large, and the horses were too tired to establish a pecking order. They wasted no time backing into the shelter which was closed on three sides.

"It's enough to get them out of the wind and snow tonight," said Señor Gonzalez. "We'll hobble them and let them graze in the morning."

Antonio and Diego brought in dry wood from the covered porch on the south side and began to build a fire. The rest of the men removed their wet outer garments and spread them on furniture that they pulled close to the fireplace.

Soon a rip-roaring fire warmed bodies and spirits. The men dug into their saddlebags for beans and dried meat wrapped in tortillas. Mauricio was glad to see Tia Anita also had packed dried cherries and plums for him. The men removed their socks and gloves and examined themselves for signs of frostbite. Mauricio was relieved when he saw only pink or red hands and feet pushed up near the fire.

"I'll make coffee," Esteban said, rummaging through his saddlebags.

Those were the first words spoken since they'd entered the casita. Mauricio chided himself for letting the enthusiasm of the other men and his desire to help Rolando get in the way of good judgment. "Men, I'm sorry. We should have waited out the storm in San Luis."

"I'm not sorry." Señor Gonzalez's bright blue eyes shone. "If we'd waited, we wouldn't be up into the mountains for another two or three days. Those boys need us."

The old man's spirit and stamina were amazing.

"It was cold, but we're a hardy people, no?" Pedro said, pulling himself up straight and tall.

Diego thrust a big log onto the burning fire. "The only thing

I could think about during all that shivering, was those poor boys abandoned on the mountain."

"I'm proud to be in the midst of such warriors!" Mauricio smiled and squatted in front of the fire, rubbing his hands together.

That evening, after checking the horses, the men pulled their bedrolls close to the fire and turned in as soon as the sun set. Already, the wind was dying down. They could get an early start the next morning.

ooooo

When Mauricio and the posse woke early Tuesday morning, there was no trace of the blizzard other than drifts of snow sparkling in the sunlight. That's how it was in the San Luis Valley. Fierce storms blew in with little warning but were over as quickly as they came.

"We'll see to the horses," Señor Gonzalez declared. He and Esteban pulled on their dusters and pushed open the hand-hewn wooden door that hung from leather hinges, shoving the snow off the casita's stoop.

Diego added a solitary log to the fire. Mauricio stepped outside to scoop clean snow into the coffee pot. He placed the muslin bag of ground coffee beans on top of the snow and put the pot on the fire to brew.

"The night of rest did the horses good." Esteban pulled the door open and stomped his feet to get the snow off his boots and pants. "They're frisky this morning."

"There's still a lot of green grass beneath the snow and dried branches." Señor Gonzalez removed his duster and laid it across a chair. "They'll be done eating, and we can leave, in less than an hour."

Chapter 38

San Luis

Caroline awoke to clear skies on Tuesday morning following the blizzard. She donned her breeches, a flannel shirt, gloves, and a duster. She said a prayer of thanks to El Señor for her warm clothes. It felt good to be thankful.

She had spent the previous day helping Señora Cohen tidy the house, even though the fine lady's house was already tidy. They also baked empanadas filled with piñon nuts and honey. The savory ones had pork, onions, and pieces of dried red chile. Señora Cohen allotted about a fourth of the empanadas for family use, reserving the rest to sell in the mercantile.

They all had been cooped up in the house for a day and a half, and Caroline felt the need to be outside. Besides, she wanted to go to the schoolhouse just in case the children closer to town tried to make it to school that morning. While the storm was over, travel through the drifts was difficult. Besides, most of the children would be needed at home to help their families clear paths to animal enclosures, sweep snow off their houses, chop wood, and haul water from streams or wells. Daily chores had ceased while the valley people waited out the storm, but the drifted snow brought new work.

Even though the schoolhouse was less than a half mile from the Cohen Mercantile, by the time she reached her destination, she was breathing hard from breaking through the snowdrifts. Sweat poured down her face as she cleared the stoop of snow and pushed open the front door.

The diligence and faithfulness of the valley people never failed to amaze her. The box next to the stove had been filled with wood, and a bucket of water had been placed on the other side. Despite the impending storm, someone had managed to ensure the basics were provided for the next time school was in session. She pulled two logs from the box and pushed them inside the stove. She dug into the side of the wood box for the small pieces of wood, placed them on top of the logs, and lit a match to ignite the kindling. Soon a fire was popping and crackling, spreading its warmth throughout the room. The ice that had formed on the top of the bucket was melted, and she used the ladle to pour herself a cup of water. She organized the books she had left askew on her desk the previous Friday afternoon when Chance's arrival had caught her off guard.

By mid-morning, the wood had nearly burned out, and Caroline was certain none of her students were venturing out. Out the side window, the sparkling white snow seemed to beckon her to dance in its crystals.

Caroline jumped when the silence was shattered by someone bursting through the door.

"I figured on a day like today the school would be empty, but instead the comely teacher is here, with a welcoming fire." A tall, skinny Anglo strutted toward the stove. "It is so kind of you to think of me." He laughed, cruelty spilling from his yellow teeth.

Caroline felt for the knife in the side pocket of her breeches. "Who are you and what do you want?" She hoped she sounded threatening.

"Why, I first thought to get me some shelter, but now I'm thinking I'll get more than that." His eyes moved from her face down her body.

Caroline felt her skin crawl, the same way she felt watching a rattlesnake writhe. She wanted to run, but the man was between her and the door. Unlike fat Sheriff McCall, whom she had seen waddling down the streets of San Luis, this man could beat her to the door.

He strode toward her, a crooked smile directed at her chest.

When he got close enough that the glare was no longer in his face, Caroline saw that his smile wasn't what was crooked. He had a raised scar that ran from his cheekbone to his jaw, giving the appearance of a smile skewed to the scarred side of his face. He was close enough that she could smell his rancid breath and the effect of not bathing for weeks.

She pulled her knife out of her pocket to stand her ground and demanded he back off.

He lunged at her. His strength and abruptness startled Caroline. She thrust the knife upward with both hands as the man grabbed her waist and pulled her to him. But he dropped his grip on her, and his eyes widened. She let go of the knife and stepped back. He crumpled to the floor, clutching the knife handle, which protruded from his lower chest. He gasped for breath, fear in his eyes. She began to tremble.

She might have gone for the doctor, but she had done enough hunting to know that the man would die. She had not intended to do it, but her knife had surely sliced the intruder's left lung.

As her eyes focused away from the wound, Caroline saw a slip of paper peeking out of his front shirt pocket. She removed it and read the hand-written note. She gasped, horrified, and shoved the paper into the pocket of her breeches.

Chapter 39

Mountains West of San Luis

Mauricio and his men moved slowly through the drifted snow, but the horses were energetic, and the temperature had returned to that of a mild autumn day.

After climbing into the mountain for about an hour, the search party began to hear faint bleating sounds. They urged their horses to move faster. They traveled down into the small valley, fighting the deep drifts, in some places higher than the horses' backs. Turning southward toward an area heavy with pine trees, they came upon the flock of sheep. Ewes, nearly-grown lambs, and a few rams pawed the snow and nibbled pine needles and bits of grass.

"Chicos, where are you?" Mauricio shouted. Then he repeated his call, hoping the young sheepherders were nearby. "¿Donde están?"

His thundering voice sent the flock running together, forming a tight group, as sheep will do when they perceive a threat. Herding sheep was something each of the men had done in his younger days, and they understood this was how the sheep defended themselves, being unable to bite, kick, or outrun predators.

Mauricio didn't know Rolando's younger brother's name, so he simply bellowed into the grove of trees, "Your brother Rolando has sent us to help you bring the sheep back home."

A teenage boy emerged from behind a large pine tree. "I'm Rolando's brother." He was clutching a short machete in his right hand.

Mauricio supposed the boy's distrust was what had kept him from being killed by the man who shot Rolando. Mauricio dismounted so that he was not looking down at the boy. "Do you have food?"

"We ran out of ammunition a while ago, so we couldn't hunt. We had to kill one of the lambs, but we finished the meat over a week ago."

Mauricio turned and rifled through his saddlebag for one of his burritos from Tia Anita. "Here, eat this."

The boy held his head high but accepted the burrito with hands red from the cold. "Thank you." He tore off several bites. "I think I should save the rest for my compañeros, no?"

"Who is with you?" Mauricio took his gloves off and handed them to the boy. "Here, put these on your hands for a while."

"Juan Valdez and Julio Romero. We've kept our flocks together since we came here in early summer." He pulled on the gloves and flexed his fingers. "My name is Emilio."

"Where are Juan and Julio?" Mauricio surveyed the dense cover of trees behind Emilio.

"They are at lookout points on either side of this little valley." Emilio breathed deeply and jutted his chest forward. "We saw you coming but didn't know who you were. Two Anglos have been tracking us, but we knew they were up to no good, so we set up a patrol schedule. I've already signaled Juan and Julio. They'll be back here soon."

Mauricio was impressed. Mere lads behaving like men. Life in the San Luis Valley had a way of growing children to adulthood quickly. *A bit too quickly at times*, he thought.

He turned toward the men. "Looks like about a hundred sheep to move and three hungry boys on foot." He sighed. "I think we'd best get them all back to their homes and leave searching for the Anglo gunmen for another time. What do you say?"

The men nodded their agreement.

Mauricio turned back to Emilio. "What is the best way out of this valley and back to San Luis?"

"There's a canyon over there," Emilio gestured in the opposite direction. "It is narrow enough to keep the sheep in a group yet wide enough that the drifts shouldn't be too bad."

Without another word, the men fanned out and began pushing the flock in the direction Emilio suggested.

"Go get your gear and your friends. You can ride behind me, and Juan and Julio can ride behind two of the other riders."

Emilio hurried back into the trees, emerging five minutes later with Juan and Julio. Each boy carried his gear in a heavy woolen blanket. Mauricio, Esteban, and Diego packed the gear into their saddlebags so the boys could wear the blankets around their shoulders. They had not been expecting to be in the mountains when the weather turned cold and did not have warm jackets. The men helped the three boys swing up behind their saddles. The warmth and movement of the horses would help keep them warm.

Chapter 40
San Luis

When the reality sank in that she had killed a man, Caroline convulsed as angry tears poured down her face. When her shaking subsided, she fumbled for the key to lock the schoolhouse door. She didn't think any of her students would make it to school so late in the day, but just in case, she didn't want them to find a dead man lying on the schoolhouse floor. She slipped the key into the pocket of her duster and sprinted as best she could to the sheriff. The new office, deeper into the downtown of San Luis, had burned to the ground the previous week, making it necessary for the sheriff to move back to the old adobe office. She had planned to go for the doctor, but when it was clear the man was dead, she decided to go for the sheriff instead.

Bursting into the office, she shouted, "I've killed a man. He tried to attack me, and I accidentally stabbed him." Then she realized her mistake in speaking Spanish, which had become second nature to her.

The pudgy Anglo the people called Sheriff McCall snarled, "Were you raised in a barn?" He rose and closed the office door. "How dare you come burst in here, speaking that disgusting language to me?"

Caroline opened her mouth to reply in English, but before

she was able, Sheriff McCall shoved her into a chair just inside the door.

"You people think you own this valley, but you can't even speak American." Salt-and-pepper whiskers indicated he hadn't shaved for several days. "Sit whilst I fetch my deputy. He speaks your language."

Caroline was about to tell him a translator wasn't necessary, but the man had insulted her; no, he had insulted all the valley people. She would let him think what he wanted.

The sheriff returned ten minutes later with a man Caroline thought she had seen about town. The deputy was Anglo, short and pudgy, a younger version of Sheriff McCall.

"Me ll ... llamo ... Deputy Regan. Porqué ... uh ... estás aquí?" His Spanish was halting and spoken with a strong Anglo accent.

Caroline answered in Spanish, "I am the teacher. A man came to the schoolhouse this morning and threatened me. I used a knife to defend myself, but when he lunged at me, the knife went into his lung and he died."

Deputy Regan's eyes widened. "Sheriff, I think she said she killed someone."

"What kind of nonsense is that? She's a woman," Sheriff McCall snorted.

The deputy turned toward Caroline and with difficulty asked, "You say there's a dead man?"

Caroline paused, deciding whether to respond in Spanish or English. She continued in Spanish. "Yes, he was threatening me. He, his body I mean, is in the schoolhouse."

"Sheriff, she said she killed a man who was threatening her and that his body is still in the schoolhouse." The deputy looked at the sheriff like a dog waiting to be petted.

For the first time since Caroline had burst into his office, Sheriff McCall seemed to understand the gravity of her announcement. "You know, Regan, when I came to work this morning, I saw Edward Clark's horse tied outside the schoolhouse."

"Is Clark that shifty drifter you hired to clear the mountain pastures of trespassing Mexicans?"

"Listen here, Regan, I know she don't understand nothing we say, but don't you ever mention me hiring Clark again!" Sheriff McCall swore and swung at the deputy, nearly falling when he missed.

Deputy Regan, who had stepped back to avoid the fist coming at him, removed his hat and nodded with gusto. "Yes, sir. Never again."

Caroline was beginning to see that the sheriff and deputy not knowing she spoke English could work to her advantage. In Spanish she said, "Come with me to the schoolhouse and I'll show you."

○○○○○

It was late afternoon when Caroline opened the schoolhouse door for the sheriff and deputy. They rushed to the body, which lay face up. The glances between Sheriff McCall and Deputy Regan confirmed the dead man was no stranger to them. The sheriff searched all the man's pockets, swearing when he found them empty.

While the sheriff and deputy were focused on the body, Caroline pretended to tend to the fire, even though it had burned out before she went for the sheriff. The men didn't seem to notice her. From across the room, she heard bits of their conversation. She heard the sheriff mutter stupid … careless … can't be traced to us. Then the voices lowered to a whisper and she could decipher nothing. Out of the corner of her eye, she saw the deputy remove the dead man's gun from the hip holster.

Caroline moved toward her desk, hoping to get a better view of where the deputy stashed the dead man's gun.

The movement caught the sheriff's eye. "Stay right there." He sprung up and rushed toward Caroline. "Turn around and put your hands behind your back."

Caroline nearly complied until she remembered they thought she understood no English. She tried her best to look like an innocent school teacher.

"Blasted people, can't understand a thing." The sheriff grabbed her arm and spun her around. She could feel him fumble for his handcuffs and struggle to put them on her. "You're under arrest for murder."

Caroline bit her lip to keep from gasping when he said 'murder.' She was glad she wasn't facing him.

"Deputy Regan, take Clark, uh, the victim to the undertaker, and I'll lock up our suspect."

The sheriff circled Caroline's upper arm with his chubby hands and pulled her toward the door. As she spun around, she saw the deputy shove something into his coat. The sheriff pushed her out the door and she heard the sound of boots being dragged across the schoolhouse's rough-hewn wooden planks.

Once outside, the sheriff drew his pistol and motioned for her to walk in front of him. The closer they got to the sheriff's office, the more he labored to breathe. Caroline had no doubt she could have turned, knocked the pistol out of his hand, and run, but her running days were over. She was determined to stay and defend herself from the charge of murder.

Caroline, not Sheriff McCall, opened the unlocked door to the sheriff's office. He was breathing so hard that she thought he might collapse onto the floor, leaving her no choice but to go for the doctor, her hands cuffed behind her back. Securing his prisoner seemed the furthest thing from his mind as he sunk into his chair and lay forward onto his desk. *If this wasn't so serious, it would be amusing*, she thought.

When his breathing slowed, he bellowed at Caroline, "You! Back there into the open cell." He swung his arm and pointed to the back of the building where two jail cells nested.

Caroline turned her back to the sheriff and raised her cuffed hands.

"Oh blasted. I'd be in trouble for shore if I left them cuffs on ya." He rifled through his pants pockets. "Now, where'd I put them keys?"

○○○○○

If not for the urgency they felt to get the boys and sheep home, Mauricio and the other men would have enjoyed the trip back. Several deer and their nearly-grown fawns pawed at the snow to uncover grass and to look for loose bark on trees. Rabbits in their silky gray coats darted through the snow.

The most difficult part was traveling through the canyon, with snow up to the sheep's bellies. Once off the mountain, they could travel faster. The brilliant reds, pinks, and golds characteristic of sunsets in the valley emerged as the sun loomed lower into the western sky, casting a magical glow at their backs. San Luis was within their view.

Mauricio and his men had been on the lookout for the Anglo gunman, or signs that he was still on the mountain, but had seen nothing. As they entered San Luis, Mauricio felt bone tired. The constant state of alert as they searched for the gunman, fighting the blizzard, apprehension that bad had come to the boys and sheep, then driving the sheep through the snow to safety had wearied him almost to oblivion. In his physical and mental exhaustion, he had almost missed it. He was instantly jolted to full alert by the sight of a Roman-nosed roan gelding tied to the hitching post outside the schoolhouse.

Chapter 41

As Sheriff McCall looked for the keys to free his prisoner's hands, the deputy burst in. "All done, Sheriff. I was dragging Clark ... er, the victim down the street toward the undertaker when some of them vaqueros came along and helped me." His yellow teeth showed when he smiled. "Don't think I could've got 'im there without the help."

"Why would a bunch of vaqueros help you drag a body to the undertaker?" The sheriff raised his eyebrows.

"One of 'em, the big vaquero who spoke English, said Clark had nearly killed his friend."

"And what did you say?"

"Told 'im I knew nothin' 'bout that," said the deputy, obviously pleased with himself. "Also told 'im we had a suspect in custody."

"And what did he say when you told him that?"

"Something about the person in custody should be released on account of 'im doin' the community a favor.'" Deputy Regan guffawed. "I didn't tell 'im it was a 'her'."

"You talk too much, Regan." The sheriff snorted. "Help me find that spare set of keys, so we can uncuff the teacher and get her into a cell."

"You're really going to hold her, Sheriff, and charge her?" The deputy's eyes went wide. "The vaquero is probably right.

The community is better off without the sick bast—"

"Now you listen to me, Regan." The sheriff's neck was red. "This town here ain't too happy with the law, now that we're havin' to remove Mexican land grant owners so the new owners can have their land. They'll be happy to see the law has apprehended, and will prosecute, a murderer." In spite of his bravado, the sheriff looked worried. "Besides, all the hoopla of a trial will take the people's attention off land disputes."

The deputy glanced at Caroline, then back at the sheriff. "I can't see anyone, white or Anglo, bein' happy to have their school teacher prosecuted for murder."

"Do as you're told, Regan. Get our suspect in a cell and remove her cuffs."

Caroline didn't know whether to laugh hysterically or cry. She had no doubt the man she stabbed would have violated her, maybe even killed her. She hadn't intended to put her knife into him. When he lunged at her, he had impaled himself on it. A sick feeling rose up in her each time she thought about the knife pushing through his chest.

Shortly after Deputy Regan locked her in the cell, he left the sheriff's office and returned with a bowl of beef stew, short on beef and long on salty water. He set the food down on the small, wobbly table with a handful of old newspapers. He poked at the newspaper pile then pointed at the chamber pot.

ooooo

The morning sun poured through the high cell window, but no one had come to the office. Caroline's hips ached from a night of tossing and turning on the wooden plank that served as a bed. She had slept more comfortably on the ground many nights, where at least there was some give in the earth, and pine boughs along with straw or prairie grass to pad her backside.

She thumbed through the newspapers, looking for something to take her mind off her predicament. A headline that read *Chinese Massacre at Rock Springs* caught her attention. She read the story about the uprising. White workers' wages had been pushed down due to the Chinese workers' willingness to work for less. Even though the massacre happened over a year earlier, she had not heard about it before. She read on with interest.

> On the 3rd of September, a telegraph message was received in Boston to the effect that armed men to the number of a hundred or more had on the previous day driven all the Chinese miners employed by the company out of the coal mines at Rock Springs, Wyoming; had killed and wounded a large number of them; had plundered and burned their quarters, including some fifty houses owned by the company; had stopped all work at the mines; had ordered certain officers of the company's mining department to leave town at an hour's notice; and now demanded, as the condition upon which they would permit the resumption of work in the mines, a pledge that the Chinese should be no longer employed. Later advices [sic] on that and the following day not only confirmed the first reports but increased the number of killed and wounded and the extent of the destruction of property. It appeared that so many of the six hundred Chinese computed to have been in the camp, as escaped massacre, had fled into the mountains and desert in the vicinity of Rock Springs, where they were in danger of perishing from terror and starvation; while the armed rioters in possession of the town threatened them with death if they returned to it.

She turned the page to finish the story but found it missing. She sighed, pushed herself to her feet, and paced the iron and adobe enclosure. The window was too high for her to peer out. From the cell she could see Sheriff McCall's empty desk.

Returning to sit on the plank, she plopped the stack of newspapers on her lap. She thumbed through them until she found one that was not yet yellowed. It was Denver's *Rocky Mountain News* from September. She scanned the front page, stopping at the headline *Geronimo Gives Up!* The article described the Apache chief's surrender to General Nelson Miles in Skeleton Canyon, Arizona, after more than a decade of fighting. Terms of the surrender included Geronimo agreeing to his tribe settling in Florida. Caroline sighed, remembering the heartbreak of Pa's people, the Cheyenne, when they had been forced first to live in agencies throughout the West and then to move to reservation land in Oklahoma. They went south, and many died from disease carried by mosquitoes.

When the Cheyenne still lived in Colorado, Pa took their family each summer to visit his relatives. Sometimes they stayed for weeks. The men hunted, Ma helped with tanning hides and drying food for winter, and the children did chores and played with their cousins and other village children. When Caroline was ten, her family had traveled to the Cheyenne summer camp to find it abandoned. After that, they never again saw their cousins. Pa learned that his people had been moved to an Indian agency. The following year, he got word from his sister—a letter written by a caring white woman who identified herself as "a friend of your sister"—saying that they were being moved to Oklahoma.

A tear slid down Caroline's cheek. She mourned the loss of her Pa's family from her life. She could have been forced to move to Oklahoma and live on a mosquito-infested reservation herself. She could have been one of the Chinese killed in Rock Springs. Instead, she had a family that loved her. She never lacked food or a warm place to sleep. Yet, she had hardened her heart and allowed herself to believe lies. She believed that no one would love her for who she was. *Never again*, she told herself.

She was startled out of her reverie by urgent pounding on the office door. Men were speaking in Spanish, but she couldn't make out the words. The pounding stopped, and she returned to the pile of newspapers.

She was startled again, this time by the sound of a key turning in the exterior door lock, then voices outside, and creaking as the door opened on its metal hinges.

"What is so blasted urgent that you must lie in wait for me?" Sheriff McCall's attitude hadn't improved with a night of rest. "I'll open my office when I'm good and ready to open it."

Then a sound like a fist slamming against the door.

"Sheriff McCall, we've been trying to get some answers about the man who shot our friend, and we find through town gossip that he has been killed and you have a suspect in custody." The speaker's commanding voice bore only the slightest Spanish accent. "We must speak with this man you have in custody."

Caroline froze. She had not heard Mauricio speak English, but she had no doubt it was him. Hadn't she been humiliated enough in front of him when she rode away from the Sanchez Estate, dishonored? She couldn't bear to have him see her locked in a cell with a chamber pot and a plank for a bed. She pulled her duster on and tipped the collar up to disguise her long hair. She sat on the plank and faced the wall at the back of the cell.

"Now, you fellas just run along and let the law take care of things," called out Sheriff McCall.

Caroline breathed a huge sigh of relief when she heard the door slam between Mauricio's men and the sheriff.

Chapter 42

Mauricio needed to leave San Luis before he lost his temper and did something he would regret. Besides, he had to check that his mother and son had come through the storm unscathed. He hadn't been home since summer. It was the first place he had planned to go when his employment with the Sanchezes ended, but the cattle drive to Denver, then Rolando being shot, had kept him away.

As he left town and rode southwest toward the ranch, muddy streets gave way to sparkling white snow dotted with cedar trees. A gray rabbit darted before him and dove for cover in a hole burrowed on the side of the path. Mauricio squinted against the brightness that made it difficult to see depth in the snow-covered path. His dependable mount was good at picking its way to the ranch, which gave him time to think about the successful rescue of Rolando's younger brother and the boy's friends who were running low on food yet faithful to look after their flocks of sheep. Mauricio gave thanks that he and his men had been able to bring them all down from the mountain without injury to boy or beast.

News of the stabbing of Rolando's attempted killer, which had delayed his return to the ranch until this morning, brought relief. But there was something unsettling about the way Sheriff McCall avoided answering questions concerning the stabbing. When Mauricio saw the corpse of the tall, skinny Anglo enroute to the undertaker, he was exactly as Rolando's mother had described him. Why would the sheriff arrest a man for killing a murderer? It was no doubt self-defense, yet Sheriff McCall offered no details about who had been arrested or the circumstances of the killing.

He determined to return to San Luis and demand answers, but not until he did some chores, like refreshing the woodpile, hauling water to the house, and seeing to the livestock. Mending fences and a new roof on the barn would have to wait until he had more time. The sun was high in the sky when he caught sight of the adobe ranch house. He loved the way it nestled at the base of the foothills. The road leading to the house meandered through knolls in the high prairie as if it were part of the mountain path.

Returning to the ranch he had called home most of his life, always flooded him with peace. His mount had kept a ground-covering pace, and within minutes Mauricio could see the steps to the front veranda that promised rest to family and visitors alike. It was his mother's favorite place. He had sipped countless mugs of strong coffee with goat's milk on that veranda in the company of his father, mother, and brother. When he married and brought his wife from Santa Fe, her complaints about the "barbaric" country had nearly ruined the leisure of the veranda. It was a mistake to have married, to have believed she would be anything but selfish and hateful. He should have seen who she really was before he married her, but he was young and besotted. Now he knew it wasn't love at all, but one-sided infatuation.

He had long since forgiven and released Teresa, but he still winced when he thought about the pain he had caused his family. Then there was Tomás. He was the one good thing that came from his brief and tumultuous marriage. Sweet, courageous Tomás. While in Denver, Mauricio had come to a decision. He would no longer take employment outside the San Luis Valley. He had to be a father to Tomás, a full-time father. He had saved up enough to pay for emergencies, make improvements to the ranch, and send Tomás to college in Santa Fe as his parents had done for him and his brother. He felt confident that if he worked smart and hard, he could make the ranch provide their food, buy supplies, and pay the tax bill.

He dismounted and hitched his horse to the rail in front of the veranda. He climbed the steps two at a time and pulled the heavy wooden door open. "¡Mamá, Tomás! I'm home!"

He heard a kettle clang in the kitchen and headed that way.

"Oh, my son, I'm so glad to see you!" His mother stepped toward him with open arms. "When I went into town for supplies last week, I heard there was trouble with some boys herding sheep in the mountains and that you were searching for them. Did you find them?" She held Mauricio with firm, strong arms, the top of her head falling below his chin. Her thick hair was peppered with white.

"Sí, Mamá, we found them. All are back home and safe now." He cupped her face in his hands. "So how are you?"

"I am happy and in good health, but most of all I am so very glad to see you home safe and strong." She smiled and ran her fingertips across his left cheek. "I need to tell you about my new friend and the help El Señor sent our way. But first you'd better find Tomás." She stepped back and swept her arm toward the door at the back of the kitchen. "He is cleaning out stalls in the barn."

Mauricio bolted out the door and sprinted to the barn. He was surprised to find the big, sliding door on the east side wide open. He hadn't been able to push open the heavy chunk of wood himself until he was nearly a teenager. From inside he heard the voice of his son and the voice of an Anglo man.

"Se llama caballo. Ca-ba-yo." Tomás over pronounced each syllable like a teacher instructing a student.

"Caballo. Caballo. Horse." The man repeated the Spanish and then used the English word.

"Horse. This is a horse." Tomás spoke English with only the slightest accent.

"!Hijo mio!" Mauricio stepped into the barn, interrupting the language lesson.

"¡Papá!" Tomás ran to his father and jumped up into waiting arms. "I missed you so much!"

"I missed you too, Son." Mauricio set Tomás back on the barn floor and squatted down onto his haunches so that his eyes were level with his son's. "I've made a decision. I'm going to come back home for good. No matter how tough things get, I don't want to leave you or Grandma again."

The boy's eyes widened. "So we can work together every day, Papá?"

"That's right, Son."

"But what about school?" Tomás looked worried.

"School? What school?" Mauricio cocked his head to one side. "When you are older, much older, I will pay for you to go to college in Santa Fe."

"No, Papá. I'm talking about school in San Luis." Tomás sported a mischievous smile. "My teacher says I'm smart."

"Well, I'm sure that is true." Now Mauricio brandished his fatherly version of a mischievous smile. "I know you are smart because I am your father, and my teachers always said I was very smart. I just didn't know the school had a teacher or that they allowed five-year-olds to attend."

"My teacher said I am a bit on the young side, but she wanted me to go, and Grandma said I could."

The joyous reunion of father and son had blocked out all else until the Anglo spoke. "Did you get the herd safely to the Denver Stockyards?" He wore a familiar, plaid flannel shirt, which Mauricio had been relieved to see once before.

"Yes. Why, yes we did." Mauricio stood and extended his hand to the man. "It was very interesting to see and learn about the buying system they have at the stockyards. Well worth the effort."

"Good, good. I'm glad." Chance Thomas still had a firm handshake. "I thought about you often after I left to come to San Luis."

"We could never have found and retrieved our cattle without you. Thank you, once again."

"We ranchers must stick together, no?" Chance chuckled.

"Is this the job you mentioned when we met near Pueblo? Working for my mother?"

"Indeed it is." Chance pointed at the roof. "Come spring, I think it is best to put a new roof on the barn, but for now I've patched it so it doesn't leak. When the weather clears, I'll get out and work on the south fence line. Part of it has fallen down, but I'm sure you know that."

"I didn't know it was that bad," Mauricio sighed, rubbing his chin between his forefinger and thumb. "It's been over a year since I've been out there, but I'm done hiring out. It's time I focus on my own ranch and my son."

"I 'spect it's time I get ready to head back home, then." Chance shoved his large hands into his pockets, his smile gone.

"No, no, you stay on. There's plenty of work for both of us." Mauricio looked like a fellow taking out his girl then finding his pockets were empty when it came time to pay. "Has my mother discussed your pay?"

"Yes. She said she has enough to pay me for at least a year from the horses she sold. I don't expect to stay much longer than that. My folks will need me back home."

"Horses? That handful of unbroken colts couldn't have brought much."

"Oh, no sirree, they weren't unbroken." Chance's look was intense. "Your ma hired my sister during the summer. She broke 'em, then helped your ma sell 'em for top dollar. My sister's really, really good with horses. She learned from our ma."

A woman who was good with horses. Realization, or suspicion, began to dawn for Mauricio. "Where is your sister now?" *But Carolina is dark. She looked nothing like Chance. It couldn't be.*

"Your ma wanted her to stay on and do ranch chores, but my sis told her she wasn't near as good with ranch chores as she was breaking horses. Besides, she had already told folks she would be the teacher at the San Luis school. That's when the two of them decided to ask if I wanted to come here to work." Chance smiled broadly, extending his arms forward, palms up. "So here I am."

It was a cold day, and Mauricio's lack of physical movement would normally have made him feel chilly. Instead sweat began to gather at his hairline. "Your sister is Carolina Vargas de Garcia?"

"No, her name is Caroline Thomas."

Mauricio thought back to the day he met Carolina and the way she had chosen a Spanish surname with the casualty of choosing a new dress. This was what she had been hiding. She wasn't Indian and Spaniard. She was Indian and Anglo. Knowing how the people of the San Luis Valley despised the Anglos taking over their land, it was no wonder she had not told him her true identity. She had trained horses for his mother, and her brother was their ranch hand. As shocking as all this was, it was his recollection of seeing the killer's Roman-nosed roan gelding in front of the schoolhouse the previous evening that made his blood run cold.

"Chance, the ranch chores will have to wait." Mauricio's hands were trembling. "Saddle your horse. We must get into San Luis to check on Carolina … on Caroline."

"Why?"

"Just saddle up. I'll explain on the way."

Mauricio turned to Tomás. "I want to make sure your teacher is safe."

"Why wouldn't she be, Papá?" The boy's eyes widened.

"I'm sure everything is fine, Tomás. Mr. Thomas and I just need to check on her. Would you tell Grandma we'll be back soon? I need you to be a good, strong boy, Son."

Tomás turned to run to the house, but not before Mauricio saw a tear slide down his cheek.

Chapter 43
San Luis

Mauricio pounded on the sheriff's door, his blows making the glass windows rattle. Chance saw the *Closed* sign in the window to the left of the door. "I think the office is closed for the day, Mauricio." Chance grasped his companion's shoulder. "We'll have to come back in the morning."

Mauricio turned, his back supported by the door, and slid to the ground. "Tuesday afternoon, three other men and I rode back into town after searching the mountains for a man who had nearly killed a friend of ours." He took a deep breath. "I've not seen the man myself, but I knew he rode a Roman-nosed, roan gelding. We saw his horse tied in front of the schoolhouse." Mauricio slammed his fist into his open palm. "I wasn't worried, because I knew the school would be closed due to the blizzard. I didn't know it was Carolina, your sister, who was the new school teacher." He rubbed his face with his weather-worn hands.

"If the schoolhouse was closed, Caroline would have been at the Cohens', no?" Color rose in Chance's face. "Let's go look for her there."

The men mounted their horses and rode less than half a mile to Cohen's Mercantile. They jumped off their horses and secured them to the hitching post outside. Mauricio turned the knob and found it locked. He knocked with insistence but with more restraint than he did at the sheriff's office.

A man opened the door and stepped back so Mauricio and Chance could enter. They spoke Spanish. Chance couldn't understand more than a dozen Spanish words, but he could understand from the red faces and emotional conversation that both the shopkeeper and Mauricio were disturbed.

Mr. Cohen disappeared through a door at the back of the shop. Chance supposed the door led to the family's quarters where Caroline lived during the week.

"What did you learn about my sister?" Chance's jaw was tight.

"It's not good." Mauricio motioned Chance to sit at one of the tables in the front of the mercantile counter. "Mr. Cohen said the word is out that Carolina killed the man who nearly killed my friend, and—"

"I know my sister," Chance said, wide-eyed. "She would never do such a thing unless it was in self-defense."

"The law will be trying her for murder." Mauricio looked down, swallowed hard, then looked back up at Chance. "The trial starts tomorrow."

ooooo

In the days since confessing the truth of her identity to Doña Maria, Caroline had come to realize what it had cost her to live a lie. It had required her to talk herself into not one, but many lies. All this time she believed she was of no value when people knew she was half Cheyenne Indian. She believed even her parents had valued her less because of her darker skin and eyes. Most of all, the lies had wrecked her soul. Until now, she believed that God was angry with her and would ignore her should she cry out to Him. Her time in the jail cell forced her to look at her life and who she had become. She didn't like it, and had tried so many times to change, but this time was different. She ceased trying to change and become 'good' on her own. She dropped to her knees and told God she didn't know how to get out of her situation, and she didn't know how she could become a good person. She told Him she was tired of striving and failing and that she wanted Him to change her from the inside out. She yielded completely to Him, even if it meant she had to die for killing the vile man in self-defense.

When she got off her knees, peace flooded her soul. She was still frightened about how people would react to the truth, and she knew the trial and sentencing would be difficult. But she also knew from the depths of her heart that she was doing the right thing and believed God would walk with her.

Ma, who had known Caroline's heart, had quoted the words of the Bible to her many times. "Ye shall know the truth, and the truth shall set you free." Knowing the truth was so much more than telling the truth; it was being honest with others and with God.

Once she had yielded her will to the Almighty, she understood what she must do when she was tried for murder. She had hidden the truth for most of her life. Why not make the truth work in her favor?

ooooo

"The Sixth Amendment to the U.S. Constitution says that any defendant charged criminally has the right to counsel." Señor Rosales, an older, scholarly man, at the request of the San Luis judge, had traveled from Del Norte to assist in Caroline's defense.

"Señor Rodrigo Rosales at your service, ma'am." He spoke in Old World Castilian Spanish, removing his gray felt bowler hat when he addressed her. It was not the habit of Hispano gentlemen to shake the hand of a lady. He tipped his head at her instead. He had traveled all night in a worn, but good quality, gray pin-striped suit. He was an inch or two shorter than Caroline. His hair was slicked back. He was graying at the temples. Ma would have called him 'distinguished.'

"I wish I were a lawyer, but I am not. I suppose it is the Anglo's way of satisfying the requirement without providing you the legal help you really need. But they may be surprised." He winked at her.

"Why do you say that?"

"For all they know, I am an old man with an education that has retired to live in Del Norte with his daughter and her children." He put his hands on his hips and jutted his chin forward. "What they do not know is that I once taught law students at a college in Santa Fe." He grinned.

"That's wonderful!" Caroline clapped her hands together. "Please explain to me what we need to do."

"The first thing the judge will ask you is how you plead?"

"Plead?"

"Yes. He wants to know if you agree you are guilty or disagree."

"I killed the man, that is for certain, but he lunged at me."

"Ah ha!" Señor Rosales clasped his right fist in front of his chest. "You will plead not guilty by reason of self-defense."

"That's true." Caroline winced. "The man would have violated me or worse. I took out my knife to defend myself."

"Yes, yes, you must tell this to the court." Señor Rosales pulled a small notebook out of his suit coat pocket. "And what do we know about the deceased? Did this man, Edward Clark, have a criminal record? What of his character?"

"I don't know. I had never seen him before he came into the schoolhouse that day." Caroline sighed. "His breath smelled like he had been drinking alcohol and he hadn't bathed in a very long time, but I guess there is no law against either of those things." She shoved her hand into her skirt pocket and pulled out the letter she had taken from Mr. Clark after he had died in the schoolhouse. "I do have this."

Señor Rosales took the paper and read it. "Señorita, this is very important evidence."

"Evidence?"

"Yes, it tells us and the jury what kind of evil man the victim was." He folded the letter and started to put it into his pocket, then he handed it back to her. "I think it is best if you keep it. I have heard about pieces of evidence like this 'disappearing'."

"If Mr. Clark was a bad man, and I killed him accidentally and in self-defense, why would I be branded a murderer?"

"The problem is, there is no one to corroborate your story." Señor Rosales scratched the back of his head as he thought. "Is there anyone I can call to the witness stand to testify to your character?"

Caroline hung her head. "I am new to San Luis. No one knows me very well." She could have added that if they did, they would know what a lie she had lived. But she didn't want Señor Rosales to think badly of her, so she said no more.

"I will ask around town for people willing to testify on your behalf and for any more information about Mr. Clark."

Caroline nodded. "When does the trial begin?"

"Tomorrow."

"Tomorrow?" Caroline shuddered.

"I don't think the court wants us to have much time to prepare." He smiled kindly, as Caroline imagined a grandfather would smile at his grandchild.

"Would you go to the Cohen Mercantile and ask Señora Cohen to send me a set of clean clothes? I board there." Caroline swallowed and looked away, then looked back at Señor Rosales. "There's one more thing. Would you send word to my brother who is working for Doña Maria at her ranch, that I will be in court tomorrow?" She choked back a sob. "I don't want him to see me ... being tried for murder ... but I need him there."

"Yes, yes, I will be glad to do this for you, señorita."

Chapter 44

The next morning, Caroline woke when the sun began to wash her jail cell with light. It poured through the high window on the east side of the building. She was surprised how well she had slept, waking only twice on the hard, wooden pallet.

She used the basin of water and lye soap to bathe. She put on the clean, pressed dress and clean undergarments the sweet Señora Cohen had sent to the jail. She braided her long, black hair, weaving in the matching ribbon. Caroline made sure to tuck the evidence letter into the pocket of her dress.

Deputy Regan brought Caroline a breakfast tray bearing coffee, stale bread, and a hunk of cheese with mold on the edges. She sipped the lukewarm, watery coffee, yearning for the steaming, rich coffee with goat's milk that she so enjoyed with Doña Maria. She knew she would need something more substantial to get her through the day, so she picked the mold off the cheese and ate half of it with the stale bread.

Without uttering a single word, the deputy returned to the cell and removed the tray.

"Time to go to the courthouse." Caroline recognized the booming voice of Sheriff McCall as he entered the cell.

She pulled her vaquero-style duster on over the dress.

"Hands behind your back so we can cuff you proper-like." The sheriff jerked her wrists back, assuming she couldn't understand and fumbled with the cuffs before she heard the snap indicating he had succeeded in locking them.

The cold took her breath away as she stepped out onto the street. The sheriff guided her from behind like he was a rancher teaching a horse to drive. The new Costilla County Courthouse was two blocks from the sheriff's office and across the street. By the time they reached the courthouse door and stepped into the outer vestibule, Sheriff McCall was wheezing.

Caroline thought it odd the courthouse was built of rough-cut beams and adobe in the style of the Hispanos, while the old and new sheriff's offices were built of wood in the style of the Anglos. Could it be that the Anglos wanted to ensure the records held in the sheriff's office were easy to destroy by an 'accidental' fire, whereas no records were yet stored in the courthouse?

"I trust you slept well, Señorita Vargas?" It was the genteel Señor Rosales. He wore a tweed suit with a vest and ascot tie. He held his brown felt bowler hat at his waist, as any gentleman did inside a church or government building.

"Yes. Yes, quite well, thank you," Caroline's voice quivered in spite of trying her best to appear strong and confident.

Señor Rosales turned to Sheriff McCall and addressed him in English. "The law requires that you uncuff a defendant before he or she enters the courtroom."

While the sheriff fumbled with the cuffs, Señor Rosales said, "I can only imagine how overwhelming this must be for you, but you should know that you have a great deal of community support." Señor Rosales swept his arm toward the door that opened into the courtroom. "After you."

Caroline's gasp was nearly audible as she entered the packed courtroom. Her students, their parents, and many other Hispano townspeople she recognized sat on the polished wooden benches. Smiling faces followed her as she willed her legs to move her across the wide, dark-stained pine floors to the front. The man from the Spanish newspaper sat on the aisle in the second row, his notebook and quill pen in hand. In the front row on the right side, Sheriff McCall, Deputy Regan, and a few men she didn't recognize were taking their seats.

When she reached the front, Señor Rosales motioned for her to be seated at the table to the left. When she turned, she saw the entire Cohen family, Chance, and Mauricio sitting in the front row, just behind the defendant's table. Her hands began to tremble and she felt dizzy. She sat with haste in the chair next to Señor Rosales.

"It seems the entire town has turned out," she whispered to her legal adviser. To herself she said, "And why is Mauricio here? Does he know my brother?"

Señor Rosales patted her hand and whispered, "You are loved by all of them, señorita. Now, you focus on what you need to say to the judge. ¿Sí?"

Chapter 45

Moments later a male clerk entered through a heavy, six-paneled wooden door in the interior of the room. He announced, "All rise for the Honorable Judge Samuel Baker."

Once the judge took his seat, the clerk instructed everyone to sit except Caroline and Señor Rosales. He had earlier explained to her that the judge would expect her to remain standing while her plea was entered.

"Carolina Vargas pleads innocent by reason of self-defense," Señor Rosales declared in heavily-accented English.

"Very well." The judge had a beak nose and stern gray eyes. "You may sit." He turned toward the man seated at the table on the right side of the courtroom. "You may present your case."

The prosecutor rose and strutted toward the section where the jury sat. Carolina searched the faces of the jury. All were Anglo. She recognized one juror, a manager at the flour mill, but no one else.

"Gentlemen, we are here today to decide a simple case. Miss Vargas killed Edward Clark, a citizen of our community, in cold blood, and left him to die on the floor of the schoolhouse. Suffering from tremendous guilt, she then ran to the sheriff's office to report her crime. Both Sheriff McCall and Deputy Regan will tell you she confessed the crime to each of them."

The prosecutor turned from the jury and strutted like a tom turkey courting a hen, stopping in front of the judge and witness stand. "The prosecution calls Sheriff McCall."

After the clerk swore in the sheriff, the pudgy man hoisted himself onto the seat in the witness stand. The courtroom was chilly, yet he pulled a handkerchief out of his shirt pocket and wiped sweat from his brow.

"Please tell us about the events that occurred December third regarding Miss Vargas." The prosecutor stepped back, so the jury could see and hear the sheriff.

"It was early afternoon. I'd taken my dinner at Susanna's Café. She makes a right fine peach cobbler. 'Course I'd had her pot roast with roast potatoes and gravy 'fore that."

Caroline glanced at the jury and saw several of the men smile and suppress laughter.

"Sheriff, let's stick to the facts of the case." The prosecutor straightened his back and gave his witness a disdainful smile.

"Oh, yes, sir. Well, shortly after I returned from dinner, that there woman," he pointed at Caroline, "came bursting into my office. She didn't shut the door. I couldn't understand a word she said. I find it despicable these people are American but can't speak American."

"What did she say?"

"I had no idea until Deputy Regan translated." The sheriff straightened in his chair. "Said she'd killed a man. Yep, that's what she said. Even led us to the schoolhouse to see the body of poor Edward, blood still oozing from his gut where she'd stabbed him."

"What did you do then?" The prosecutor looked both hopeful and frightened, like a mother taking a young child to church, hoping he wouldn't blurt out anything embarrassing.

"Why, I arrested her for murder." Sheriff McCall looked smug. "What else could I do?"

"Yes, yes, indeed. Thank you for your testimony, Sheriff." The prosecutor returned to his chair and sat.

"Do you have any questions for this witness?" Judge Baker

turned in the direction of Señor Rosales and Caroline, but failed to look directly at them.

Señor Rosales stood. "Not at this time, sir."

Caroline looked at her legal counsel with wide eyes.

"Don't worry, señorita," Señor Rosales whispered into Caroline's ear while Deputy Regan was sworn in. "Let them dig a deeper hole for themselves. We can always recall them later."

The deputy's testimony was as brief as his boss's, not untrue but far from complete. Then Deputy Regan took his seat.

The prosecutor marched to the front of the courtroom, just below where the judge sat. "Your Honor, we'd like to call Ned Wilson." The prosecutor put his hand on his hip and his nose in the air. "Mr. Wilson has been sequestered."

The double doors at the back of the courtroom swung open, and a man whose attitude and demeanor reminded Caroline of Edward Clark, stood. There were gasps from people in the courtroom and surprised looks on the faces of the jurymen.

Someone among the people whispered loudly in Spanish, "That's the man. The one who shot me."

Caroline turned just enough to see the whisperer was Rolando, who had worked for Mauricio at the Sanchez Estate and who had been recovering recently from a gunshot wound.

"Order in the court." Judge Baker pounded his gavel on a block of wood. "We'll not have further outbursts in this court. Do you understand?"

Ned Wilson approached the witness stand, and the clerk instructed him to place his left hand on the Bible and raise his right hand.

"Sure. Why not?" Mr. Wilson chortled his response and climbed into the witness seat.

"Mr. Wilson, did you know the victim, Edward Clark?" The prosecutor glanced at Caroline.

"Shore did. Me and Ed, we've been friends a long time."

"In what capacity did you know him?"

"Huh?"

"How did you know him? Did you work together? Were you kin?"

"Well, yeh, you could say we worked together," Wilson snickered. "Guess you could even say we was like brothers, ol' Ed and me."

"Tell us about Mr. Clark's character."

Wilson looked confused.

The prosecutor was careful to enunciate each syllable. "Was he a good man?"

"Shore was. Rumor's been going round that he tried to assault her." Wilson pointed at Caroline. "But she really ain't his type."

"Thank you, Mr. Wilson." The prosecutor's eyes flared. "We've heard enough. That will be all."

"Do you have any more witnesses?" Judge Baker asked.

"No, the prosecution rests." The strutting had deteriorated into shuffling, as the red-faced prosecutor took his seat.

Señor Rosales stood. "Your Honor, the defense would like to call Señor Cohen."

Señor Cohen was sworn in and took his seat in the witness stand.

"Your Honor, members of the jury, Prosecutor: Señor Cohen is much more comfortable speaking Spanish." Señor Rosales turned toward the clerk. "We will ask an impartial person to translate his words into English."

"Very well." Judge Baker beckoned his clerk to come forward.

"Señor Cohen, please state your occupation and in what capacity you know the defendant." Caroline's counsel pointed to her.

"My wife and I own and operate Cohen's Mercantile. We have been merchants since we moved to the San Luis Valley a decade ago. My three children met Señorita Vargas in the town square last spring. They brought her to our home to meet Señora Cohen and me. We liked her immediately. It is the same reaction most people have when meeting Señorita Vargas. Everyone loves her. In fact, this courtroom is packed with townspeople and her students and their families. They are all here to support her."

Caroline brightened. *They are here to support someone like me?*

After hearing for the English translation, Señor Rosales continued, "How did the defendant come to be the San Luis school teacher, and where did she live?"

"She lived with us. We insisted. She was very kind to our children and helpful to my wife. When we learned that she had training as a school teacher, we were thrilled. We thought the school would not open this year because we had no teacher. Señorita Vargas's students will tell you she cares about each student, and her teaching methods are creative. The students are inspired to learn."

Caroline let the generous and sincere words soothe her heart.

When the translator missed a sentence, Señor Rosales prompted him.

"One last question, Señor Cohen. Can you imagine that the defendant could murder someone?"

"Preposterous! She is strong and quite capable with weapons. I have no doubt she could defend herself. But murder? Never!"

"Thank you for your testimony." Señor Rosales smiled. "The defense now calls Mauricio Córdoba."

Caroline gasped. She covered her mouth, hoping no one would hear her ... or notice her reddening face.

Chapter 46

Señor Rosales moved to the witness stand and turned toward the jury to ensure they heard his questions. "Señor Córdoba, please tell us your occupation and how you know the defendant."

"I am a rancher. I live and ranch near San Luis. Until recently, I was ranch manager at the Sanchez Estate south of San Luis. I met Señorita Vargas when I went to a neighboring ranch to buy horses for my ranch hands."

It all makes sense. Mario is a nickname for Mauricio—Doña Maria's son! Caroline swallowed hard. *Mauricio knows my secrets, at least some of them.*

He continued in nearly perfect English, "Señorita Vargas is a very skilled horse trainer, and I later learned she is also a teacher. Since my employer would never have allowed a woman to train horses for her, I offered the señorita a job teaching the children of the Sanchez Estate employees. She accepted."

Señor Rosales asked, "How would you describe the character of the defendant?"

Caroline winced. Above all things, Mauricio was honest. *How will he describe the character of someone who has deceived him?*

"She worked very hard, also achieved more than she promised. She is smart and talented, but also humble."

Caroline stared at Mauricio through her tears.

Then he looked directly at her, and his eyes bore into hers. "She is one of the finest human beings I have ever met."

Caroline almost forgot she was in a courtroom, being tried for murder, until Señor Rosales said, "I hate to malign the dead, but the defendant's fate depends on it. What can you tell us about the victim?"

"I saw him. My men and I helped the deputy carry his body to the undertaker. He was exactly as my friend Rolando described the man who shot him. His horse—a Roman-nosed roan gelding—was found tied outside the schoolhouse the afternoon Clark was killed. Furthermore, when Mr. Wilson stood to testify, Rolando, who is sitting right there…" Mauricio pointed, and Rolando nodded. "He whispered to me that Wilson was with Clark when he shot Rolando."

"One last question, Señor Córdoba." The retired professor crossed his arms in front of his chest. "Do you think Señorita Vargas killed Edward Clark?"

"If she killed him, it was only because she feared he would kill her." Mauricio again looked square at Caroline. "There is no other explanation. She's a kind and loving woman."

Caroline smiled at Mauricio. She used her kerchief to dab at the tears coursing down her cheeks.

Judge Baker leaned forward. "Are both the prosecution and defense ready for closing arguments?"

Señor Rosales held up his right hand, palm open. "Your Honor, the defense wishes to call the defendant, Señorita Carolina Vargas."

"Very well." Judge Baker turned to his right. "I'll call my clerk to swear her in and interpret."

Caroline slid onto the seat in the witness stand. She raised her left hand and poked her right hand into her skirt pocket to feel the paper evidence. She sighed with relief, then pulled her right hand out of her pocket and put it on the Bible the clerk held.

After she swore to tell the truth, the whole truth, and nothing but the truth, Señor Rosales spoke to her in Spanish. "Please state your name for the record."

"Before I do that, I need to explain." She folded and unfolded her hands in front of her. "I want to thank you all for your kindness and support." Caroline sat up straight and leaned forward, speaking in Spanish. "You have all known me as Carolina Vargas, the school teacher, but my real name is Caroline Thomas." She paused while the clerk translated.

Caroline saw surprised expressions and heard people whispering in Spanish, but was unable to make out the words. She continued, "I am half Anglo and half Cheyenne Indian. My parents are good people, but I was ashamed of my heritage. When I came to the San Luis Valley, people thought I was Hispano. It felt good to feel like I belonged. I had learned Spanish from a friend of my mother's in Denver who was born in the valley. She said I spoke with only the slightest accent. When I came here, everyone just assumed I was a daughter of the valley."

The courtroom was silent.

She looked down at her hands, then out at the people seated in the back rows. "I am so sorry I deceived you."

Judge Baker scratched the right side of his head, then folded his arms in front of him, while turning toward the witness stand. "Miss Vargas, ah Thomas, if English is your native tongue, why not speak it now?"

"I understand, sir." Caroline said in English, her tongue feeling thick, similar to what she had felt when she began learning Spanish. Besides speaking to Chance and teaching her students English, she had spoken only Spanish for more than two years. "I just have one request. If I continue speaking English, I want my words translated into Spanish."

"That's a reasonable request." Judge Baker turned toward his Anglo clerk. "Are you able to translate English to Spanish?"

The man nodded.

"Very well. We shall proceed."

Her counsel cleared his throat. "Miss Thomas, please tell us what happened the Tuesday afternoon you encountered Edward Clark."

Sheriff McCall and Deputy Regan squirmed in their seats. That just gave Caroline more courage. "It was the day after the blizzard. I wanted to make sure no students had made the trip to the schoolhouse, so I left the Cohens' house early in the morning. With no one at the schoolhouse, I decided to do some cleaning." Caroline paused for translation of her words into Spanish. She felt all eyes on her.

"I think it was shortly before noon when I heard someone on the stairs. I thought it was a student, but then an unkempt man burst through the door. He leered at me in a most uncomfortable way. He was inebriated."

She put the open palm of her right hand against her upper chest. "I asked what he wanted, and he said, 'Why, I first thought to get me some shelter, but now I see I can get more than that.' Those were his exact words."

"Then what happened? Take your time. I know it is very difficult to tell." Señor Rosales patted her left hand and nodded.

"I told him to stop, but he kept coming toward me." Caroline's lips curled. "His eyes were moving from here to here." She pointed at her clavicle and swept her hand downward. "I always keep a knife in my skirt pocket, so I took it out and held it in front of me with both hands." Caroline put her fists, one on top of the other, in front of her. Moisture was gathering at her eyes.

"What happened next?"

"I yelled at him to stop, wielding the knife to push him away, but he didn't stop. He lunged at me and impaled himself on my knife." Caroline covered her face, not able to choke back the sobs.

The prosecutor jumped to his feet. "I'd like to cross-examine the witness. That is, after she has composed herself."

"Very well. That is your right." Judge Baker leaned forward, turning his head to make eye contact with Caroline and waited until she regained control.

The prosecutor paraded past the jury and toward Caroline, shoulders erect, chin held high. "Señorita Vargas, or is it Thomas? Do you expect us to believe a man would purposely fall onto a knife so clearly displayed?"

"I don't know why he did it. Maybe he thought he could knock it out of my hands that way." Caroline straightened in her chair. "I am certain, though, that he would have violated me and maybe even killed me if I had not killed him."

"I'm sure you were very frightened, but there is no way of knowing what he would have done. Besides, how can we believe a woman who doesn't even tell the truth about her identity?" The prosecutor walked toward the jury, then stopped and tipped his head toward Caroline. "Why didn't you go for the doctor after you stabbed him?"

"I thought about that, but his mouth hung open, and I could hear wheezing coming from inside. I have hunted enough to know, by that sound, that the knife had punctured his lung." She looked down. "There was nothing to be done by anyone, even a doctor."

"One more question, Miss Whatever-Your-Name-Is. If you told the story you just told to Sheriff McCall, why didn't he testify to that?"

"The sheriff had hired Edward Clark and Ned Wilson at the request of some Anglo land investors to get Hispano families to vacate their land. The investors also wanted the Hispanos off the common ground the people of the valley use to hunt, fish, graze, and cut timber."

Caroline paused for the clerk to translate. He looked at her, eyes wide. "Please translate exactly what I said." He nodded.

When the clerk had translated, the courtroom which was buzzing with chatter from the Anglos, exploded in angry outbursts from the Hispanos.

Chapter 47

Order, order!" Judge Baker slammed his gavel on the wooden block, and the courtroom became silent.

"How can you say such an awful thing about Sheriff McCall?" The prosecutor's eyes shot darts at Caroline.

"Because I heard the sheriff and his deputy talking about it. They assumed I could only understand Spanish."

"That is preposterous! You expect us to believe a woman who kills a man in cold blood and even lies about her own name, rather than a man of the law?"

"No, sir, I do not expect you to believe me." Caroline looked at Señor Rosales, who nodded. She pulled the letter from her pocket and opened it. "But I do expect you to take into consideration a letter written to Edward Clark and Ned Wilson in Sheriff McCall's own hand."

Señor Rosales shot to his feet. "Your Honor, we request this letter be read and submitted into evidence." He could barely be heard over the talk in the courtroom.

Judge Baker brought his gavel down, calling for silence. All obeyed, save the sheriff and his deputy.

"I told you to get that letter off Clark's body." Sheriff McCall's face was red and dripping with perspiration.

"I tried, but I couldn't find it." Deputy Regan's eyes were wide, and Caroline thought she saw a tremor in his face muscle.

When McCall and Regan realized the courtroom had silenced, and they had been heard, they bolted toward the door.

"Apprehend those men!" Judge Baker spoke to his bailiff and clerk and scowled at McCall and Regan. "No one leaves the courtroom until this evidence is considered."

After McCall and Regan were ushered back to their seats, Caroline asked, "Would you like me to read the letter?"

He nodded.

"It is in English, so I will read in English."

21 August 1888

Dear Misters Clark & Wilson,

A group of landowners, who wish to remain anonymous, request your services to clear their holdings of all Hispano land claims by whatever means necessary. On their behalf, I will pay you fifty dollars up front and another two-hundred dollars when their deeds are free of all outside claims. Please meet me tomorrow evening at the café to discuss details.

Sincerely,
San Luis Sheriff George McCall

Caroline feared the clerk would faint, so she translated the letter into Spanish herself. Again, the courtroom burst into an uproar.

This time, Judge Baker pounded his gavel five times before the noise subsided. "Ladies and gentlemen, please sit. I'll not have such disorder in my courtroom."

The prosecutor jumped to his feet, all dignity forgotten. "Your Honor, the defendant by her own admission, has lied about her name, her identity, her ... well, just about everything." He tugged on his suit vest. "I ask for proof this is an authentic letter."

"You heard Sheriff McCall himself ask his deputy why he hadn't removed the letter from Clark's body," said Judge Baker. He tapped his upper lip with his right index finger. "But you are correct, we need to confirm that the signature on that letter is Sheriff McCall's." He turned toward his clerk and held out a piece of blank paper. "Have the sheriff sign his name on this piece of paper."

"Objection." Señor Rosales rose to his feet. "Knowing that you want to compare signatures, Your Honor, the sheriff will disguise his true signature. If we compare it to his signature on the court documents, that will provide us with a more accurate comparison, no?"

"Excellent suggestion." Under his breath the judge muttered, "I wish I'd thought of it myself."

"Sir, may I pass both signatures to the jury for inspection?" Señor Rosales beamed.

"Yes, please do, Señor Rosales. And when they have finished, please bring the signatures to me."

The jurymen nodded as they compared the signatures, then passed them to the next juryman. When all twelve had examined the signatures, Señor Rosales carried the court paper and the letter to Judge Baker.

"Does the jury have any doubt the two signatures were made by the same man?"

All heads shook back and forth.

"Well, we've got to have it on the record. Who is jury foreman?"

The man from the flour mill stood. "I am, Your Honor." He looked to his left and to his right at nodding heads. "We agree the signatures match."

"I concur with the jury," the judge said, and his steel-grey eyes began to soften.

There was a scuffling in the first row, as the sheriff and deputy tried to leave, this time sneaking into the side aisle.

"Bailiff, take the sheriff and his deputy into custody. These two will help us get to the bottom of who it is that hired killers to intimidate law-abiding citizens." Judge Baker cast a sympathetic glance at Caroline and Señor Rosales. Then he added, "I'll not allow such illegal and immoral schemes in my district."

The clerk translated the judge's assertion into Spanish for the courtroom to hear.

Señor Rosales stood. "I request the defendant be declared not guilty by reason of self-defense and released, Your Honor."

Judge Baker slammed his gavel against the wood block. "You are free to go, Miss Thomas." He nodded at Caroline, who released a deep sigh. Maybe it was the breath she'd been holding since she left home more than two years ago.

Chapter 48

San Luis, Christmas Eve 1886

M y feet hurt. And it's cold outside," Ana wailed as Señora Cohen wrapped her daughter in a bulky, gray woolen serape. "Do I have to go out?"

"Of course, you must go tonight." Señora Cohen draped the brown cotton robe around her daughter over the serape and overlapped the front of the robe, tying it closed with a white satin waist sash. "How can the people of San Luis celebrate Las Posadas without the Virgin Mary?"

Caroline squatted so she was eye-to-eye with Ana. "Don't you remember when I asked the students who they wanted to play the part of Mary and Joseph in Las Posadas, and you were so excited to be chosen?" She cradled the impetuous Ana's pouty face in her open palms. "Tonight is the last night. It is Christmas Eve. After we finish, we'll go to a special Christmas service and then have tamales at the church. Won't it be fun to break the piñata in the back of the new church?"

"I guess it will be fun. Will you help us break the piñata?" Ana grasped Caroline's hand.

"I will watch you and the other children try to break it. You know, the piñata will be in the shape of a star, because it was a star that led the Wise Men from the East to visit baby Jesus."

"Bueno." A cautious smile replaced Ana's pout.

"Now stand still for your mother to put on the headscarf to make you look like Mary." Caroline winked at Señora Cohen. "Remember, being the mother of the baby Jesus is a big responsibility."

Ten minutes later, Caroline and Ana stepped out of the Cohen house, gloved hands entwined. The sky was clear and displayed hundreds of twinkling stars, but the absence of cloud cover offered no protection from the biting cold.

Caroline had agreed to take Ana to the church so Señora Cohen could come later with her tamales and the piñata.

The Sangre de Cristo Church had been completed the past summer, and it contained an adobe oven in the vestibule. Caroline and Ana stomped their feet and scraped them against the rough sisal mat just outside the door so they wouldn't track the muddy snow into the church.

"Oh, there's my little Mary." Father Valdéz, a short, plump, jolly man reminded Caroline of the drawings she'd seen of Saint Nicolas, save the white beard and hair. His hair was still black and his closely trimmed beard was peppered with just a few bristles of gray. "Please, come warm yourselves by the fire."

They required no further urging but removed their gloves and held their hands close to the logs that glowed red.

"When the ladies bring the delicious Las Posadas foods, we'll put the dishes here along the hearth to keep warm." Father Valdéz's eyes danced with excitement.

Caroline had only met the priest once before, but both times he had impressed her as someone who truly cared about his parishioners.

Within a few minutes Joseph, the angels, and a group of faithful townspeople had arrived.

"Is everyone ready for our Christmas Eve posada and celebration?" Father Valdéz asked. He smiled warmly. "Well then, vamos."

The procession shuffled out of the church vestibule and into the town square just a few blocks away. They stopped in front of the Pacheco home, a stylish adobe with painted wood shutters and patio railings.

As he had done for the past eight evenings, Juan, who was playing the part of Joseph, knocked on the door of the 'inn'. "Have you room for us to stay? Mary is going to have a baby."

Señor Pacheco bellowed, "You poor peasants go away. We have no room for you."

Then, as they walked back toward the church, the group of parishioners sang a song about the couple's travails finding lodging.

On the previous night, Juan had asked for lodging at the Vigil home across the square from the Cohen's Mercantile. The window in the tidy, new, stucco home framed a lit, seven-candle candelabra in the front window. A shy teenaged girl wearing a pink, Western-style shirtwaist had answered the door.

"Have you room for us to stay? Mary is going to have a baby," Juan had asked in a clear, polite voice.

"No," the teenaged girl responded, then covered her mouth, embarrassed, and turned around where an elderly woman prompted her.

The girl turned to the crowd and looked up before stating the rehearsed words. "No, we have relatives from out of town. We have no room for you to stay."

Now, once Ana, Juan and the other parishioners were inside the church, they recited the rosary.

"Let us pray," Father Valdéz said. "We thank Thee, our Señor, for the many blessings you have bestowed upon us. Let each one experience the joy and peace of this Christmas season. We ask that you bless and provide for those in need. In the name of the Father, the Son, and the Holy Spirit. Amen."

"Friends, if you will form a line, you may pass by the stove where the ladies who have prepared us this special Christmas food will offer you tamales and other treats." The priest winked. "Make sure you leave a tamale or two for me."

People shuffled into some semblance of a line while continuing to visit.

"We are so happy you are teaching our children again after that awful man tried to hurt you." Juan's mother stood directly in front of Caroline, grasping her forearms. "No one ever thought you killed that man intentionally. We're so glad the judge saw the truth."

The kindness warmed Caroline's heart. "Thank you, señora. Juan and Felicia are delightful, smart children."

The señora gave Caroline's arms a gentle squeeze before moving on.

"We also thank you for exposing the evil ways some of the Anglos are trying to steal our land." It was Luis's grandfather speaking. Though he appeared feeble, his voice was strong and bold. "Before I went to your trial, I thought all Anglos were the same. But the judge restored my confidence in the American judicial system."

"My ma and pa always told me that with any group of people, there are bad ones and good ones," Caroline replied. She smiled at Luis's grandfather and the others listening in. "Let's remember they were right as we keep fighting to protect your farms."

After joining the food line, she felt a hand on her back. She had no need to turn to see whose hand it was. Heat radiated up her spine and into her cheeks.

"Do you think if I stand behind you, they'll give me a tamale, even though I was not part of the procession?" Mauricio whispered.

"Certainly not!" Caroline stamped her foot as she turned to face him. Her eyes moved from his chin to his eyes. She blinked. "Well, maybe I could split mine with you."

He laughed mischievously, and then his expression turned serious. "I really had planned to make it in time to be part of the procession, but we had a ewe go into labor this afternoon. The first lamb was breech, and the second had its head turned back. It wasn't easy to get them out, but all three seem to be fine now." He winked at her. "Don't worry, I took a good bath before I left."

"Why didn't you have Chance help you?"

"If it's not a cow or a horse, he's helpless." Mauricio cocked his head to one side. "Besides, his hands are too big to deliver lambs."

Señora Cohen gave Caroline a tamale and a bowl of hominy, red chile, and pork stew called posole. She gave Mauricio two tamales and a bowl of posole. They moved to a pew in the sanctuary to eat the steaming, spicy food.

"I'm not sharing this with you," Caroline laughed, bringing a second spoonful of posole to her lips. "It's delicious!"

"Then I'm glad Señora Cohen had mercy on me and served me my own tamales and posole." His smile faded, and his eyes looked away from her, then back. "Would you allow me to walk you home to the Cohens?"

Caroline swallowed, "I'd like that very much, but I brought Ana, and—"

"I hope you don't think me presumptuous, but I already spoke to Señora Cohen, and she assured me she would prefer that Ana stay after the piñata is broken, to help clean up." He cocked his head to one side and the impish smile returned. "So, what do you say, Señorita Thomas?"

"I'd like that very much. Let me clean out our bowls and return them." She stacked their bowls and marched to the bucket of warm soapy water by the big oven. She washed the bowls with trembling hands.

Chapter 49

Mauricio held Caroline's arm as they walked toward the Cohen residence. She liked leaning on him, but her mind went blank. She could think of nothing to say, then she decided to ask about the origins of Las Posadas.

The organizers had explained to her that she needed to select one honorable boy to play Joseph and one honorable girl to play Mary. She had assumed it was a Christmas play like children enacted in small churches on the Eastern Plains where she had grown up. After participating in Las Posadas of San Luis for nine days, she needed more explanation.

"Las Posadas started in Spain hundreds of years ago. It was a play to teach the peasants, who were illiterate, about the coming of the baby Jesus." Mauricio held onto Caroline with his left arm, gesturing as he spoke. "When the Spaniards came to Mexico, the priests wanted to find a way to teach the Indians about their faith. The Aztec Indians were in the habit of holding a festival in December to celebrate the winter solstice and the birth of their sun god. So the priests and missionaries used Las Posadas to weave Christianity into a celebration that already existed. And it continues to this day in Spain and Latin America, even here in Colorado."

As she focused on Mauricio's story, Caroline felt the nervous-
ness subside. "Wasn't that confusing for the Indians, not knowing
exactly which event and which god they were celebrating?"

"I suppose it might have been, but the Catholic missionaries
in those days had seen or heard previous generations talk about
how the church in Spain had forced Jews and Muslims to convert to Christianity or be exiled or killed." The light-heartedness
in Mauricio's voice was gone now. "Maybe merging Christianity
with another religion wasn't the right thing to do, but I believe
they had seen persecution and wanted people to know that God
is love, that He doesn't force people to believe in Him."

"That makes sense." Caroline pushed her hands deeper into
the pockets of her coat.

They entered the town square and passed the Vigil home.
She remembered her puzzlement with the candelabra. "Why do
so many valley people have that sort of candelabra in their windows?"

"I doubt most of them know. It is a tradition carried on by
many generations. My father told me it is a Jewish tradition, but
I don't know why Catholics display them."

When they arrived at the Cohens' door, Mauricio opened it
for Caroline to enter first. "The best person to ask about the candelabra is Señor Cohen."

She turned to thank him for walking her home, then Señor
Cohen called out, "Are you finished already?"

"It's just me ... Caroline ... and Mauricio, who has been so
kind as to walk me home."

Señor Cohen was at the door. "Please, do come in. Have some
coffee and warm up before you have to go home." He addressed
Mauricio. "Are you going back to the ranch tonight?"

"No, no, I'm staying over at Tia Anita's inn."

"Glad to hear that. Well, please, have a seat." He gestured
toward the chairs arranged snugly around the fireplace, between
the kitchen and living room.

Caroline had become accustomed to the heavy, dark-stained

wooden chairs, featuring intricate carving on the backs and legs. Señora Cohen had told her when she first came to live with the family, that the chairs were made by her grandfather as her wedding gift and traveled with the Cohen family when they moved from Santa Fe to the San Luis Valley.

"Caroline asked me about the candelabra that many people in the valley display in their windows, especially at Christmas time." Mauricio pulled off his coat and placed it in Caroline's outstretched arm. "My father told me it is a remnant of the conversos, but I don't know much more about it."

"¿Conversos? What's that?" Caroline had hung her and Mauricio's coats on the pegs beside the front door. All three sat facing the fireplace.

"Yes, yes, you are right that the candelabra and a lot of other customs came from the Spanish Jews. They called them conversos because even though they converted—some forcibly, some by choice—to Catholicism, they were never viewed by the old-time Spaniards as legitimate Christians."

Señor Cohen crossed, then uncrossed his legs. "It is not a joyous Christmas story, but one of great evil. You see, in the latter part of the fifteenth century, a man by the name of Torquemada launched the Spanish Inquisition, convincing King Ferdinand II and Queen Isabella that Jews and Muslims—even the ones who had converted to Christianity—were a threat to Catholic Spain." He drew in a deep breath and released a sigh. "Jews, especially, were forced to leave Spain or convert. Even if they did convert, they were considered 'New Christians' and never totally trusted. Can you imagine what it was like to have your every action scrutinized? That is how it was during that horrible time. Anyone suspected of not being a 'true Christian' could be tortured until they supposedly told the 'truth,' which was anything the inquisitor wanted to hear. The same fate awaited friends and neighbors who sympathized with those who were suspect."

"That is awful." Caroline wiped a tear. "My father's people were killed because the whites didn't understand them and were afraid of them; and to be honest, his people killed a lot of whites because they hated them coming into their hunting grounds."

Señor Cohen patted her on the back. "Caroline, your trial gave many of the residents in this valley hope that there are honorable people among the Anglos and that we might be able to live together in peace."

"Thank you. I'm glad for that." Caroline nodded her head. "So, what does the Spanish Inquisition have to do with the candelabras we see here in windows?"

"Torquemada wasn't the only or the last inquisitor. Over time, many people—whether they were still secretly Jewish, had been Jewish, or were afraid of being accused of being Jewish—decided to leave Spain." Señor Cohen rose to his feet. "But I think the coffee is ready." He returned with three full mugs and a pitcher of goat's milk.

"So what you are saying is that a lot of people with Jewish blood came to the New World to escape an inquisition?" Mauricio asked, speaking slowly and looking thoughtful.

Señor Cohen nodded. "Either to escape an inquisition or to live without worrying who was watching them. It is not a thing people talked about. Even today, many are afraid to talk about their Jewish ancestry. As a result, few really know." He paused to add more milk to his coffee. "My family is very Spanish and has been Catholic for generations. Yet, my parents passed on to me some traditions with foods and a blessing that we say on Friday evenings."

"Oh, it's the Jewish Sabbath or the beginning of it, no?" Caroline scooted to the edge of her seat. "My mother taught me about some of the Jewish traditions in the Bible."

"That's right. I'm quite certain the candelabra is one of those traditions that people do without knowing why."

"I've always wondered about your surname, Cohen," Mauricio chuckled. "It's not a Spanish name at all."

"No, it isn't. I remember my grandfather saying that at least in this country he didn't have to be afraid to use his real name."

"I'm going to ask my mother if she knows about our family having Jewish blood. I hope she's not still afraid to talk about it. Thank you for sharing this history of the Spanish people. It will remind me not to be judgmental of others," Mauricio said.

He stood and began to pull on his coat and gloves. "I really must be going. I don't want to arrive after Tia Anita pulls the lock down on her door. She likes me, but she would not like to get out of bed to open the door for me," he chuckled.

Señor Cohen stood. "Thank you for bringing Carolina home. You know, she's become a bit like a daughter to me."

Mauricio winked at Caroline. "I hope to see you soon."

She thought it sounded more like a question than a statement.

Chapter 50

San Luis, February 1887

*H*e may have hoped to see me soon, but he has made no effort to do so.

Caroline huffed aloud, drawing glances from a few of her students, who were reading silently.

She had insisted the school purchase an assortment of children's novels. Just a few months into the school year, most of her students had begun to enjoy reading—with various levels of fluency.

A few weeks after Christmas, between debilitating blizzards, Chance had called on his sister at Cohen's Mercantile.

"With Mauricio back home, Doña Maria doesn't really need me. I helped put a new timber roof on the barn and completed a few other chores that were best done with two sets of hands." His smile was broad and his eyes merry. "I think it's time I got back to the Bijou Basin, to Ma and Pa. Truth is, I'm more of a homebody than you are, Sis."

Caroline had bid him farewell. She would miss him, but she felt no desire to leave the San Luis Valley and return to the Bijou Basin with him. Telling the truth to the kind and generous people of the valley during the trial had caused them to generously open their hearts and homes to her. The San Luis Valley was her home now. Knowing she belonged brought a warm glow to her soul.

The sun pouring through the schoolhouse's western windows

created lengthening shadows. It soon would be time for the children to make their way to their homes. She always made sure to dismiss school in time for the children traveling from outlying farms to reach home before dark.

She had turned to face the students when she saw a hand waving for her attention. It was Tomás. A teacher wasn't supposed to have favorites, and she supposed she adored each of her students in a certain way, but Tomás worked so hard. At just six years old he was reading a Spanish translation of *Pinocchio*.

Caroline went to his desk and leaned over him. "Do you like the book?"

"Oh, yes, Miss Vargas." He sat up straight in his seat and pointed to a word. "What is this word 'huérfano'?"

"Huérfano is a child with neither a mother nor a father."

"Oh." Great sadness darkened his face. "Was Pinocchio so bad that his mother left him?"

Caroline felt her throat constrict. "I'm going to dismiss the rest of the students, then we can talk about this."

She instructed her students to pack up their belongings and return their books to the bookshelf. "See you Monday. Be careful going home. Hasta luego." She bid each student farewell.

Returning to Tomás's desk, she placed her hand on his shoulder. "Do you think your mother left you because you were bad?"

"Sí." He looked up at her with tear-filled eyes.

"No, no. I'm sure that is not it at all." She lowered herself onto her haunches and placed her arm around him. "You are a smart, handsome and kind young man. I can't imagine a nicer boy. Truly, Tomás!"

"Really?" A smile began to spread across his face. "Thank you, Miss Carolina."

"I like you very much." She arched her eyebrows. "In fact, sometimes I am tempted to steal you away from your papá and abuela. But I can't do that. They love you and would miss you so very much."

He giggled. "I love you, Miss Carolina." He wrapped his arms around her neck.

"I ... I love you, too, Tomás." A few tears trickled down her face. Then she straightened and gave him a bright smile. "Are you ready to walk to Tia Anita's or do you want to wait here for your papá?"

Tomás was boarding with the kindly woman during the week. Since Mauricio had returned home, Caroline no longer spent weekends at Doña Maria's rancho. Each Friday evening Mauricio picked up his son and brought him back to school each Monday morning.

Tomás slid his hand into hers. "It's getting late. Maybe you should walk me to Tia Anita's. That is where my father will go to look for me."

ooooo

For the fourth time this month Mauricio was at the San Luis telegraph office. Chance told him the Bijou Basin was many miles from a telegraph office and that he should be patient. Now, finally, a telegram was waiting for him from the Bijou Basin. With trembling hands he opened the sealed message. It contained one word: *Yes.*

He sprang up onto his buckskin and clucked the horse into a lope, holding the telegram in his right hand. He was nearly out of town when he realized he had not stopped at the school to pick up Tomás. He stopped and turned his horse back toward town.

As Mauricio neared the schoolhouse, he saw it was dark and that no smoke rose from its chimney. Tomás would be at Tia Anita's.

A few minutes later, Mauricio picked up Tomás and swung him around. "Hurry, get your things, Son. Abuela will be waiting for us."

"See you Monday," Tia Anita called to Mauricio and Tomás as they bounded out the door.

ooooo

Father and son rode double to the livery, where Mauricio had left Tomás's horse, Frost. The little mare with the frost-bitten ears that looked angry all the time, had been rejected by buyers in both Denver and the valley. Frost was the mare Carolina rode when Mauricio first discovered that the odd vaquero who worked wonders with horses was really a beautiful woman. Looking back, he realized Carolina's love of the dejected mare had captured his heart. Now, it wasn't that he couldn't sell Frost; he didn't *want* to sell her. Keeping her was his way of holding on to a small part of Carolina. Besides, Frost made a perfect mount for Tomás.

Frost and Mauricio's big buckskin were fit and used to navigating through snow and ice. They loped the pair to within a mile of the ranch before dropping to a trot to let the horses catch their breath and cool down. It was dusk when they pulled into the ranch yard and headed to the barn to unsaddle, groom, and feed their mounts.

"My hands are cold, Papá." Tomás hunched over in the saddle. "And I'm hungry."

"We always feed our animals before we eat, Son." Mauricio swung off the buckskin and came to help the much shorter Tomás dismount. "Move your fingers and rub your hands together like this." Mauricio patted his gloved hands together.

"Sí, señor." Tomás mimicked his father's actions.

"Besides, with all the nice things you told me Miss Carolina said about you today, don't you also want her to think you're courageous?"

"¡Sí!" Tomás said, tugging with gusto to loosen the leather latigo that held his saddle in place.

Mauricio lifted his son's saddle and carried it into the tack area. "It's good to be willing to ask for help; just don't expect someone else to do what you can and should do yourself. Alright, Son?"

Tomás nodded. He handed Mauricio the saddle blanket and bridle.

"Papá, can we leave the horses in the barn tonight?" Tomás asked with concern. "I don't want them to be cold."

"We'll leave them in the barn to eat some extra hay and their grain." Mauricio scooped up Tomás and moved him to his right hip. "Before I go to bed, I'll come out and open the door so they can join the other horses in the corral or stay in the barn. Horses are pretty good about deciding what they need to stay safe and healthy."

"I think letting them out of the barn before bedtime should be my job, Papá." Tomás straightened his back and lifted his chin. "A man must act like a man, no?"

The moment Mauricio opened the back door to the house, the smell of beef roasting with herbs and onion wafted over him. He released Tomás's hand and instructed him to wash up at the sink.

"Let me get that," he said to his mother, who was bent in front of the oven, pulling out the roaster pan. "It smells magnificent. I'm starving." He took the potholders she handed him and pulled the pan out of the oven and slid it onto the table. "What else do you need me to do, Mamá?"

"Nada, nada. Estoy listo." She smoothed an escaping strand of hair back into the bun at the back of her head. "Please, let's eat."

Along with the beef, they ate roasted carrots and green chiles and homemade whole wheat tortillas.

Tomás licked his lips when his grandmother finally removed the cloth from the fresh-baked empanadas and slid the plate to the center of the table. She poured cups of coffee for herself and Mauricio, then set the coffee and a pitcher of goat's milk on the table.

Tomás poured himself some milk and slid two flaky pastries onto his plate. "My favorite! Pine nuts with honey and cinnamon."

When the six-year-old had sufficiently stuffed himself with empanadas, he announced he would let the horses out of the barn before going to bed.

"Good, Son." Mauricio winked and picked up the two cups. After refilling them with the simmering pot off the stove, he returned to the table.

Doña Maria reached across the table to pat his forearm. "I've not seen you this happy since before … well, for a very long time."

"I am very happy. I love being back at the ranch. I love being a father to my son." He stretched his arms out in front of him and brought them back, folded, to the table in front of him. "And, there's one more thing." He swallowed and folded his hands. "I'm going to ask Carolina to marry me."

"But how will you ask for her hand when her family lives so far away?"

"I've already done it." He slapped the opened telegram on the table. "Before he left, I asked Chance what he thought. He said he would welcome me into his family. So I penned a letter to Carolina's parents, asking for her hand in marriage." Mauricio poked at the telegram. "Today I got the answer!"

Doña Maria abruptly rose and left the kitchen.

"Mamá, I thought you would approve." He drummed his fingers on the table until she returned. "Are you angry because she's not Hispano? Or, because the church may not recognize our union?"

"Don't be ridiculous. You know me better than that!" She held a pouch as she sat back at the table. "The only thing that would make me angry is if you let such a beautiful young woman slip away. She's smart, hard-working, loving, and expects nothing."

"Gracias, Mamá," Mauricio released his breath in a long sigh.

Doña Maria opened the pouch and pulled out a large, expertly-cut emerald encircled with small diamonds that hung on a heavy gold chain. "Judge Charles Beaubien, or Carlos, as the Hispanos knew him, gave these to me because your father and I protected his wife during the Taos Revolt over three decades ago." She then pulled out a set of earrings, each with a smaller, though beautifully-cut, emerald surrounded by diamonds. "It is a lovely and valuable set. After moving to the valley, I felt it too expensive to wear. So I packed it away and determined to give it to my daughter-in-law someday."

"But you didn't."

"Carolina is the first, the only, young woman I ever wanted to have this set." She pushed the necklace and earrings toward Mauricio, sliding them on the table with care. "You may use them as an engagement gift. She is a woman who will truly cherish them."

Mauricio fingered the necklace, then picked it up. "It's beautiful. Thank you, Mamá ... if you're certain?"

"I am." She stood and gathered the cups and milk pitcher off the table. "We can talk tomorrow about where you plan to build your house."

Chapter 51

Cohen's Mercantile, San Luis

Caroline paced back and forth between the Cohens' living room and kitchen.

"You're going to wear a hole in our floor," Señora Cohen chuckled.

"What?" Caroline started. "Oh, I'm sorry." Her thoughts had raced since yesterday afternoon when she had returned to the Cohens' house after delivering Tomás to Tia Anita's. With a knowing smile, Señora Cohen had handed her the tooled leather horse's headstall and note.

Caroline first thought the headstall was from the Washington family. She knew Mr. Washington worked in leather, creating saddlebags, lady's purses, and other pieces of tack used by vaqueros. However, as she examined the headstall closer, she saw that it was not an ordinary piece of work. The heavy piece of dark-stained leather was sturdy but pliable. An expert hand had carved a decorative pattern along both edges, giving the headstall an elegant yet practical feel. The leather felt rich in her hands.

She couldn't imagine any of her students' parents giving her such a fine gift. With heightened curiosity, she opened the note. It read:

Please accept my gift to you of a proper Spanish headstall. Azúcar deserves to be treated as the fine mare she is. I thank her for transporting and protecting you all these months when I did not. May I have the honor of your company tomorrow? If your answer is yes, saddle Azúcar, dress warmly, and leave the barn door open to show me you accept my offer. If the barn door is closed, I will ride on, and you can know that I will be forever in your debt for all you have done for my mother and my son.

Caroline's hands trembled as she refolded the note and slipped it into her skirt pocket. She tossed and turned all night, unable to sleep. In the pre-dawn hours, she disassembled Azúcar's bridle, untying the worn mecate headstall, replacing it with the beautiful tooled leather headstall. She reattached the mouth bit and mecate rope reins. Maybe it was Caroline's imagination, but she thought Azúcar smiled when she slipped the beautiful, soft leather head-stall over the mare's ears.

Caroline could groom, saddle, and bridle a horse with one arm tied behind her back, yet she kept checking and re-checking her work to ensure she hadn't missed anything. Azúcar and the Cohens' horse were tied in the barn. No wind blew. She flung the barn door open wide and secured it with a rope before returning to the house to change into clean clothes and brush her hair.

Gloriana and Ana were in the kitchen helping their mother prepare breakfast, so Caroline had the bedroom to herself. She hesitated for a moment while considering the calico dress she wore for special occasions, but opted for the more practical breeches, and woolen socks and sweater. Her oiled duster and hat hung from the coat tree she shared with the two Cohen girls.

When Ana called everyone for breakfast, Caroline went to the table and sat at her usual place. She picked at the eggs and tortilla that comprised their breakfast that Saturday morning, worrying that the barn door had somehow slammed shut.

Any time now, she thought as she paced back and forth,

peering out the window next to the door, then returning to the kitchen. After Señora Cohen made the comment about wearing a hole in the floor, Caroline sat at the table, where her pacing was replaced with fidgeting. She flinched when she heard the knock at the door.

"It's Mauricio," the señora called.

Caroline pulled on her duster and pushed the hat onto her head, her shiny, long black hair cascading over her shoulders and down her back.

"Buenos días." Her hands trembled but her voice was steady.

"Are you ready to ride?" Mauricio spoke with a formality she had not observed before.

"Sí." Caroline stepped out onto the front veranda. She could see that Mauricio held the reins of both his big buckskin gelding and Azúcar.

"I brought Azúcar from the barn for you. I hope you don't mind."

"Of course not. Thank you." She smiled at him.

The muscles in Mauricio's face relaxed. His answering smile warmed her.

Caroline pushed her boots into Azúcar's sides to cue the mare to follow Mauricio and his mount. They slow-loped out of town and toward the ranch. Caroline felt a twinge of disappointment. She wanted to spend the day with him, only him.

Several miles before they reached the ranch, though, Mauricio pulled his buckskin to a walk. Their horses walked side-by-side. "Have you heard the story about the chapel of San Acacio?" He pointed to the little chapel nestled among the scrub oak and piñon pine trees.

"Yes, the Cohens told me the story."

She followed him to the entrance of the chapel. For the first time, she noticed the stained-glass windows on both sides of the otherwise unremarkable, flat-roofed, adobe structure. They dismounted, slipped rope halters onto their horses, and tied them to the hitching post in front of the chapel.

The heavy, dark-stained wooden door on leather hinges protested as Mauricio pulled it open for Caroline.

The interior was every bit as magical as Gloriana had described it. A carving she assumed was San Acacio stood at the entrance. Rough-hewn wooden benches sat perpendicular to the center aisle. At the front of the little church a large, splintered cross stretched from just below the pitch of the roof to the floor. Several feet in front of the cross was an altar of sanded, stained wood. The altar had intricate carvings on the front and sides, scenes of Jesus' birth, the feeding of the five thousand, and the crucifixion. A tarnished set of silver candlesticks sat on the altar. Caroline gasped when she saw the way the light filtered through the stained-glass windows in the morning sun. Green, blue, pink and gold beams of light streamed down onto the altar and the benches on the east side of the chapel.

Mauricio's hand on her lower back guided her forward. "Just as the angel warriors protected the people of this settlement, I will always protect you, Carolina."

He dropped to one knee.

AFTERWORD

Prairie Truth is a work of fiction, but it is heavily researched and includes many actual events, people, places and cultural traditions.

The killing spree of the Espinosa Brothers and Tom Tobin's capture and beheading of the remaining brother and nephew, are factual. Hispanics sympathized with their plight. Anglos found them nothing more than vicious murderers.

U.S. General Stephen Kearny, Narciso Beaubien, Judge Charles Beaubien, Maria Paula Lobato, the surrender of New Mexico by Governor Manuel Armijo and the Revolt of Taos in January 1847 are actual people and events as written in history books.

Rights afforded by land grants from the Spanish and Mexican governments, including the Sangre de Cristo Land Grant in *Prairie Truth*, have been contentious, with the people of the San Luis Valley believing they were cheated out of land. History tends to agree with them. Unscrupulous land grabs occurred, as did arson to destroy historical records showing Hispanic Americans' legitimate claims to land. In addition, legal suits throughout history often went against the original land grant settlers. In the defense of the American government, the system of land grants, whereby one titled individual was granted ownership of a huge tract of land with the stipulation that he must get settlers into the area in a set amount of time—usually two years—was a system completely foreign to American laws. Often the land grant owner had never actually seen the land he owned. This contrasted sharply with the U.S. Homestead Act, which granted smaller parcels of land to each of many owners and required that they live on and improve the land. Spanish and Mexican land grants featured common land for grazing, hunting, fishing, and harvesting lumber. This type of common-use ground was an unfamiliar concept to Americans during this time.

A variety of immoral and illegal tactics were used to discourage the Hispanic population in southern Colorado from claiming the rights afforded them by the Spanish and Mexican land grants. They were often at a disadvantage, because many of them were not fluent in English and did not understand Anglo customs and U.S. laws. Attempts have been made to right the wrongs of land taken from Hispanic grantees. In 2018, heirs of the 1860s Sangre de Cristo land grant had their rights to use ground reaffirmed by an appellate division, which upheld the Colorado Supreme Court decision in 2002 to allow heirs access to the Taylor Ranch. This ranch in 2002 occupied approximately 83,000 acres and was part of the original Sangre de Cristo land grant.

In the 1990s, when I was working for National Farmers Union, I learned about the probable Jewish heritage of people who settled in the San Luis Valley of Colorado. We were working with farmers in the area to explore the feasibility of starting a Kosher meat processing plant. They brought in an East Coast rabbi and discovered that many of their processing practices already conformed with Kosher processing. There were other habits, such as displaying menorahs in living-room windows that hinted at Jewish roots among this very Catholic population. Years later, I read about research on a specific type of breast cancer prevalent in Jewish women. Sadly, women of Hispanic heritage in the San Luis Valley were being diagnosed with this same cancer. Genetic studies of the descendants of the early Mexican/Spanish immigrants to southern Colorado, then Mexico, clearly show Jewish heritage.

During the Spanish Inquisition, Jews who had been earlier welcomed into Spain, were demanded to convert, leave Spain, or die. Getting as far away from Spain by settling in the New World allowed them to escape death, while remaining Spaniards. While most Jewish Spanairds integrated into Catholic Spanish life, customs and sayings often remained. Even today, menorahs are seen in windows in San Luis. In *Prairie Truth*, the Cohen family, whose surname was taken from historical documents of families who were early immigrants, symbolizes the melding of Jewish traditions into Catholic Hispanic homes.

The partido, the use of a sheep flock in exchange for labor, was a customary system whereby older shepherds got free labor, and young men were able to start their own flocks. It is also a historical fact that when non-Hispanics came into the San Luis Valley, they changed the terms of the partidos to their financial advantage. Often these new terms were spelled out in English-language contracts that unscrupulous issuers knew the Hispanic shepherds could not understand.

The official stockyards owned by the Denver Union Stock Yard Company, and the Livestock Exchange, opened in 1886. The competitive bidding on livestock was a major factor in ranchers getting fair prices for their animals. Out of the stockyards grew the world-renowned National Western Stock Show, still held each year in Denver.

Greeley, Colorado, was founded originally as Union Colony and known for its hide-tanning industry.

The story of San Acacio, a small settlement in the San Luis Valley named after Saint Acacio, the Greek centurion who was martyred for his faith, is historically accurate. San Acacio women prayed to the saint to be delivered from Ute warriors who threatened them while the men were away from the settlement. People of the Valley know of this story from 1853. The San Acacio Chapel still stands there today.

Las Posadas, in which townspeople reenact Mary and Joseph's search for a place to stay overnight in Bethlehem, is a Hispanic Christmas tradition played out in towns throughout the Spanish-speaking world, including towns in southern Colorado.

AUTHOR'S ACKNOWLEDGEMENTS

Many thanks to all who advised, read, proofread or otherwise contributed to the final manuscript of *Prairie Truth*. Historian Richard Olivas y Cordova, whose family heritage in San Luis goes back to the days when New Mexicans settled land grant property, provided me a bibliography for my initial research and also made (non-exhaustive) suggestions on the final manuscript. Thanks to my manuscript proofreader Sue Carter, and to Christina Slike at Cladach Publishing for her very thorough job of editing.

Other contributions came from members of the two book critique groups of which I was a part over the time I wrote *Prairie Truth*. Thanks to authors Laura Bartnick, Tonya Blessing, Charmayne Hafen, Jaydine Rendall, and Alice Longaker and aspiring author Penny Sebring for their suggestions and edits.

I would also like to thank Daymn Montoya for allowing me to read his family history, written by his father Vivian Montoya. Daymn's and Vivian's ancestors were early settlers around San Luis, settling in southern Colorado under the Sangre de Cristo Land Grant. This charming family history confirmed many of the surnames, places and history obtained in other research.

ABOUT THE AUTHOR

Marilyn Bay grew up on a crop and sheep farm in Northern Colorado, near the land homesteaded by her great-great grandparents. As a child, she learned that she was a small part Native American. This information motivated her to read and research Native Americans, as well as the origins and historic treks west by the settlers with whom they interacted, and, in some cases, intermarried.

Marilyn operates Prairie Natural Lamb, raising lambs and marketing them directly to her forty-plus customers. She enjoys riding and training horses, and is a certified Colorado 4-H horse-show judge and level rater.

She has written and edited newsletters and magazines and also has handled public relations and promotions for a list of clients that includes the National Bison Association and the American Grassfed Association. She serves as executive director of the Colorado Fruit & Vegetable Growers Association.

Prairie Truth is the sequel to Marilyn's first novel, *Prairie Grace*, a work of historical fiction set in 1864 Colorado Territory. In addition, Marilyn and her mother, Mildred Nelson Bay, wrote *All We Like Sheep: Lessons from the Sheepfold*, an autobiographical devotional book featuring stories of the mother-daughter duo's collective seven decades of sheep-raising experience.

Marilyn is the mother of two adult daughters, Kelly and Shannon.

Connect with Marilyn online at her Website:
    http://www.MarilynBay.com
and Facebook page:
    https://www.facebook.com/MarilynBayAuthor/

CPSIA information can be obtained
at www.ICGtesting.com
Printed in the USA
JSHW022337130819
1083JS00002B/12